SEP 0 7

DATE DUE

GAYLORD 234   PRINTED IN U.S.A.

PENUMBRA

This Large Print Book carries the
Seal of Approval of N.A.V.H.

PENUMBRA

CAROLYN HAINES

THORNDIKE PRESS

An imprint of Thomson Gale, a part of The Thomson Corporation

THOMSON
—★—™
GALE

Detroit • New York • San Francisco • New Haven, Conn. • Waterville, Maine • London • Munich

Copyright © 2006 by Carolyn Haines.

Thomson Gale is part of The Thomson Corporation.

Thomson, Star Logo and Thorndike are trademarks and Gale is a registered trademark used herein under license.

LIBRARY OF CONGRESS CATALOGING-IN-PUBLICATION DATA

Haines, Carolyn.
    Penumbra / by Carolyn Haines.
      p. cm.
    "Thorndike Press large print reviewers' choice" — T.p. verso.
    ISBN 0-7862-8823-X (hardcover : alk. paper) 1. Women detectives — Mississippi — Fiction. 2. Racially mixed people — Fiction. 3. Race relations — Fiction. 4. Mississippi — Fiction. 5. Kidnapping — Fiction. 6. Large type books. I. Title.
    PS3558.A329P46 2006b
    813'.54—dc22
                                              2006012280

Published in 2006 in arrangement with St. Martin's Press, LLC.

Printed in the United States of America on permanent paper
10 9 8 7 6 5 4 3 2 1

For
Rebecca Barrett
and Jan Zimlich

ACKNOWLEDGMENTS

With each book there are always many people to whom I owe thanks. The usual suspects: Renee Paul, Aleta Boudreaux, Stephanie Chisholm, Susan Tanner, and Thomas Lakeman-the members of the Deep South Writers Salon. For fifteen years this group has read my first drafts, offering advice and constructive criticism. I owe them all a great deal.

My agent, Marian Young, is an indispensable part of the process. I trust her judgment and her knowledge and value her friendship.

A special thanks to Roscoe Sigler, who helped me with the technical details of the funeral business. When we were children, we played hide-and-seek on the grounds of his family's funeral home. Perhaps it was during this time that the seed for this novel was first planted.

And a big thanks to Kelley Ragland and

the entire St. Martin's gang. It is a pleasure to work with such a dynamic and enthusiastic group.

1

The black Cadillac convertible churned down the dirt road, whipping whirls of dust behind it. The car, low-slung and fast, disappeared behind a stand of dark pines, leaving the landscape unexplainably barren. In a pasture beside the road an old mule grazed on grass burned dry by a merciless sun. From the shadow of a leaning barn came the low of a cow. The car sped by them, almost a vision, leaving only the settling dust and the taste of scorched dirt.

Behind the wheel, Marlena Bramlett pushed dark sunglasses higher on a perfect nose. A white scarf protected her hair, except for her bangs, which bobbed in hairsprayed curls on her forehead. The red-and-white-striped shirt she wore hugged her breasts; darts emphasized her narrow waist. She drove as if her profile were the masthead on a ship.

Beside Marlena, standing in the middle of

the seat, a six-year-old girl faced the wind. Brown pigtails, tipped with white bows, fluttered wildly behind the child.

"I see him!" Suzanna pointed up the road, her childish voice rising in excitement. "He's there. He's waiting for us."

"Sit down," Marlena told her daughter. "You act like a heathen."

"Will he have olives? The ones with the red things inside?" Suzanna bounced up and down on the seat.

"I don't know." Marlena passed the back of her hand over her forehead, smoothing the blond curls that, only half an hour before, had been pinned to lie just so.

"Big Johnny lives on a red dirt road, and he tastes like chocolate," Suzanna said.

"He *gives* you chocolate," Marlena corrected. "And he thinks you're very smart. But that's our secret, remember? If you tell anyone, I mean anyone, you can never come with me again." The car fell into shadow as it entered a thick grove of pines. The road narrowed, and sand grabbed at the wheels.

"I won't tell." Suzanna glanced at her mother, hurt. "I'd never tell on you."

Marlena slowed the car, finally stopping. She pulled her daughter to her side. "I know you won't tell. You're the one who loves me best." She kissed Suzanna's cheek, then quickly brushed the fine dust from her daughter's skin. "If I didn't trust you, I wouldn't bring you. Now let's make sure we look good." She turned the rearview mirror so she could check her ruby lipstick.

"Does Big Johnny really think I'm smart?" Suzanna twisted both pigtails in front of her chest. "He says I'm pretty, like you."

"Does he really?" Marlena's attention focused on the man half-hidden in the shadow of the car. She drove slowly abreast of the two-toned Chevy and stopped. The man sitting behind the wheel was tall, his black hair Bryllcremed back, white shirt unbuttoned at the collar. The ringless hand on the window was long and tanned, the nails neat. One finger thumped a rhythm.

"You're late," he said.

"I couldn't get away. Lucas brought someone home for lunch."

Suzanna felt the tension between the two adults. Big Johnny was angry. He looked hot, inside and out. His olive skin was slick with heat, his black eyes burning. If Johnny acted ugly to her mother, Marlena would be upset for days.

"I can count to a hundred," Suzanna said.

"I'm sorry we're late," Marlena said. "I came as quickly as I could."

"We brought some iced tea," Suzanna

said. Big Johnny loved iced tea. She held up the heavy gallon jar, lemons floating on top and ice rattling against the glass. "I've got glasses, too. And Mama dug worms for me." At last she had Big Johnny's attention.

"You brought worms?" His voice strained in an effort to be jolly. "Worms for Susie-Belle-Ring-o-ling." Big Johnny got out of the car, his white teeth showing in a false smile. In his hand he carried a leather satchel. He went around to the passenger door and got in. Suzanna stood on the seat between the two adults, feeling suddenly trapped. Marlena put the car in gear and slowly drove away.

"I've missed you," Marlena said, her hands on the wheel and her gaze on the dirt road that wound ahead of them through the pine forests. "Where've you been?"

"Up to Mendenhall and Magee, Collins and Hattiesburg. I had to take Lew's route when he came down with the fever. I would have called, but I can't." His voice was bitter. "Your husband might answer the phone."

Marlena glanced at him, and Suzanna saw the pleading in her eyes. "I'm sorry. That's just the way things are."

"I'm tired of the way things are." Big Johnny stared straight ahead, his voice low.

Suzanna leaned against the seat. She could feel the hot leather, now dust-coated. She didn't like it when her mother and Big Johnny were angry. She liked it when they laughed and teased each other, then her mother's blue eyes sparked and she was beautiful and alive. When they were angry, the fun left her mother and only the hard, cold shell of her body was there.

"Mama said we could go fishing today," Suzanna said. Usually Big Johnny liked it when they went fishing.

"I don't have time." Big Johnny's voice was punishing.

"Please, Johnny." Marlena turned to him. "I made an excuse to stay out for three hours. It's hard for me to find that much time away."

"I feel like I'm renting you. Watch the road," he snapped.

"Don't say things like that."

"That's the reality. I feel cheap." Johnny pulled a cigarette from his pocket and lit it, the air from the moving car pushing the smoke behind them. His laugh was harsh. "Isn't that the best? *I* feel cheap. I want more, Marlena."

There was a long silence that made Suzanna furious. She hated Big Johnny and she hated her father. They were stupid jackasses. She'd learned that word at school, and she was proud of it.

Finally, Marlena spoke. "I don't have more to give right now, Johnny. If you'd like, I can take you back to your car."

Suzanna watched the corner of her mother's mouth, the tiny tuck in the lips and flesh. Her chin was trembling and in a moment her mother would be crying. In a flash of fury, Suzanna turned on the man beside her. "I hate you!" She drew back her foot and kicked, catching the man in the ribs. He made a strange sound and leaned forward.

"Suzanna!" Marlena slammed on the brakes and put the car into a skid. The Cadillac turned sideways, wheels making the sound of tearing as they slewed through the sand.

"Goddamn it!" Johnny leaned across the seat and grabbed the wheel. He gave it a vicious jerk. The car swung heavy and fast, then righted itself and stopped in the center of the road. "You could have killed us all!" His arm was around Suzanna's legs, holding her as she braced her hands against the top of the windshield. "She would have been thrown out of the car if I hadn't caught her."

"I'm sorry, I'm sorry, I'm sorry." Marlena's head dipped to the steering wheel. "I don't know why I'm alive," she said. "I want to die."

"Mama!" Suzanna struggled free of the man's grip. "Mama, it's okay. Don't cry." She hugged her mother's shoulder and felt hatred again for the man beside her. She glared at him. "Fix it," she demanded.

Johnny got out of the car and moved around to the driver's side. Marlena slid over and leaned her face into Suzanna.

The car started smoothly and Johnny kept driving. He didn't turn around. He didn't say anything. He put one arm on the door and drove, the wind drying the sweat on his forehead.

Suzanna saw the shaded timber trail ahead even before Johnny slowed to turn. This was her favorite place to fish. The two-track road, wallowed out in mud holes, wound to the river. It was a slow, brown river with deep places darkened by rotting leaves and the trunks of trees caught in a swirl of currents and forever doomed to remain there. The day was hot enough to wade in the shallows, if her mother would let her. She couldn't swim. No one had time to teach her.

After the car stopped, Suzanna got the fishing pole from the backseat and the worms in a can from the floorboard. She hated threading the worm on the hook, but Big Johnny had taught her how to do it, and he would mock her if she acted squeamish. She took the cane pole and the can of worms to the bank of the river.

"What was the Indian tribe that lived on this river?" Johnny asked her as he lifted his satchel from the floorboard.

"The Chickasawhay Indians. They were Choctaws," Suzanna answered, unable to hide the thrill of being right. Every time they met, Big Johnny taught her something new, and then the next time he would quiz her on it. She always knew the answer, and she liked the way he smiled when she was right. "Mama, can I wade?"

Marlena walked to the edge of the river. About four feet from the bank a sandbar beckoned just below the surface of the lazy water. "No further than the sandbar," she said. "And wear the life jacket."

Suzanna's jaw locked into place. "I hate that thing. It stinks. I can't hold the fishing pole good. I won't —"

"Then sit on the bank." Johnny's voice bit into her complaint.

She was stunned. Big Johnny never talked to her that way. That was how her father spoke to her. "I want to go home," she said. She threw her pole to the ground. "I want to go home now."

"Baby, you can wade to the sandbar," Marlena said. She flashed a look at Johnny.

"I'm not wearing the life jacket." Suzanna dared them to defy her.

"Okay, but don't go any further than the sandbar." Marlena got the jar of tea and a blanket. Johnny picked up the picnic basket that was covered with a cloth on the floorboard of the backseat. "We're going to set up the picnic. We'll eat after you catch three fish. Remember, call out to us before you come, okay?"

Suzanna nodded. She liked for them to leave so she could be alone. She sat on the bank of the river and removed her Keds. They were brand new, the white rubber around the soles still pristine. She'd gotten them at Marcel's, the only clothing store in Drexel. The shoes had been a special present from her mother, something to wear for the rest of the summer.

She heard Johnny's deep laughter and the sound of her mother's squeal. They weren't angry anymore. She turned back to the water. She was going to catch a mess of bream, but first she had to bait the hook.

She got a worm from the can, gripping the writhing creature tightly. Johnny had told her to cut the worms in half with a piece of broken glass, but she didn't want to do that. She hooked the night crawler three times and threw the line into a dark pool by the bank. The red and white cork floated under a hanging branch where a huge fish swirled, hungry, in the dark water. Squinting her eyes against the glare on the water, she waited.

A copse of thick briars, dogwoods, privet, and huckleberry bushes hid her mother from view, but she could hear Marlena's low laugh, the soft sound of pleasure she made. Suzanna knew to stay away. Big Johnny wouldn't give her the treats he'd brought in his satchel if she disturbed them. Once, she'd asked her mother what they were doing. "I have a terrible pain, right here," her mother had said, taking her hand and putting it between her breasts. "Sometimes, Johnny can touch that spot and make it better."

Since that time, Susanna had worried that her mother would die. It was a fact that Marlena sometimes had trouble breathing in the woods. Susanna had heard her, more than once, heaving for air and making sharp noises in her throat as if a bone was stuck.

Suzanna's cork bobbed in the water and she jerked it, pulling up a five-inch bream. The silvery fish arched and bucked as it dangled from the hook. A tiny drop of blood oozed down the silver scales of its head, fluttering in the moving gills.

Johnny had taught her to put the fish on the ground and to step on it with her shoe so that the sharp dorsal fins couldn't prick her hand. Instead, though, she grasped the fish between her thumb and forefinger and worked the hook out of its mouth. There was a torn place below the bony structure of the lip. The fish opened and closed its mouth, gasping, losing the fight to live in the oxygen-rich air. She drew back her arm and threw the fish to the middle of the river. She'd lost her desire to catch dinner.

Putting her pole on the ground, she eased through the dead oak and sycamore leaves, finally dropping to her knees to crawl up to the huckleberry bushes. She'd promised never to do this. Had promised to keep all of this a secret from everyone, especially her father. Now her mother and Big Johnny were quiet. There was the sound of a long sigh, an exhale of contentment. She knelt at the base of the bushes and worked her hand into the dense foliage. When she pulled the lower branches aside, she saw her mother leaning against a tree trunk. Big Johnny's head was dark against the pale white of her mother's stomach and thighs. Her large breasts tipped toward his face, and as Suzanna watched, Big Johnny took one nipple in his mouth. Her mother tilted her head back, exposing the long, white throat that she covered each night with a milky lotion.

"My God, that feels good," Marlena said.

"Let me show you what feels better," Johnny said, his voice strangely full. He sat up and pulled her farther down the blue picnic cloth.

Suzanna gasped.

Big Johnny's head came up, coyote eyes narrowed as he scanned the undergrowth. "Where's that kid?" he asked. He rose to his knees. He still wore his pants but was shirtless. "If she's not at the riverbank fishing, I'm going to give her the spanking she's needed for the last five years."

Suzanna backed out of the shrub and ran to the riverbank. She snatched up her baitless hook and threw it into the water, the splash of the cork sounding just as a limb crackled behind her.

Big Johnny didn't say anything. She felt him standing behind her on the bank, towering over her. Suzanna kept her gaze focused on the water, thinking how the submerged sandbar was exactly the shape of her mother's rounded hip.

Behind her another stick crackled. There

was a grunt and the sound of someone crashing down the bank. She started to turn, intending to confront Big Johnny and tell him that she wanted none of the candy or bribes in his black satchel. She was going to tell her father about the fishing trips, and then Big Johnny would never dare to threaten her with a spanking again. Defiant, she turned, one pigtail brushing across her chest. She opened her mouth to speak.

A hand covered her mouth, the grip so hard it felt as if her jaw would pop out of place. Another hand grabbed her hair and snatched her off the ground. The cry that was smothered in her throat was part rage and part fear. She struggled against the cloth sack that was thrust over her head, and when she choked and sneezed at the flour that invaded her eyes and nose and mouth, she heard laughter.

"She's a little hellcat," a man said. She didn't recognize the voice.

"Shut up and bring her." Another man she didn't know spoke. Where was Big Johnny? Where was her mother?

And then she was lifted, her back pressed to the man's chest, his arm around her, squeezing too tightly. She started to scream, to cry out for her mother, but the cry was choked back in her throat by the cruel fingers of the man who held her. She flailed her arms and legs, finally jamming her heel as hard as she could into the man's crotch. He doubled over in pain, but his grip didn't loosen.

"You little bitch," he ground into her ear.

The other man laughed. "Shut her up," he said. "We don't want the brat to spoil our surprise."

2

Jade Dupree stood alone in the chilled tile room. The body on the table before her was still, lifeless. She hesitated, dizzy with the smell of putrefaction and a strange, sweet scent that she'd never before associated with death. Horace Bradshaw was dead, and his earthly remains awaited her beneath the sheet. Still, she didn't move. She crossed her bare arms on her chest, straining the back of the fitted pink polka-dot dress, a sliver of summer that pierced the embalming room.

Jade closed her eyes and tucked her chin. The overhead light haloed her dark, curly hair, worn scandalously short. After a moment, she stepped forward. Behind her, the gravity bottles filled with colorless embalming fluid swayed slightly on their poles.

Her high heels, a spotless white, clicked on the tile floor as she walked to the porcelain table. It was going to be bad. She'd heard the talk. Kobe had come running into the beauty salon telling her to "come quick. Mr. Lavallette needs you fast. Got him an emergency." And she'd left Mrs. Moss, her gray hair pin-curled, under the big bonnet dryer.

Promising to be back in twenty minutes, she'd raced the four blocks to Rideout Funeral Home. There'd been the tang of tragedy in the air all afternoon. She'd smelled it in the perm solution she'd put on Betty Johnson and the dye she'd worked into Letty Wells's auburn hair. Doom hung over the town when she stepped out back of her salon to hang the towels she'd washed. Now, here it was, lying in front of her. Death. It was never simple, and even when it was sought, it left damage behind. She did not want to look upon this dead body. The smell was enough to tell her that only a miracle would make this one presentable.

Taking the sheet in both hands, she pulled it back to reveal what had once been Horace Bradshaw. As she watched, several ants staggered out of his left nostril. Or what remained of the nostril. She knew the odor then. She'd smelled it during the summer when she cut across Billy Dee's cow pasture. It was the smell of the rags Billy Dee hung from trees for the cows to walk under to kill the flies that tormented them. Insecticide. Junior Clements, the county coroner, must have doused the body in something to kill the ants.

She brushed the insects away, assessing the ruin. The eyes were gone, the swollen lids sunk into the skull. The tender flesh of the lips had also been eaten, revealing yellowed teeth below a partially consumed nose. The remaining flesh was blotched and swollen. Even the top of the head, visible through thinning gray hair, was bitten and ravaged. She'd heard talk that Mr. Bradshaw had lost his mind, that he'd taken to wandering over to his daughter's neighbors in only his boxer shorts, touching himself and shouting obscenities. Sometimes the old got cranky. It was part of the cycle. Age changed everyone, even bankers.

Jade heard the door to the embalming room open. Expecting Elwood Lavallette, she looked up. Instead of the man she worked for, she saw Junior Clements. Her gaze dropped to his hands. They were always blistered and covered in scabs and sores, a reflection of his soul, and she struggled not to show her disgust. She tried to stay out of Junior's way, especially when she was alone.

"Mr. Elwood says the family wants an

open casket."

Jade could hear her own slow breathing. She lowered the sheet, shielding the dead man from Junior's curious gaze. "I see."

Junior stepped deeper into the room, closing the door behind him. The smell of the insecticide was suddenly unbearable. Jade backed away from the table.

"Folks say you talk to the dead," Junior said. A thin string of spittle moved between his lips when he talked. "They say that late at night, the dead come back here to help you. Is that true?"

Jade directed her gaze to the floor. She'd learned long ago not to show her feelings to men like Junior. Her contempt triggered their fear, and their cruelty. "The dead don't always leave this earth right away," she said. "Sometimes they linger. When their hearts are heavy."

"Are you trying to spook me?" Junior asked angrily.

"Not me," Jade said. "No, sir."

"Sh-it," Junior said. "I'm not afraid of no corpse." He took three strides to the table. His crusty hands pulled back the sheet. "Look at that mess. Poor bastard laid out in that ant bed at least three days. His hip's broke so he couldn't get up. Now the family's all cryin' 'poor daddy, poor daddy.'

Poor daddy my ass. They more likely afraid of a charge of criminal neglect." He shifted so that his gaze lingered on her breasts. "How you gonna make him look human in his casket?"

Jade didn't answer. She turned away. "I'll need some marbles. Some wax. Some putty." She would work with the corpse after she finished at her beauty shop, after her clients had gone. "It'd be best if we could get a hat." Through the thinning gray hair, the red eruptions of ant bites were too obvious. "And a pair of gloves. Whatever kind the family thinks he would have worn. Or we can cover the hands with some kind of floral arrangement." She spoke to the floor. "Could you tell Mr. Lavallette those are the things I'll need?" If Junior had an errand that gave him importance, he would leave.

"Sure. I'll tell him." Junior walked to the door and opened it. "You wait right here."

She didn't look up. "Mr. Clements, the thing you have to remember is that the dead see. They look and they know. They remember." She lifted her face, her green eyes bright in her pale face. "And they come back to visit sometimes when they got a score to settle."

Junior vanished out the door. Jade was smiling when she stepped out of the room and into the hallway. Junior wouldn't bother her anymore that day. The fright would wear off in a day or two and he'd be back, but for a while she'd bought some peace. She had to get back to the beauty salon and tend her customers, but first she had to speak to Mr. Lavallette, reassure him that she'd be back in the evening and do her best for the dead man.

From the embalming room she took a corridor that ended in a huge wooden door. She cracked the door and listened. Most folks in Jebediah County knew she tended the dead. Some folks asked for her special, wanting her to use her skills to roll back the years or soften the agonies of illness and death on a loved one. There were others, though, who wouldn't feel right that a Negro had touched their dead. Mr. Elwood was good to her, and she didn't want to make trouble for him. Folks could be mighty superstitious when it came to the dead.

In the front parlor, she heard voices. There was the low, gentle cadence of Elwood Lavallette. She couldn't hear what he was saying, but she knew it by heart. It was the language of release. It was Elwood Lavallette's job to help those who remained on this side of the River Jordan to let go of those who had passed over.

She tiptoed across the hardwood floor to the expensive wool rug that whirled in burgundies and golds. Now her footsteps were absorbed by the thick carpeting and she could make better time. She started toward the front door, thinking she'd call Elwood later on. She had to get back to the beauty shop. She heard what sounded like a screen door, rusted and ill used, being wrenched open. The sound fell down the scale, back to human register, before it turned into a sob.

"Daddy!" The woman screamed the word. "Daddy! Where's my daddy!" There was the sound of a chair overturning.

"Miss Cora, you don't want to see him like he is." Elwood's voice was soothing, kind.

"I have to see him. Junior told me he was eat up by ants!" The voice rose high, quivering, then broke. "By ants! My daddy laid out in an ant bed, Mr. Lavallette. He died in a bed of fire ants."

"Now, Miss Cora, that's not the way to remember your daddy. Think on the time when you got that brand new Ford. Remember? I saw you driving through town like queen of the parade. Your smile was bright enough to blind me. Your daddy was so proud that he could get that car for you."

The keening moans of the woman had begun to settle down. Jade stepped into one of the visitation rooms. Mr. Lavallette and the woman were between her and the front door. She hesitated, not wanting to intrude on the woman's grief.

"I think you were dating Duke Farley, weren't you? Yes, that's right." Elwood's voice shifted up and down, lulling. "Duke was such a bright boy. I hear he's doing real well up at Canton."

"Who's gone fix Daddy up for the casket?" The question was asked with a few hiccups of emotion. "I want him to look like himself. Like he did before he lost his mind."

"Miss Dupree is with him right now," Elwood said. "She's the best in the Southeast. You just rest easy on that question, Miss Cora, and let us handle this situation."

Jade heard the scraping of chairs. Mr. Elwood was seating Cora in the front parlor. Jade was about to retreat when she heard Cora speak again. "Jade can fix him. That nigger gal can work miracles. If she lived in New Orleans or some big city, she'd be rich."

The words were a spell, binding Jade to the floor. But she didn't live in a city. She lived in Drexel, Mississippi, a crossroads town in the heart of the pine barrens. Her life was a straw house of ifs. If she'd been born in a big city, she could pass for white. If she moved to a big city, she could start over as a white woman with dark hair and eyes the color of the most expensive jade. If her mother's husband hadn't forced a pact of silence on the community, Jade would have been the acknowledged heir to a timber fortune, a fortune now lost at the gaming tables. If frogs had wings, they wouldn't bump their asses on the ground. "If" was a tiny word with the power to destroy. "If only" were two words that could corrupt a soul.

Jade needed to move, to walk, to put Cora Bradshaw and her summation of Jade's life far behind her. Junior was undoubtedly at the rear exit near the ramp where they rolled the bodies into the back of the funeral home. Mr. Elwood was near the front door. She'd have to try the side exit. She made her way there and slipped out the door under the portico where the hearse parked during services. Trumpet vine, thick with leaves and flowers, covered the portico and created dense shade. A dozen of the orange flowers had fallen to the shell drive. Jade stepped around the flowers, thinking how much they look like splotches of blood on the dry bones of the shells.

She stepped out of the shade and into the August heat. The salon was only four blocks away. She'd walked because her car had been blocked in the alley by some of her customers, but it was going to be a long four blocks back in the afternoon humidity. The hour between three and four was the hottest of the day.

She started across the parking lot, realizing too late that the heels of her shoes were sinking into the overheated asphalt. The shoes were expensive, her best pair. She considered walking barefoot, but if she were seen it would only add to the body of gossip about her. Folks would use it as proof that despite the fact that she looked white, she was a field hand in costume. It only took one drop of Negro blood to make a nigger. She stood, storklike, as the sheriff's car pulled into the lot.

Sheriff Huey Jones passed her as if she weren't there. Deputy Frank Kimble, in the passenger seat, leaned into the window to watch her. She used her leg muscles to pull her heel free and started walking. Two car doors slammed behind her.

"Miss Dupree, wait up," Frank called out to her.

She turned and watched the sheriff hurry up the brick steps and into the coolness of the funeral home. Frank came to her side and offered his arm. His black hair was thick, his gaze touched with worry.

Jade hesitated, then put her hand on his arm and allowed him to help her across the asphalt. His large feet were in no danger of sinking. At the edge of the lot, she turned to him and smiled. "Thank you, Mr. Frank." She wondered why he had come back to Drexel. He'd been a paratrooper during the war. On a secret mission in Germany he'd been captured. The women in the beauty shop talked about him, especially the young ones. They said he was haunted by dreams and visions of the dead, and for a split second, Jade thought she could see torment in the lines around his mouth.

"You're welcome, Miss Dupree, but please call me Frank." He wiped sweat from his forehead. "If you can wait for a ride, the sheriff'll let me take the patrol car."

She was surprised that he treated her like she was white. "Call me Jade," she said. "What's going on?" Her curiosity had been piqued by the sheriff's rush as he strode into the funeral home.

Frank looked beyond her and considered his answer. "I don't want to upset you, but Mr. Bramlett called the sheriff and said his wife's missing. The little girl, too."

Jade felt as if a wire had been inserted into her spine. "Marlena is missing?"

Frank nodded. "I'm sorry. I know you're . . . close. Lucas said Marlena took off with the kid after lunch. She was supposed to go to the church and help sort clothes for the poor. She never showed up, and she's nowhere to be found." His hand grasped her elbow. "You okay?"

"Sure," Jade said, but a nest of wasps was buzzing in her brain. She had never been Marlena's confidante, but it was unlike Marlena to leave without telling her husband where she was going.

"Do you have any idea where Marlena might have gone?" Frank stared into her eyes as if he could read the answer.

Jade hesitated. There was something in his question. "I don't know."

"You baby-sit the little girl sometimes. Folks say she's a difficult child."

Jade was too aware of Frank's hand on her flesh. She thought about the six-year-old girl with braids so long she could sit on them. Folks in town thought she was a brat. In truth, she was, but Jade had a special bond with her. "Folks in Drexel say a lot of things. Suzanna's not so bad if she's treated like a person."

"You care for her," Frank said.

Jade didn't respond. She walked a careful line where Marlena and Suzanna Bramlett were concerned. Her affection was private.

"Marlena's new car is missing, too." Frank wiped his forehead with his hand. "She probably went to visit a friend or took a long drive."

"Sure enough," Jade agreed, though she didn't believe it for a moment. Something was wrong. Terribly wrong. In the back of her nostrils was the smell of burning. A bad omen.

"Are you sure you're okay?" Frank's other hand moved to support her back.

She'd known tragedy hung over the town. Doom. Not Horace Bradshaw but something more, something worse. "I have to get to the shop," she said, remembering the hair dryer and Mrs. Moss's curls. They'd be burned to a frizzy gray crisp. She pulled free of his grasp and walked hurriedly away, worried about her half-sister and niece and unsettled by Frank Kimble and the questions he had not asked.

3

The setting sun struck the two-tone Chevy, glinting in a red metallic gleam that spilled like angry blood onto the sandy road. The car was parked in the ditch. Two men stood beside it, black splinters against the western horizon. Frank Kimble heard the sheriff grunt as he pulled the patrol car into the ditch, like he intended to block the Chevy in case it decided, on its own, to make a getaway.

"Sure enough looks like a scene from hell," Huey said, the folds of his neck hiding most of his collar. He spat tobacco juice out the car window. "Let's see what we got."

Frank watched the sheriff push himself out of the car, spit again, and heft his gun belt from where it had sunk, along with his pants, to halfway down his ass. Looking through the windshield, Frank could now make out the features of the two men standing by the abandoned car. Junior Clements and Pet Wilkinson. Junior's dust-coated pickup still ticked and knocked, showing that he had driven it hard and relentlessly so he could later say that he was the first man on the scene. The scene of what? An abandoned car? Casting an eye on the two men, Frank got out and followed the sheriff.

Pet stood beside Junior, his hand on a holstered pistol. Pet was another wanna-be. He'd been given the ludicrous nickname by his mama, who Frank felt knew what she was doing the first time she'd uttered the one-syllable sobriquet. Pet had no legal authority to carry a gun and no criminal record to keep him from it. It made the skin between Frank's shoulder blades itch when he looked at the gun and Pet's dirty fingers tapping on the cross-grained butt.

"What's in the car?" the sheriff asked Junior, reaching for a door handle.

Frank stepped in front of the sheriff. "Maybe we should see if there are any fingerprints," he suggested. Huey was an elected lawman, not a trained one. The fingerprints were probably futile. More than likely Junior and Pet had touched every inch of the car, taking anything of value left lying around. On every scene where they were present, things went missing. Frank didn't understand why folks continued to vote for

Junior as coroner when everyone knew he was a petty thief. The joke around town was he robbed the gold fillings out of the corpses he transported to the funeral home.

"Run the tag," the sheriff said. "It's Forrest County. Old man Eubanks said the car has been parked here since just after lunch. He didn't see who was in it. He said when he went up to the high field to check his beans, the car wasn't here. Coming back, it was in the road and nobody around it."

Frank walked back to the patrol car and pulled the radio up. He gave the tag number and car make and model to the dispatcher, who would call it in to Forrest County. It would take a little while, but if the tag on the car was valid, they'd know who owned it. It was only a hunch, but he figured this car somehow played into the disappearance of Marlena Bramlett and her daughter. Frank couldn't say why he thought such a thing, but he'd learned to rely on his instincts. He was alive because he did.

"Looks like some clothes hanging in the back." Huey pointed to a suit and five laundered white shirts on hangers suspended from a metal pole in the back seat.

"Yes, sir." Frank nodded. Huey was a master of the obvious. To Frank, the clothes told about the driver of the car. He was male, and he traveled for a living. The driver had a job where he needed to look pressed and clean. Probably a salesman of some sort.

There was the sound of another car bumping over the washboard road. Frank recognized the big Lincoln. He wasn't surprised that Lucas Bramlett had arrived; Huey reported every move he made to Lucas. Frank watched the subtle shift in the postures of the men around him. Huey stepped forward and waited for the car to stop and the tall man to get out from behind the wheel, red dust pooling around the legs of his black suit and his polished black wingtips.

"We're checking it, Mr. Bramlett," Huey said.

"Is my wife here?" Bramlett looked around, his hawklike gaze possessing everything it touched.

"No, sir. Not so we can tell," Huey said, his finger loosening his collar. "We'll find her, Lucas. You've got my word on it."

"You think she's somewhere around here?" Lucas asked, and Frank couldn't tell if he had a better idea where his wife might be.

"We're just checking this here abandoned car. I'm sure Marlena's just fine," Huey said, his jowls going all jolly. "Probably got too far from home and maybe had car trouble or something. We'll hear from her."

"The car is new," Lucas said.

Huey shut up. He looked at Frank. "Find some evidence," he ordered.

Frank had been back in Drexel for two years. When he'd joined the army and gone to Fort Benning, Georgia, to be trained as a paratrooper, he thought never to come back. He'd gotten on the bus, his clothes in a suitcase held together by an old belt, and ridden north. That whole long bus ride through Missisippi and Alabama, he'd never once turned to look at what he was leaving behind. He'd only looked ahead. For the first time in his life he'd seen the soft range of the Smokey Mountains, the bluish mist that clung to them and gave them their name. He'd met other cracker farm boys from other towns just like Drexel. He'd grown hard and tough and learned to kill. He'd picked up the pieces of his friends in brace works and foxholes after the explosion of a mortar shell. In Paris, France, he'd kissed girls who were glad to be alive. He'd done all of those things without ever a thought of going back home to the wet wool summers of Mississippi. Yet here he was, discharged from a hospital where they told him he'd healed from wounds that no one but himself could ever see.

"Frank!"

He turned to look at the sheriff.

"Mr. Bramlett says his wife was wearing a red-and-white blouse and white slacks."

He wondered what he was supposed to do with this information. "Okay."

"Her shoes were sandals with three straps across the top."

"Okay," Frank said, because there was no other response. "I'm going to walk down the road," he said. He had no real goal in walking, but it would get him away from the knot of men who were so busy kowtowing to Lucas they'd forgotten why they were on a little-used road at sunset.

There were indentations in the sand, wallowed out dips that had begun to collect the falling night, but the sand was too soft to hold any useful impression. He followed them for half a mile along the ditch, saw where they crossed the road and disappeared in the thick pinewoods.

He felt a sensation on the back of his neck, like someone breathing on him. He swallowed and stepped into the pine trees. Darkness touched him, a cool promise. He moved deeper into the trees, seeing how the trunks were black against the shafts of slanting golden light. His footsteps were swallowed by the thick layer of pine needles. Once, long ago, the land had been covered with hardwoods. Those trees had been felled and harvested, floated down the area rivers. Pines, trees that matured in thirty years instead of a hundred for an oak, were planted instead. He thought of the saw that hung on his back porch. His grandfather Gustave's double-handled saw, the one he'd used with his brother Alfred when they were young men.

He was still thinking of the saw when he noticed what looked like a white dove. The light in the woods was dim, and he moved closer to the bird. It hovered on the ground, moving gently and making sounds like a low warble.

He stared at it hard and realized it wasn't a bird. It was a foot. He began to run through the underbrush. He heard the moaning then. He angled through the trees so that he saw her body, white hip rising from the bed of pine needles, long legs tapered, breasts floating gently amidst the blood that covered her torso and throat.

She was alive.

Marlena Bramlett's face was beaten beyond recognition. The eyes were swollen shut, the skin purpling and split around her mouth.

"Marlena," he said, kneeling beside her. His hands moved over her cool flesh. She'd been cut on both breasts and sliced from her sternum to her pelvis. The wound didn't appear to be life-threatening, but blood had seeped all over her. There was blood between her legs and all over her thighs, but he couldn't tell the source of it.

"Marlena," he said again.

"No," she said, shaking her head, her blond curls stained with her own blood and particles of dirt.

He scooped her into his arms. She struggled for a moment and then stopped, her head hanging back behind him as he carried her out of the woods.

He walked through the woods for most of a lifetime. He made his way down the road, the burden of the woman making him think each step. In the middle of the road, the men turned, one by one. Frank ignored Huey and Junior and Pet. His gaze was on Lucas Bramlett. Even when Frank was close enough for Bramlett to recognize his wife, he didn't move.

"Good Lord Almighty," Huey said. He rushed to the patrol car and radioed the dispatcher to send an ambulance.

Frank stood with Marlena in his arms. Junior and Pet were openly staring at her, their eyes devouring her nakedness.

"There's an old blanket in the back of the patrol car," Frank said. "Get it." He spoke to Lucas, but it was Pet who jumped to get the blanket, Pet who draped it over the unconscious form of the woman as Frank held her, arms and legs dangling as blood dripped slowly into the thirsty sand of the road.

4

The old Kimble house had once been the showplace of Drexel. Alfred and Gustave Kimble, two brothers who'd emigrated from the economic hardship of a Finland under the thumb of Russia, had used their brawn to build a house of whimsy, a total contrast to their unsmiling faces and compulsion to work from sunup to sundown. The brothers had built the house together, as they did everything. The plan was to marry and bring their brides to the turreted house trimmed with ornate gingerbread and gilt shingles that glowed in the morning sun. To entertain their wives, the brothers constructed hidden staircases and a library filled with classics, biography, and verse. The large kitchen held two stoves, two sinks, and countertops spacious enough to accommodate two cooks. The brothers planned and built, using the timber they felled with their own hands, selecting only the heartwood. By the time the house was finished, the brothers were in their forties. They were handsome men, tall and straight in posture and morality. When they decided to marry, they did so together. Alfred found his bride first, a darkling girl with eyes the color of a winter sky. Her name was Anna. The bride that Gustave found could not have been more opposite. Greta was tall and blond and filled with laughter. They held a double wedding, and the brothers married amidst red roses and white lilies, flowers symbolizing the two brides.

For the first five years the Kimble house was the center of culture in the town. And then Greta got pregnant. Stories began to float around the town that Anna had lost her mind with jealousy. Alfred's wife began to look unkempt, her dark hair, always worn in a shining coronet, hung about her shoulders, unwashed.

Greta began to leave the house early in the morning, walking into town to shop and visit with her friends. She said she was afraid of her sister-in-law, afraid to remain in the house when Gustave was working. There were arguments that ended in tears from the women and blows from the men. By the time twin boys, Thomas and George Kimble, were born, the brothers no longer spoke to each other. The house had been divided. A thin peace was restored, until the morning that Greta and Gustave awoke to find one of their babies missing. Greta and Gustave searched high and low on their side of the house. There was no sign of the baby. The sheriff was called. Baby George was found dead in the arms of his aunt. His neck had been broken.

Gustave lost his mind. He took his pistol and shot his sister-in-law in the heart. Then he turned the gun on his brother, shooting him in the forehead. Gustave, at last, turned the gun on himself, leaving his widow to raise the only heir to the Kimble name. Greta packed her things and the baby and moved to Sumrall, where she had a sister.

The house remained empty for years after that, until Thomas grew old enough to marry and return to Drexel. He brought his new bride to the house where they shut off two thirds of the place and made their life in the first-story rooms. Frank Kimble had been born in the house. He'd grown up there, and it seemed he'd spent his boyhood watching for the true owners of the house to return. His grandfather and great-uncle and -aunt hid in the dark corners of the unused second and third floors. For most of his childhood, the house had terrified him.

After the war, he came back to the house. He was not so easily frightened, and Drexel was his only option.

The old house was dark when Frank pulled into the yard. He walked up the steps, noting, as he did every time he came home, that the porch needed painting. The first summer he'd come home from the war, he'd sanded and painted the entire exterior of the house. He'd taken different shades of green and redone the shake shingles that fronted all of the turrets. He'd painted the gingerbread a gleaming white. Somehow, though, he'd never gotten to the gray boards of the porch.

The interior contained the furniture he'd known as a boy. He entered the front door, letting the screen slam behind him. The sound woke the ghosts. He caught them out of the corner of his eye, the slender form of his great-aunt Anna, the body of an infant in her arms hiding the blood that spread across her chest. He kept walking to the kitchen. He went straight to the sink where he washed his hands, the blood rinsing pink against the white porcelain. An ambulance had transported Marlena to the hospital. She'd been delirious, unable to tell him what had happened to her.

There'd been no sign of the child, Suzanna, or the owner of the Chevy abandoned on the side of the road. But Frank had begun to put a picture together. Someone had nearly killed Marlena and snatched Suzanna. If his hunch was right, there would be a demand for ransom in a few hours.

Marlena was in surgery now. The doctor had said she had severe internal damage. It would be hours before she'd be able to talk, and there was the possibility that she'd never be right in the mind. The doctor had said the blows to her face and head were severe, enough to cause brain damage if there was any swelling inside her head.

Marlena's ruined face was still in his mind when he walked to the parlor and poured whiskey into a cut crystal glass his grandmother Greta had once used for her entertainments. He drank the whiskey fast, then poured another. In the far corner of the room his uncle Alfred stood watching, the bullet hole in the center of his forehead like a third eye. Frank ignored his great-uncle. He carried his drink to the bathroom where he shaved, took a hot bath, and redressed, preparing to go to the hospital.

The hospital was a one-story brick building with a tin walkway over ramped cement where the ambulance parked. The injured were pulled out of the ambulance, the legs of the collapsible stretcher extended, and rolled up the ramp and into the emergency room. Two hard-backed chairs had been placed in the corridor for those waiting on emergency victims or those with a loved one in surgery. Jade sat on one chair, waiting for Lucas Bramlett. After he'd called her to the hospital, he'd disappeared. Marlena was in surgery, struggling to live.

When Lucas reappeared from behind a partition, his gaze found Jade and lingered. "It might be a blessing if she died," he said.

Jade kept her face carefully blank. "What about Suzanna?"

"Marlena never said a word. Whoever attacked her must have taken Suzanna." He sat down and put his elbows on his knees. "They don't know if my wife will ever be able to talk again." He stood up, as if he couldn't bear to relax. "Will you stay with her, Jade?"

"I'll stay tonight," she said.

"No, I mean permanently. She's going to need someone to care for her. She can't even eat. Marlena's been good to you. She —" He stopped abruptly.

"I'll stay tonight. We can think about this tomorrow." Jade felt her bones against the chair. She was tired. She'd worked all day in the beauty shop, then gone to the funeral home and helped Elwood prepare Horace Bradshaw for his funeral. She was just finishing up there when Lucas had appeared, wanting her at the hospital.

"I'll see about a cot," Lucas said.

"They won't give you a cot for me," Jade said. "Make sure there's a chair."

He left her, going to the nurse's desk where he could fire orders at the two middle-aged women in white uniforms. Jade leaned her head against the wall. She had an image in her mind of Marlena on her wedding day. Jade had been hired to help with the wedding. She'd dressed the bridesmaids' hair and helped Marlena twist her long blond curls into a more sophisticated look.

The wedding dress had been a white satin sheath with a long train sewn with tiny crystals that caught the light. The veil floated over Marlena's face, concealing the glint of victory in the bride's smile. Marlena, a seventeen-year-old girl, had caught the most eligible bachelor in Jebediah County, in the whole southeastern corner of the state. Marlena had the two-carat diamond on her finger to prove it, and within the hour, she'd have the band of gold that sealed the marriage. Jade had not talked to Marlena about her prospective husband. She hadn't repeated the stories she'd heard from two black girls who sold their bodies for white men's pleasure. Jade had not told Marlena because she knew Marlena didn't have a choice. Lucas Bramlett had been selected for her to catch. Now she had him, and Lucille Longier, Marlena's mother, could go on with her role as the first lady of Drexel. Lucas's money would buy that for her.

She heard the door of the operating room open, and Dr. Nelson McMillan stepped into the hallway. His expression was grim, his shirt soaked with blood. "Where's Lucas?" he asked.

Jade rose to her feet, the white shoes she'd once valued so highly pinching her toes in a cruel grip. "He was at the nurses' desk." But he was gone. He'd left.

"I have to go home and get some rest," the doctor said. "Tell him I'll be by tomorrow around noon."

"How is she?" She held him with her words. She did not call Marlena her sister — had never said the words aloud. Jade cared about Marlena, and she pitied her. Jade felt a need to protect her, from both Lucas and Lucille. The two people who were supposed to love her most seemed unable to love anyone, and Jade never failed to thank the fates for Jonah and Ruth. "Can I see Marlena?"

The doctor looked at her, something dark bubbling in his tired eyes. "Her injuries are severe. It's a wonder she's alive."

"Will she be all right?"

He considered, that restless look stirring. "I don't know."

"Her little girl. Did she say anything about Suzanna?"

He shook his head. "She hasn't said anything. I don't know if she can. If she's lucky and she does regain consciousness, she won't remember much." His mouth twisted. "The bastards raped her with a pine limb. They tore her cervix and her uterus. She'll never have another child. There's hemorrhaging in the retinas of her eyes. She may be blind. The good news is that the cuts she sustained weren't life-threatening. Of course, it took over two hundred stitches to close her up, but that's minor compared to the rest."

Too angry to remain, the doctor walked away. Halfway down the hall, he threw his mask and surgical hat to the floor.

Jade returned to her chair and was still there when the stretcher bearing Marlena was wheeled out of recovery and pushed down the hall. Jade followed to a private room. No one spoke to her. The nurses arranged the drips, turned on the fluorescent light above the bed, and left.

The hospital room was tinted green, a color that made the blood in Marlena's hair look black and the blond look cheap. The only sound was the shush of Marlena's breathing, the only movement the rise and fall of her chest. Outside the partially opened door, the shoes of nurses squeaked on the waxed linoleum.

Jade moved from the shadows, picking up a white washcloth and filling a basin with water. She wrung the cloth with both hands and gently touched it to Marlena's temples and forehead, working at the crusts of blood. She pushed aside the hospital gown. The black stitches ran in a straight line from her sternum to her pelvis. It looked like someone had tried to gut her. There were more stitches on both breasts, Xs outlined with black stitches.

Jade rewet the cloth and wiped more, thinking that Marlena would no longer wear her black-and-yellow bikini at the summer parties she held at her private swimming pool. A lot of things had changed for Marlena.

5

Early morning light filtered through the yellow curtains of the second-floor bedroom window. A fly buzzed against the screen, its electric green body thumping, demanding entrance. Dotty Strickland turned her face, catching the light full on her cheek. She examined her reflection in the mirror, searching for the faint crinkling of skin at the corner of her eye that would mark the beginning of the end. Satisfied, she put on lipstick and fluffed the curls she'd just taken down from foam curlers. She examined her reflection one last time, thinking that Jade Dupree had been right. Cutting her hair had taken at least five years off her appearance. The golden blond, from a bottle, had been her idea. Dotty ran down the stairs to the kitchen, her bottom lip caught between her teeth.

Heat blasted her face as she pulled the metal casserole pan and a baking sheet of biscuits out of the oven. She put the pan on the top burner, peeled back the tinfoil, and nodded in satisfaction at the perfectly browned crust of cheese. There wasn't a man alive who could refuse her sausage, eggs, grits, and cheese casserole.

She put the hot biscuits in a basket and covered them with a cloth, picked up the pan, and headed to her car, an older model Ford. No traffic was stirring as she drove through the main street of Drexel. Her watch showed half past six. She was right on time.

One hand fluffed her curls as she left Drexel behind and drove two miles down the main highway to the two-story gray house where her best friend Marlena lived. A frown touched Dotty's face. Marlena was in the hospital. She'd been attacked and nearly killed. The talk was all over town, and the details coming out of the hospital were just awful. Someone had raped Marlena with a tree limb. It was just horrible. And they'd cut her. They'd sliced her like a gutted cow.

Dotty forced that image from her mind and concentrated on the task at hand. As Marlena's friend, Dotty was trying to help out by making breakfast for Lucas Bramlett. Lucas wasn't a man who would know his way around a kitchen. He'd been raised with a silver spoon in his mouth. He liked to eat at six-forty-five sharp. Every morning. Marlena had told her that with a roll of her eyes. "Like the whole world will end if he doesn't have hot food in front of his face at six-forty-five."

Dotty had ignored Marlena's sarcasm. Marlena didn't appreciate having a man like Lucas. Dotty was Marlena's best friend, but there were things that Marlena did that were just pure-dee self-destructive, like complaining about making breakfast for the man who kept her in such style and comfort.

She stopped her car in front of the house and got out, admiring the gray paint job with the white trim, green plants, and white wicker lawn furniture on the front porch. It looked like something out of a magazine. Marlena complained all the time about keeping the plants alive. She said they drank more water than a thirsty field hand. The plants made the porch, Dotty could see that. As she walked across the wooden floor she touched the frond of a fern. The plant needed water. She'd be sure to bring some out. With Marlena in the hospital for God knew how long, Dotty decided on the spot that she'd come over and water the plants so they wouldn't die. It was bad enough that

Lucas had to worry about his wife hurt so bad and his little girl taken. He shouldn't have to worry about plants, too.

Her knock was answered by Lucas himself. For all his grief and worry, he was impeccably dressed. "I brought you some breakfast, Lucas," she said, inching the hot pan she held with a baking mitt toward him.

"Dotty," he said, his voice not even surprised, "what a kind thing to do. Come in." He stepped back so she could enter.

Dotty took the hot food to the kitchen, talking over her shoulder as she walked. "Any word on Suzanna?"

"None."

She didn't have to see his face to know that he didn't want to talk about his missing daughter. "Let me fix you a plate. Just take a seat at the table, and I'll serve you. Is there coffee made?" She looked at the untouched percolator. "I'll put some on." She loved working in Marlena's kitchen. Everything was spotless, and there were all the latest appliances to work with. Cooking meals in such a kitchen would be a pleasure, not a chore like Marlena made it sound.

She put water and coffee in the pot and plugged it in. While it was perking she got a china plate and loaded it with a heaping serving of her casserole. She got the fresh butter that Joe Mergenschoer's wife churned every other day and put chunks in two still-hot biscuits. She picked up silverware and a clean linen napkin from the drawer and took it all to the table where Lucas waited.

She put the food in front of him and allowed her hand to flutter over his shoulder, barely registering the feel of the worsted wool suit jacket. "I know this isn't as good as Marlena can make, but I tried."

Lucas laughed. "Marlena does good to scramble an egg without burning it. I didn't marry her for her talent in the kitchen."

Dotty stepped back. Marlena had never discussed her sex life with Lucas. Not because Dotty hadn't tried to lead her that way. In fact, Dotty had often fantasized what it would be like to climb between the sheets with Lucas Bramlett. There was just something about him that made her imagination gallop. He had an air of command, like he'd do whatever he felt like doing. That excited her. She wanted to feel helpless and ravished, forced to climax by a ruthless man. Lucas played a large role in her fantasies as she lay alone in her bed each night.

She realized he was talking to her.

"Jade stayed with Marlena last night. Could you manage to sit with her today? I have work at the real estate office."

"Sure," Dotty said. "I'll do whatever I can to help you. I mean, Marlena's my best friend."

Lucas assessed her as if she'd suddenly spouted the formula for a successful stock buy. After a moment, he said, "I can see you want to be helpful."

She felt the area below her bellybutton tighten, as if the muscles had suddenly bunched into a fist. Under the common words he spoke was another message. "Yes," she answered, her voice breathless. "I want to help."

She could tell that he knew how he was affecting her. His smile was nothing more than the lift of one corner of his mouth.

"Do you really want to help me?" he asked, putting his napkin on his barely touched food.

"Yes." The word was hardly a whisper. She pressed her thighs together beneath the full skirt of her navy dress. She had the strangest idea that he could see up her skirt, see that she'd worn her fanciest panties with the white lace panel that covered the entire front. Her pubic hairs were a triangle of darkness beneath the lace, looking mysterious and feminine.

"Dotty, I know you're Marlena's best

friend," he said, scooting his chair back so he could face her, hands relaxed on the arms of the chair. His expression was mildly curious. "And you want to help me, is that right?"

He was playing with her. She knew that, and she liked it. "Yes," she said, her thighs pressing against the sensation that crept through her lower body. She stood only two feet away from him, unable to move closer or away.

"Take off your clothes," he said. "Lean over the table."

The trees caught Frank's attention first. He stood in the spot where Marlena had been found. He knew it was the exact spot because he found darkened earth where her blood had pooled. Had he not had the mental picture of her bloody body, he would have found the place beautiful. Old oak trees, limbs draping to the ground, created a circle. The morning sun slanted through the mossy limbs and gave it the look of a place where an ancient ritual might have been held, some Druid rite, he thought.

There was no sign of the Cadillac, but there was evidence that Marlena had stumbled through the underbrush until she'd fallen, unable to go farther. As he began to examine the ground more closely, he found traces of the story he sought. Her footprints led back to the river. Marlena had come up from the water, her right foot dragging slightly as she stumbled along.

He read the trail in the pine needles and thought about Totem Joe, a wind talker in the 101st Airborne, a unit that took heavy casualties during the war. Joe had been only a kid, a boy of eighteen whose real name was Joseph Longfeather. Totem Joe had been a nickname, one given in spite and accepted in friendship. Joe had taught Frank the art of tracking. Frank could still hear his soft voice with the rustle of cottonwood trees in it. "The earth tells many stories, if a man is patient enough and observant enough to read them." Frank had decided that he would be such a man. Even though he was five years older, Frank had become a student of Joseph Longfeather. The two of them had done a good bit of tracking in the war. Joe had used his strange pecks and taps to send information he'd observed back to army headquarters. Totem Joe had saved a lot of lives, but not his own. Joe had been hit by shrapnel. Frank looked up and saw Joe partially hidden by one of the old oaks. He stepped forward, his hands holding his stomach where the shrapnel had cut him wide open. Blood and pink tissue peeked from beneath his fingers.

Leaving Joe behind, Frank followed Marlena's trail to the sandy bank of the river. Her footsteps had left hollow indentions in the sand and finally disappeared in the brown current of the Chickasawhay. She'd come from up river, he could tell that by the angle of her footsteps as she came out of the water. She was trying to make her way east, toward Drexel, maybe. Or maybe toward the Chevy car, which he'd learned was registered to one John Hubbard. That was a long leap, but so far, no one had come forward to claim the car, and in Frank's experience, folks didn't just up and lose a mostly new Chevy on the side of a little-used dirt road. Marlena's attack, the abduction of the girl, and the car were all tied together.

Thinking about the Chevy sent his thoughts to the Cadillac convertible. Lucas hadn't said a word about the missing car. Of course, Lucas hadn't been around to make statements of any kind, and the sheriff had ordered Frank not to go to the Bramlett house. On the two trips that Frank had made to the hospital yesterday evening and early this morning, he'd seen only Jade in the room. One time Jade had been sleeping while she sat in a chair, her head tipped back against the wall. The last time she'd been wiping Marlena's face with a cool cloth. Even from the doorway Frank could tell that Marlena was not awake. He'd left without talking to either woman. He thought about that, about how he felt in the presence of Jade Dupree and her half-sister Marlena Bramlett.

The resemblance shared by the two women was uncanny, more a type of glow than a physical trait. One was lemon sherbet and the other burnished like pale wood. He couldn't say which one was the more beautiful. That would be like trying to say what tasted better, steak or fried chicken. Jade was the older by two years, but it seemed to make no difference. They both had large eyes, one had a blue set and the other that impenetrable green. They were both slender, with graceful arms and hands and pretty legs. Marlena was blond, a pale ash shade that said money. Jade's short hair was a cluster of brunette curls. He thought of the story *Black Beauty* when he looked at the two of them. It didn't make much sense, but he always thought of Beauty and the other horse, Ginger. Inseparable, and when they were parted, one died. The women were like elegant horses of two different colors, but both thoroughbreds who could go the distance.

They lived within four miles of each other, yet Marlena had never been allowed to acknowledge her half-sister. Jade had been in the Bramlett house, but as a servant. She'd baby-sat the girl, Suzanna, and cooked for special events, and done Marlena's hair. Almost like real sisters, but Jade had been paid for these services. That fact was well known in town. Lucille had made sure of it.

The unacknowledged kinship between the women was another indication of the power that Lucas, and through him Lucille, held over the town. Lucille Sellers Longier had slept with a black man, had borne him a child, yet folks pretended it never happened. With Jade standing right in front of them looking like a dark shadow of Marlena, they pretended she belonged to Jonah and Ruth. It was downright amazing.

Frank stepped into the deliciously cold water of the river, moving slowly so he could examine the bank. Once he found Marlena's entry point, he'd be close to finding the scene of the abduction and attack.

As he moved upriver, his thoughts remained on Jade. He still had to wonder how Lucille had pulled off having the baby of a

Negro and not been run out of town on a rail. The only thing he could figure was that folks were busy trying to survive the Depression. He moved steadily against the current, his gaze on the riverbank, his mind on the past. The 1920s had been hard for everyone, especially those who made their living from timber. Bad storms had leveled vast tracts of pines, wrecking the timber industry. Lucille's family had not suffered, though. They'd hosted big parties with music and liquor. The way he heard it was that Lucille had taken to carrying on with a café au lait trumpet player from New Orleans. She got pregnant, and when she began to show, her folks sent her away, saying she'd gone to the Meridian School for Young Ladies. Before she came back, though, an infant girl appeared in the home of Jonah and Ruth Dupree, a childless black couple who worked for the Sellerses, and then later the Longiers.

Most folks had put two and two together, but nothing was ever said in public. Lucille, properly subdued by her experience, married Jacques Longier, a newly arrived Frenchman who hadn't had time to hear the seamier rumors of the town, or maybe heard them and didn't care because the Sellerses were wealthy and Lucille their only

66

child. In truth, Jacques had been a poor businessman and a worse gambler. But Marlena was born during the second year of the marriage, thereby sealing the bargain.

Frank had traveled several miles upstream when he noticed several ferns had been uprooted on the bank. He waded over to make a closer inspection. Something had been dragged over the lip of the small bank. He moved a few leaves with a pencil. There was a dark stain in the sand. Blood. Using a tree limb he pulled himself up the bank, stopping when he found a cane pole thrown into the shrubs beside the river. He didn't touch it, hoping he could lift some prints. His heart rate increased. He was closing in on the place where everything had gone wrong for Marlena and Suzanna. He was glad he was alone.

6

For a long time the hospital room had been quiet. Dawn had crept through the blinds on a window that gave a view of a patch of brown grass and two old water oaks, leaves hanging listlessly in the heat. Jade had watched the sunrise, finally turning to stare at the woman so still in the hospital bed. Marlena's profile seemed to drink the morning light, glowing softly in the semidarkness of the room. The drip had given out after midnight, and a nurse had come to replace the bottle, the tiny bubbles chasing up like silver beads at a rate of thirty-seven a minute. Jade had counted the bubbles, periodically making sure that the pace was steady. She imagined that each tiny drop sent more strength into Marlena, more will to fight. Her imagination, though, wasn't quite strong enough to banish the comparison of the drip to the gravity bottles that pushed embalming fluid into the dead, preserving them against decay.

When the nurse came into the room, Jade had asked what was in the drip, but the nurse hadn't answered her. She'd lifted her nose only half an inch, but enough to tell Jade she was beneath an answer. She might look white, but she was just a pale nigger.

After the nurse left, Frank visited. Jade had pretended not to see him as she wiped Marlena's face, but she'd seen him. She'd caught his outline in the doorway and knew exactly who it was just by the way he stood. He'd assessed the scene and then left. He had questions and Jade had no answers. Marlena hadn't told her anything. She'd slept all night, moaning on occasion, but never uttering a single comprehensible word.

Jade turned to adjust the blinds, and in the window's reflection she saw Marlena shift. A frown moved across Marlena's face. She said something so softly that Jade leaned forward, her head cocked so that her ear was only inches from Marlena's lips.

"Help me," Marlena said.

Jade felt a sweep of relief. She'd watched Marlena throughout the night and wondered if she'd be able to talk, or even if she'd live. She'd imagined that Marlena's blond beauty had begun to cool and decay, so that in a few days she would be at Ride-out Funeral Home and Jade would put the last lipstick on her rubbery lips.

"I'm here," Jade said. She watched the eyelids flutter and then open. Marlena looked at her without recognition. "It's me, Jade," she whispered.

"Suzanna." Marlena said the word as if she wasn't certain what it meant. "Suzanna." She said it again, this time with more emphasis.

"It's okay," Jade said, pulling the call bell from beneath the pillow and pressing it hard. Marlena had the look of someone waking from a nightmare yet still caught in fear.

Marlena looked around the room, now lit by the morning sun. She started to sit up but cried out in pain and sank back against the pillows. "Su-zan-na!" She shouted the word, each syllable with equal emphasis.

Jade put her hands on Marlena's arms. "It's okay," she said again, pressing hard to hold Marlena still. "You have to be careful. You've been hurt."

Marlena stared at her without recognition. "Suzanna," she said, and Jade began to fear that she didn't really know that Suzanna was her daughter, that the name had simply become the only word Marlena could utter.

"Suzanna," Jade said back to her.

"Taken," Marlena sighed, and then she began to cry.

The black Cadillac was hidden behind a thick wall of huckleberry bushes. Frank found it without difficulty. He'd followed signs of a struggle on the riverbank until he came upon a pair of brand-new Keds. They were sized for a child, not an adult. He studied the ground, the knocked-over can of worms, the fishing pole cast into the bushes by the side of the river, the pine straw and scrub oak leaves scuffled in places. The marks in the ground told a distinct story. Suzanna had been fishing when someone came up behind her and grabbed her.

About fifty feet from the scene of the abduction he found a place where something had crushed the delicate wild ferns that grew in sandy soil. The area was about the size of a child. He could assume that Suzanna had been subdued in some manner and left on that spot, perhaps while the attacker went after Marlena, or went to join his cohort, if there were two. But what was Marlena doing that a man, or two men, could sneak up on her? The last anyone heard from Marlena, she'd told Lucas she was going to the church to help sort clothes for the poor. She'd never put in an appearance. There was something wrong with the story.

He began to walk a circle around the area. He moved slowly, taking his time, thinking once again how glad he was that he was alone. Huey would bring tracking dogs in another hour and destroy any chance of finding clues. Huey was a man of action. He wasn't smart, but he was smart enough to know that to the voters, action looked like he was doing something. Long ago, Frank had learned that small actions often counted most.

Briars gripped the laces of his shoes, and he stepped carefully out of their clinging embrace. He moved around the Cadillac until he came to the picnic cloth. He surveyed the scene from a distance of fifteen feet. Ants had taken over the food, but he could see the ruin of chicken salad sandwiches, a jug of tea, dark at the bottom and clear at the top with lemon slices floating. A swarm of yellow jackets made a bowl of potato salad look alive. Beside the sandwiches was a wicker basket. Moving carefully, he walked to it and nudged it open with his toe. Three plates and forks were inside. The number was troubling.

The picnic cloth was crumpled, and when he knelt down to look more closely he saw the blood. It sprayed in tiny drops across the lower corner of the cloth. There were other stains, too. Sex and blood. The story he read from the picnic scene didn't jive with anything he'd been able to put together.

He broadened his circle, looking for anything. About twenty feet from the picnic cloth he found six bags of Big Sun potato chips. He picked up a stick and moved three of the bags, thinking of the Chevy abandoned on the road. Forrest County had reported back. John Hubbard, the registered owner of the Chevy, was a traveling salesman for Big Sun, a company that stocked small rural stores in Mississippi with chips and candy bars, beef jerky and pork rinds. Frank pulled a paper sack from his back pocket and scooped up the chips, setting them aside on the picnic cloth. He began his search again, this time faster because he was looking for something larger. A body.

The house was set back off the road a little piece, enough to keep the chickens that persisted in getting out of the pen safe from the occasional car. Once the house had belonged to Emma Grey, but she'd passed on, and Miss Lucille had bought it after her daughter married into the Bramlett money. Not that it was the most expensive house in town, but it did sit on a hill and caught the infrequent summer breezes. No, it wasn't a real expensive house, but there was just something about it. Jonah Dupree knew that if he could have his pick of all the houses in the world, it would be this one.

He waded through a dozen Rhode Island reds as he went to the porch. He'd worn his best suit, the pants pressed so many times the crease was shiny like a blade. Miss Lucille had sent word that he was to drive her to the hospital today.

He'd heard the talk about what happened to Miss Marlena, and his heart was sorely troubled. Marlena had never hurt a living soul, as far as he knew, excepting maybe herself. On the day of her wedding to Lucas Bramlett, Marlena had stepped off the edge of a cliff. Pouring drinks for all the teetotalers in town, Jonah had watched the couple say their vows in the outdoor garden of the house Lucas had already bought and decorated. His bride was the finishing touch to the décor, her blond looks the perfect complement to the life Lucas had so carefully designed. Jonah had stood in his starched shirt and black bow tie and watched Lucas slip a gold ring on Marlena's trembling hand, and Jonah had felt that an inevitable tragedy had been set in motion. Marlena looked more dazed than happy, and he understood why. Lucas Bramlett had been an ambition, like a college degree or a certain job. Marlena had got him. Now she would have to be his wife, and she wasn't prepared for what that meant. That had been sixteen years ago. Marlena had been married to Lucas for almost half as long as she'd been alive.

Jonah blinked the past out of his eyes and was frowning when he went around the porch that circled three sides of the house and knocked at the side door by the kitchen. Miss Lucille would be there, having her coffee and toast. He saw his wife, Ruth, at the stove, the dripolator in her hand. She poured a steady stream into the cup in front of Lucille, but her gaze was on Jonah.

"Press my teal dress," Lucille said to Ruth, her voice sloppy at the end of the sentence.

Jonah stood at the screen door, waiting until the currents of the room were established. If Miss Lucille had been drinking, things would be a lot different than he'd imagined as he came up the road from Drexel.

"Yes, ma'am," Ruth said in her Sunday voice.

Jonah didn't know what to make of that. Ruth hated Miss Lucille with a pure flame. For thirty-seven years, though, she'd never missed a day of work. She came and she cooked, cleaned, and tended the woman's needs. She listened to her talk and her bragging. Not once, in all that time, had Ruth ever let on how she really felt. Jonah considered that and realized there were things about his wife that frightened him.

He'd worked for Lucille Sellers Longier for nearly forty years. Had, in fact, met his wife at Miss Bedelia Sellerses' Christmas party in 1915, back when her pale gold daughter's dream of catching a rich man had not yet been tainted by her actions. As it was, in 1918, Lucille had married Jacques Longier, a man forty-two years her senior. A foreigner, Longier hadn't cared that Lucille had a scandalous past. He'd married Lucille, taken over control of the Sellerses' money, and bought the town's silence with total ruthlessness.

Old Lizzie Tolbert had found out the price of a loose tongue. She'd made it a point to call Lucille a slut and a nigger-lover. Two days later, the Tolbert house burned to the ground. Lizzie's son had died in the flame.

The Tolberts left Drexel. Jacques bought the Tolbert homestead and donated the property to the Mt. Pleasant Baptist Church, a black congregation.

That lesson had never had to be repeated. Folks began to focus on who Lucille was now, not what she'd been in the past.

In a strange way, Jacques had been Jonah's benefactor. The Frenchman had come on the scene shortly after Lucille had gotten herself in trouble. Had Lucille wanted to raise the baby girl who was the product of her penchant for drink and a black jazz man, she would have lost Jacques. So Jade — a gift worth any amount of suffering — had been given to him and Ruth, and Lucille's honor had been restored.

Jonah felt his wife's hot glare on him, and he watched as she left the kitchen, going to iron, as Miss Lucille had directed her. Jonah tapped on the screen door. "Miss Lucille, I'm here to drive you whenever you're ready."

"Come in, Jonah," she said, her back still to the door.

He stepped into the coolness of the house, amazed anew at how this one house seemed to keep out the August heat. He stopped halfway across the kitchen, not knowing exactly where he should go.

"Sit down," Lucille said, waving at the chair across from her. She had her makeup on and her hair fixed, but she was still in her turquoise dressing gown. She'd always favored bright colors. Her lipstick was bright, too, a contrast to her pale skin, which sagged around her jawline.

Jonah felt apprehension seep into his bones. Lucille was not a woman who asked her hired help to sit at the table with her.

"Pour yourself a cup of coffee," she said.

He made no move to get a cup. "What time you want to go to the hospital?" he asked. "I could work on the scuppernong arbor until you're ready to go."

"Sit down," she said.

He eased into the chair, his hands on his thighs. He looked into her eyes, the blue of a morning sky. His heart was beating too fast, and he tried to find something of the past in her intense gaze. It was gone, though, just as the fresh beauty that had once held him spellbound was gone. Miss Marlena had captured that beauty, and he wondered for the first time if Lucille hated her own daughter.

"How long have you been working for me, Jonah?" she asked.

"Close on to forty years," he said, knowing that there was something behind the question. Miss Lucille had become an expert at making layers of things.

"And Ruth, how long for her?"

"Thirty-seven years." Jonah decided to say what he knew. Not even Miss Lucille could change a fact.

"How is Jade?"

The abrupt change in the subject alarmed Jonah. In all the years that Jade had lived with them, Miss Lucille had never asked about Jade's well-being. Other than to say do this or do that, he didn't think Jade's name had ever passed Lucille's lips.

"She's doing just fine." That was enough. Just an answer, no details.

"Lucas called me this morning. He wants Jade to stay with Marlena. On a permanent basis."

There it was. The daughter Miss Lucille had kept needed care. "Jade's got a business to run." It wasn't really an answer, just a statement of fact.

He saw the subtle shift in Lucille's expression, more a tightening of the flesh around the eyes. "It would put Jade in a good light to help Lucas out."

Jonah saw the way she was going to play it. Not an outright order, but a subtle application of pressure. She'd learned that from her first husband. Old Jacques had been an expert at such tactics. Jonah shrugged. "That's up to Jade. She's plenty grown."

Ruth came back into the room with the freshly ironed dress hanging from a wire hanger. She stopped so abruptly the dress swung on the hanger like a gust of wind had entered the room. "What's up to Jade?"

Jonah kept his eyes fixed on Lucille. "They want Jade to sit with Miss Marlena while she heals."

"Jade has a business to run." Ruth's tone said that was the end of it.

"Folks tend to do better in business when they have Lucas Bramlett behind them." Lucille's hands had pulled into fists so tight the big ruby ring she wore seemed to glow against her white skin. "She should be happy to tend to Marlena."

"We're all real sorry about what's happened. Jade is fond of Suzanna, and Miss Marlena, too." Ruth hung the dress on the molding over the door. "I'm sure Jade will do what she can when she isn't working." She smoothed the hem of the dress, focusing on the teal material. "I think I'm coming down with something, Miss Lucille. I'm gone go home and rest up. Might be I can help some with Marlena if it turns necessary."

Ruth walked across the kitchen and out the side door. There was the sound of her too-big shoes clapping on the porch boards, and then she was gone.

Jonah thought about offering to give his wife a ride, but he knew it was best to let Ruth walk, even if she felt bad. Ruth wouldn't want to be in the car with Miss Lucille, and Jonah surely wouldn't get the car unless its owner was riding with him. He thought he heard his wife's footsteps in the dirt, and then there was only the sound of Miss Lucille's breath. He tried not to hear it, tried not to remember another time when her breath had come all rushed and fast. She'd been different then, and it had almost ruined her.

"I would have thought Ruth would be more concerned about Marlena," Lucille said, anger in her voice.

Jonah thought about the last forty years. Lucille had not been bad to work for. She was demanding, and sometimes so self-involved as to be comical. But she'd given him something that was more valuable to him than his own life. For that, he would always owe her. "Ruth is worried, Miss Lucille. She's worried about your daughter and her own."

There it was, just out in the open. He held

steady, forcing his gaze to meet hers. She lifted a hand as if she intended to strike him. There had been some of that, too, in the past. He saw she remembered it and lowered her hand.

"How dare you speak to me in that way," she managed.

"The day you gave Jade to us, Ruth and I knew there would never be a way we could repay you. We've tried, through the years, to show our gratitude. Ruth has never missed a day of work. I've missed two, when I hurt my hand in the car motor. But the hard truth is, you never wanted Jade. Never. Neither did her daddy. He was on the road and gone before you could tell him you were in trouble. Ruth and I were more than glad to take that precious baby girl and raise her. What I'm getting to is that Ruth don't owe you anything. Neither does Jade."

Jonah saw the shift in her eyes. "I've paid you for every day you've worked. And Jade, too. Everything she's ever done for Marlena and Suzanna, she's been paid for." Lucille's voice quivered.

"Because that's how you wanted it."

"I can't believe this conversation. I've never known such ingrates. I can't remember a time when I've been more shocked."

"I'll tell you what I remember. I remember

a time before Jacques Longier."

The shock of his words caused her to inhale sharply. "I should fire you."

At last he understood. "Yes, ma'am, you probably should." But she wouldn't. He finally had hold of the truth of it. She kept him because he reminded her of the past. He'd thought for so long that she hated the past, but now he saw that she didn't.

"You gave me your daughter," he said quietly, "and then I gave her to herself. What Jade does is her choice. And that's the way it's going to be."

He got up from the table and walked out the screen door. When the door slammed behind him, he turned back. "I'll be getting the car ready for when you want to go to the hospital to see Miss Marlena."

7

The sun was halfway up the sky by the time Jade got to Hollywood Styles. Dotty Strickland had been nearly two hours late in arriving at the hospital, and Jade hadn't even had time to go home and take a bath. She parked her secondhand Hudson, bought in Mobile from the only colored car lot in the southeastern part of the state, and walked to the front door of her shop. The sign in the window, a bright pink, was the only neon in Drexel. The first word was block letters, like the ones on the hillside in Los Angeles, while Styles was cursive, fast and sleek. The sign had been crafted by a glass worker in Gulfport and was Jade's biggest extravagance. It had paid for itself nine times over. Drexel was as far removed from Hollywood as it was New York City, but the women of the small town craved cosmopolitanism. They wanted to look glamorous, or at least elegant, while retaining the privilege of provincialism. The sign allowed them to bask in the idea of Hollywood without keeping company with the actors and actresses they viewed as deviants and moral degenerates.

Jade unlocked the door of her shop and stepped inside. Large photographs of Veronica Lake, Marilyn Monroe, Joan Crawford, Grace Kelly, Bette Davis, Deborah Kerr, Joan Fontaine, and the most popular, Vivien Leigh, hung around the large room. Jade had written the various movie studios and asked for the poster-sized black-and-white photos of the stars. No one in town could figure how she'd gotten them, and it gave the beauty shop another little boost of exclusivity.

From a picture in a magazine, Jade had gotten the idea for the black sinks and fixtures, the black-and-white tiled floor. In Drexel, the decor was thought of as deliciously avant-garde. Titillation was a large draw in a population that believed pleasure to be a trap of Satan.

Jade had long ago given up thinking about the perversity of her clientele. Women who considered her a social inferior begged for hair appointments, and within the confines of the shop, she was their superior. They deferred to her judgment and taste. Jade had come to believe that she was lucky. There had been no mirror of society to reflect her image, so she'd learned at a young age to see herself. The women whose hair she cut and styled had no clear picture of themselves. They depended on others to tell them who they were and what they should look like. The movies shaped their view of glamour; men defined their sexuality and their roles as wives and mothers. Having lived outside society, in a world where she was neither black nor white, Jade had developed a unique sense of style that took into account only the shape of her own face, her skin, her hair, and her eyes.

She worked alone in the shop because no white woman would work for her, and her clients wouldn't allow a "real" Negro woman to touch their hair. Jade was an anomaly. Her talent wasn't necessarily styling hair or choosing cosmetics, though she was good at that, it was being able to see another's fantasy and then bridge the gap between that and the reality of what she had to work with. Women who snubbed her in public left her shop feeling that she'd touched them with magic. Two of her clients were women who drove the forty miles from Mobile once a week for a cut and style. Jade long ago accepted that vanity was stronger than prejudice. This knowledge was just one of the many reasons that she remained in Drexel against her parents' wishes. It wasn't that Ruth and Jonah didn't love her. Her adopted parents had given her every ounce of love they had, to the point that there was nothing left to give each other. She recognized that in many ways, she was the spoke that kept the wheel of their marriage rolling, just as she was the counterweight that gave balance to Suzanna Bramlett's life.

She thought of the little girl and felt dread squeeze down so hard that she leaned against the back of a chair for support. To most folks, Suzanna was an ill-behaved and spoiled child. They saw her as the daughter of the wealthiest man in town, with a doting mother who gave into the child's every whim. They had no real idea of Suzanna's life. The young girl was a ghost in her own house. She flitted from room to room, maybe breaking something valuable or banging on the piano, or screaming and kicking. She did that because no one saw her. Lucas and Marlena looked right through her. Jade understood, probably better than most, what that felt like.

Jade pulled down the penciled note that Jonah had taped to the glass, proud of her father's penmanship, his neat letters and proper grammar. "Jade is at the hospital," was all the note said. She went to the appointment book and made a list of the women she'd have to call and apologize to. Her clients were mighty particular about their hair appointments. There would be tears, perhaps ugliness. Dependency often created anger. She read down the list of appointments. Coming in at ten-thirty was Betsy McBane. Jade sighed, blowing the breath up so that her soft bangs lifted for a moment. She thought about putting the note back up, locking the door, and hiding until Mrs. McBane left. She didn't, though.

The chemical odor of perms was overpowering. Jade opened the windows and the back door, hoping a cross current would pull the smell into the street. She had a full day, one appointment after the next without even a lunch break, and she was bone tired. It was better to stay busy, though. That might keep the worry about Suzanna at bay, at least enough for her to get through until she heard something from Frank. Once he knew something for positive, he'd come and tell her. Frank might not understand her affection for Suzanna, but he knew it was there. He'd tell her what he knew, even if Marlena's husband wouldn't remember to.

Thinking about Lucas was a waste of good

energy. Jade had never shown the discomfort he made her feel. She was afraid if she did, he wouldn't allow her to baby-sit Suzanna. Lucas had never done a single thing to make Jade uneasy, but she felt his gaze on her when her back was turned, and there was strong emotion in it. What upset Jade the most was that she recognized her likeness to Lucas Bramlett. He lived as he chose, because he was strong enough to do so. Most folks thought it was money that gave Lucas his power, but Jade knew differently. The money was part of it, but mostly it came from his character. Like her, he was outside the bounds of society.

Lucas never hesitated to call Jade when he wanted someone to keep Suzanna for an afternoon, or an evening, or a weekend, or a three-week cruise. Would he bother to tell her if there was a ransom demand? She doubted it, but Huey Jones couldn't keep his mouth shut to save his life. If there was a ransom demand, it would be all over town.

It occurred to Jade that Lucas wouldn't pay for something he didn't value, and she felt a surge of desperation. Public opinion would force him to pay the ransom, though. He was outside society, but not inured to it. That thought brought a bit of comfort, even when she knew that Lucas had never shown the first glimmer of joy at his daughter. Not at her birth and not at her first step. Not when she did well in school or excelled at the piano. Nothing the little girl did could capture his praise or pleasure. Sadness like a weight pressed on Jade's chest. Folks were always making the comment that she could do better in a big city. Even Ruth had joined in that refrain. Ruth wanted her to marry and have babies. In Drexel, she was too white for the black men and too black for the white. In a place like New Orleans, she could have her pick of either.

The front door of the shop was open for ventilation, and Jade was busy with her call list when Mrs. McBane walked in. She strode to the counter where Jade sat.

"You missed five appointments this morning." She set her black patent leather handbag with the gold clasp on the counter with force.

"Yes, ma'am, I know." Jade put the pencil down. She reached for the telephone. "If you'll have a seat, I need to call one more person."

"It's ten-thirty."

Jade looked at the clock on the wall. "It's ten-twenty-three. I just need to make this call."

Mrs. McBane didn't move. "What's Marlena Bramlett to you, anyway?"

Jade knew perfectly well that Betsy McBane knew they were half-sisters. She wasn't asking about a blood relationship; she was asking about something else, something that involved Jade's right to care what happened to Marlena and her daughter.

"I'm fond of Suzanna," Jade said. "I may be the only person who is."

"She's a brat. I'll bet if someone did take her, they'll pay Lucas good money to take her back."

Jade felt an unfamiliar flash of anger. She was so used to her clients that she seldom took anything they said to heart. She picked up the phone and began to dial.

She completed the call with Betsy McBane standing over her. She put the phone down and stood up. "What would you like today, Mrs. McBane?" she asked, pointedly looking at the clock, which showed ten-thirty.

Betsy took a seat in the beauty chair, Jade standing behind her. "Something special. I want to look good in case there's a funeral." Her smile was tight as she looked into the mirror and into Jade's eyes. "If that little girl is dead, do you think you'll work on her at the funeral home? I hear you did a fine job on Horace Bradshaw." Her gaze in the mirror was eager.

The idea of Suzanna, dead, made Jade step back.

"I'm sorry, Jade. That was thoughtless of me." Betsy held Jade's gaze.

"What makes you think Suzanna is dead?" Jade asked, not bothering to wonder if it was thoughtlessness or the opposite.

"I happened by the hospital this morning. You know, Marlena is just the darling of the town, and I wanted to see how she was doing. Your father was waiting outside at the car, and he told me Lucille was terrified her granddaughter was dead. He looked right sick himself."

"Did you see Marlena?" Jade wondered if she'd come around and begun to talk. After the incident where Marlena had called her daughter's name and tossed on the bed, the nurse had administered more morphine. Marlena hadn't said anything helpful. At least not while Jade was there.

"No. Those fool doctors won't allow anyone but family members." She watched the mirror as Jade picked up lank strands of brown hair and held them out. "Do you have an idea for a new style?"

"What about something Olivia de Haviland-ish?" Jade asked.

Disappointment crossed Betsy's face. "Isn't she sort of a secondary character?"

Jade kept her face serious. "She was the one who got Ashley Wilkes, after all."

Betsy brightened. "That's right."

Jade set to work. Once she started concentrating, she could shut out the sound of Betsy's voice. All she had to do was nod and make an occasional sound of agreement. Betsy did the rest. In a few moments, Betsy would be under the dryer.

"Huey's gone up to Quincy to get some tracking dogs," Betsy said. "He's probably in the woods right now with them."

That caught Jade's attention. So they were looking for Suzanna. "Uh-hum," she said, hoping to encourage Betsy more.

"Huey said those dogs can pick up a trail that's three days old and follow it through water."

"Uh-hum." She started cutting.

"They didn't call the FBI in yet. They said they have to be able to prove that Suzanna was carried across a state line for it to be a federal matter."

"How will they know whether she's across a state line or not?" Jade asked.

Betsy shrugged. "I personally think Huey wants all the credit. Frank Kimble was out at the crack of dawn. Heck, it's a good thing Frank's on the case. Huey couldn't find his way out of a paper sack."

Jade realized that Betsy was staring into the mirror, watching her expression. "Frank's a good detective," she said.

"Yes, he is. And a handsome man," Betsy prompted. When Jade didn't respond, she continued. "You sat with Marlena all night. What all happened to her? I've heard the most terrible things. That she'll never be able to have a baby again. Is it true?"

Jade cut faster, knowing that her only salvation would be the dryer.

The two hounds lunged on their leather leashes, pulling Nathan Ryan forward a step at a time. He held them, the corded muscles in his arms showing the strain as he waited on Huey to give the word to turn the dogs loose on Marlena's trail in the hopes that it would lead to Suzanna. Frank knew the trail was empty. He'd backtracked it from the point where he'd recovered Marlena, up the river, and finally to the place where he'd found the Cadillac. Now he waited for Huey to make a decision. The sheriff had shown up with Ryan, the dogs, and five volunteers, among them Junior Clements and Pet Wilkinson. Several of the volunteers stood smoking under one of the oaks.

If they found Suzanna Bramlett, Huey would have money to run his campaign for sheriff for the rest of his life. Frank could almost see the dollar signs in Huey's eyes as he pointed down the trail and talked to Ryan.

"The dogs'll be trailin' Marlena," Huey repeated what Frank had told him. He waved Frank over. "The little girl could be anywhere in these woods. What we're hoping is that Marlena's trail will bring us to Suzanna. Should we show the blouse to the dogs?"

Lucas had dropped one of Marlena's blouses by the sheriff's office, an unnecessary gesture because the dogs would strike a trail where they found it. But it was also a telling gesture, and one that made Frank consider what Lucas Bramlett truly hoped the outcome of the search would be.

The blouse was navy blue with a sailor collar and white tie, expensive. Marlena had worn it at the Fourth of July picnic. Now it was lying on the front seat of the patrol car. The vague scent of a light perfume still clung to the cotton fabric and filled the car with a whisper of Marlena.

"The dogs don't need the blouse," Frank said. Twenty yards away, the two bloodhounds were desperate to follow the scent. They lunged and bayed, acting as if the quarry they sought was in immediate danger.

"Frank?" Huey said.

Frank nodded. "Let them go."

Ryan allowed the dogs to drag him forward at a fast jog, their noses to the ground and tails pointed out behind them. Huey and the volunteers took off in pursuit. The sheriff looked over his shoulder. "Frank, are you coming?"

"There's something here I want to look at," Frank said. He nodded reassuringly. "I'll be along directly." Frank did not mention the chips, not in front of Junior and Pet and the other volunteers. He would tell the sheriff later, when they were alone. Aside from the chips, Frank had found something else, a different trail, one that led to the south. This was a trail Frank wanted to follow on his own.

The array of chips wasn't proof, but they had led his thoughts to a certain conclusion. The second trail belonged, he believed, to the third member of Marlena's picnic and the owner of the Chevy that had been towed to a Drexel garage. John Hubbard. If his assumptions were correct, Frank had to try and understand why Hubbard had run in a different direction than Marlena.

In his methodical investigation, Frank had

found some interesting facts about the Big Sun salesman. He'd been arrested once in Hattiesburg for drunk and disorderly involving a bar fight. He'd pled guilty and paid a fine. He lived at 2121 Kenner Street off West Fourth in a modest shingle house with a one-car garage. Lieutenant Lloyd Hafner of the Hattiesburg P.D. had been very helpful. The Hattiesburg officer had done a little digging and found out that Hubbard was a single man who lived alone. He drove a two-tone green Chevy. His neighbors said he was quiet and gone a lot. He spent a lot of time polishing his car, and for a single man he led a solitary life. He hadn't been home for the past few days.

John Hubbard was missing in action with Big Sun. Frank had spoken to an irritable man whom he visualized pulling a beard as he talked. The Big Sun manager had told Frank that Johnny, as he called him, had covered a route for another salesman during the first of the week, and that he'd taken up his regular route to New Augusta, Beaumont, McLain, Lucedale, State Line, Leakesville, and Drexel. John Hubbard should have reported in Thursday afternoon. He had not.

Frank moved slowly, carefully along the trail. Whoever had gone this way had been in a hurry. Leaves were stripped from limbs and there were places where a shoe heel had dug deep into the soft ground. He came upon a footprint and knew he had the best evidence of the case so far. What troubled him was that he couldn't even form a supposition as to why John Hubbard, if this was indeed his trail, had run in a different direction from Marlena. Why hadn't he gone to help her? And why had Suzanna left no trail?

Frank considered the possibility that he was following the trail of Suzanna's abductor, and that he had carried the child in his arms, but Frank didn't think so. This way led to the river and the swamps. Someone carrying a child would have gone to the road to be picked up in a vehicle. That assumption was based on an abductor who wanted to keep Suzanna alive. If John Hubbard had killed the child, or if she'd been taken by some deviant, some sick pervert who had other plans for the child. . . . He stopped that thought before it could go further. There was sickness in the world, that much he knew. He'd come from a family of it, and he'd seen it across the United States and Europe, most especially in the POW camp in Germany where he'd been held. There, he'd come to accept that human beings were capable of inflicting terrible pain for the pleasure of it. That knowledge darkened his hopes for Suzanna. And for Marlena, too. She would pay with guilt and grief for whatever happened to her child.

The trail he was following came to a swamp where yellow flies swarmed him in a cloud. The footprints he'd been following disappeared in a mud slick covered with a half-inch layer of rancid water. Frank hesitated. He did not believe the man who went this way could have carried the weight of a child, and pursuing the fleeing man through the swamp would take all the resources of the Jebediah County sheriff's department and a host of volunteers. As interesting as it would be to find Hubbard and question him, Frank knew that finding Suzanna was his primary goal. Punishment could come after Suzanna was found.

8

The hospital room was small and smelled vaguely of pine cleaner and Clorox. Dotty felt a headache begin at her temples. In another half hour it would be pounding, and there was nothing she could do about it. Walking out of the hospital and into the fresh air was the only thing that would help, and she couldn't do that. She'd promised Lucas she would sit with Marlena and listen, on the chance that Marlena might say something that would help the searchers find Suzanna.

The little girl was dead, and that's all there was to it. Dotty knew that. If a ransom request were coming, it would have arrived by now. And what was Marlena doing out in the middle of the woods with Suzanna anyway? Marlena wasn't some tomboy. She'd never hunted or fished, to Dotty's knowledge, and Dotty pretty much knew everything there was to know about Marlena. What Marlena was was a spoiled rich woman who didn't know which side her bread was buttered on. Dotty had told her that again and again. Told it to her face, not behind her back. She'd done everything she could to help Marlena see how lucky she was.

Dotty shifted in the wooden chair and felt the soreness in her bottom. Lucas had put it to her with force and a hint of savagery that she'd found more than exciting. He'd taken her from behind the first time, right there on the dining room table. He'd leaned his weight down on top of her, pinning her to the cool wood. When he'd entered her, he'd been brutal and punishing, acting like he wouldn't be satisfied until she begged for mercy. He had no restraint. Her hand went automatically to her right shoulder, and she pressed until the pain made her gasp. He'd bitten her so hard she had a bruise in the shape of his teeth. What would Betsy McBane and Sharon Bosworth think about that? She giggled softly to herself as she thought of their scandalized reactions. Of course, that only hid the fact that they really wanted rough sex themselves. Whenever anyone talked about sex in front of Betsy and Sharon, they pruned up and acted horrified, but Dotty could see how much they wanted it. And feared it. What would they reveal about their secret selves if they dropped the shackles of propriety? They were terrified of that answer.

Marlena's head shifted on the pillow, and Dotty stood up, causing a delicious little pull throughout her pelvic region.

"Suzanna," Marlena mumbled.

Dotty listened with a tingle of horror. The bones around one of Marlena's eyes had been damaged, and the doctors had done something to her mouth to stabilize that side of her face. "What happened to Suzanna?" she asked, leaning forward and putting her hand on the sick woman's forehead. "Tell me." Marlena was hot, burning to the touch. The doctor said infection was a probability. There had been dirt in her internal wounds.

"Two men," Marlena said, tears leaking out of her swollen-shut right eye. "Took her."

Dotty's hand slipped beneath the pillow and found the nurse call and pressed it six times as hard as she could. Someone else had to hear this. Something Marlena said might lead to Suzanna's recovery, and Dotty wanted to be sure she got it straight. She didn't want Lucas to waste time grieving for his lost daughter, though he hadn't seemed overly upset this morning.

"Tell me," Dotty said, picking up Marlena's hand and holding it. "What did the men look like?"

"Hoods." Marlena's first tears plopped on the starched pillow. Soon, there was a wet spot so large the tears no longer made a sound but were silently absorbed. "Help her." Marlena pulled her hand free and made an effort to push herself into a sitting position.

"Easy," Dotty said, trying to help her. "Be easy, Marlena, you've got stitches everywhere."

Marlena frowned, finally focusing her one eye that would open on her friend. She slowly turned her head. "Where am I?"

"At the Drexel Hospital. You've been hurt real bad." Dotty felt the tears spring into her own eyes. Marlena would never have a child again. There would be no replacing Suzanna if she was gone.

"Suzanna?" Marlena made fluttering motions with her hands on top of the white sheets.

Dotty's gaze was captured by the hands, the perfectly manicured nails and the huge diamond ring. The attackers hadn't taken the ring! Dotty forced her gaze up to meet Marlena's. "They've got tracking dogs in the woods now. They'll find her." There was no conviction in the last sentence. "Marlena, do you know who took her?"

Before Marlena could answer, the nurse appeared in the door, a frown crossing her face when she saw Marlena half-sitting.

"Lie back down. You'll pull your stitches."

"My baby." Marlena's hands made bigger loops against the sheets, like something trying to escape. "Find her."

"You'll do nothing of the sort. You aren't fit to walk across this room. Now settle back down and try to heal. That's the best thing you can do for your child and your husband."

Marlena blanched. "Lucas?"

"He's gone to help hunt," Dotty lied, patting Marlena's shoulder. "Calm down. I'll try and get word to the searchers. You said there were two men? What did they look like?"

"One big. One slender." Marlena's face crumpled. "Mean." Her voice broke, and her face took on a look of terror. "He —" She hiccupped. "He hurt me." She turned her face away. "Don't tell Lucas."

Dotty's tears were real. She lifted a shoulder to wipe her eye and felt again the pain of the bite. It would be a long time before Marlena could give Lucas the kind of loving he needed. It was a good thing that Dotty was around, available for Lucas to slake his lust on. A man had needs, and when a wife couldn't fulfill them, a marriage sometimes fell apart. That couldn't happen. No man would have Marlena after what had been done to her. Besides, Dotty knew that Lucas would never marry her. She wasn't the kind of woman a man like him married. But he could help her financially. And he would. He had plenty. She would be rewarded for being a good friend to Marlena in her time of trouble.

The Buick stopped beside the Cadillac, and Jonah Dupree got out. Frank watched as the light-skinned black man came toward him, his eyes direct and unflinching. "Miss Marlena's come around," he said. "They want the sheriff up at the hospital to see what she knows. From what Miss Strickland could tell, Marlena says there were two men who hurt her. They wore hoods."

Frank observed things about people, and what he saw in Jonah Dupree made him stop and consider. Jonah wasn't simply delivering a message. He was emotional. That made a number of questions pop into Frank's head. Frank knew that Jonah worked for Lucille Longier, and Lucille was

Marlena's mother. Jonah had known Marlena as a little girl. He'd been on the fringes of her life since the day she was born. Jonah had raised Marlena's half-sister as his own child, and it was obvious he cared deeply for the brutalized woman and her missing child.

"Sheriff Huey is following a trail," Frank said. "I'll go to the hospital and talk to Marlena."

Jonah nodded. "That would be for the best."

Frank didn't press him on that statement. Even the black folks knew that Huey wasn't a very good lawman. His forte was politics, shaking hands and kissing babies, and making the womenfolk feel safe when their husbands were out of town. Huey had a regular little route that he drove every evening, stopping by for a cup of coffee and a slice of apple pie or blackberry cobbler. He'd check the windows and doors for the widow women and those whose husbands were out of town on business. If it was necessary, he'd feed the cows and horses, slop the hogs, whatever it took. In many ways, Huey was a kind man, if not bright. Frank enjoyed working for him, because Huey most often left him alone to solve the public drunks, disorderly conducts, burglaries, and infrequent stabbings that were the crimes of Jebediah County. Huey was involved only so much as to *appear* involved in the actual investigations.

The sheriff hated walking in the woods, sinking up to his knees in mud and muck, stumbling upon the timber rattlers that could get up to seven feet in length and as big around as sinewy Nathan Ryan's upper arm. Huey preferred his late evening rounds of pie and palaver. As soon as Lucas was convinced that Huey had done everything possible, Huey would turn the investigation over to Frank.

The trail Huey was working was a dead end. Frank knew it, and he suspected even Huey knew it. They would find the spot where Frank had found Marlena. There would be no sign of the girl. She'd gone with the abductors, and they had left in a vehicle, not on foot. He'd ruled out the possibility that she was with Johnny Hubbard. The route man's trail was too fast, too reckless for a man carrying a child, but he was carrying something else. The truth about what had happened to Marlena and Suzanna.

"When are you coming to the hospital?" Jonah's voice brought Frank back from his thoughts.

"I'm going there now," he said. "Was Marlena able to give any kind of description of the men?"

"One was big and the other slender. That's all they told me. They said to tell you to come talk to her, ask her the questions you need to know."

"Who's with her now?"

"Miss Dotty," Jonah said, his gaze falling to the ground.

Jonah wasn't the only one who didn't understand the friendship between Marlena and Dotty Strickland. Frank knew the plump and vivacious Dotty. He knew her well. She didn't seem to have a thing in common with Marlena Bramlett.

"Is Miss Jade at the beauty shop?" Frank asked. He needed to talk to her. Dotty didn't have sense enough to come in out of the rain, but Jade had sat all night with Marlena. If something of importance had been said, Jade would remember.

"Yes, sir, she's there. She's busy all day."

"Will she sit with Marlena tonight?"

Jonah sighed. "Most likely. She should go home and rest, but she'll stay with Miss Marlena if they ask."

"Thanks," Frank said. "I'm headed back to town now." Jonah got in the Buick, reversed expertly, dodging the pines and oaks, and headed back to town.

Frank watched the car disappear. Lucille Longier must have been desperate to get word to Frank if she let Jonah have the car without her riding with him. It was just another thing for Frank to ponder.

9

Lucille sat rigid in the passenger seat of the Buick, her gaze straight ahead, hands folded on her lap. Since coming out of the hospital, she hadn't spoken a word, and Jonah knew to let it lie. She'd talk when she was ready. Once, she'd been very different. There had been a time when she flaunted propriety, when she'd laughed at the idea that what others thought had any control over her. And then she'd gotten pregnant with Jade.

The Buick's engine was big but quiet. Its sound was interrupted only by the wind whipping past the open windows. The sun burned down on the paved road, sending up little shimmers of heat in the distance that made Jonah think of childhood. When he was a boy, there'd been no paved roads, just dirt. Mules had pulled wagons, except for a few rich folk, who had horses. Mules plowed the fields where timber had already been cut and the land bent to the will of the farmers. Mose Dupree, Jonah's father, had an appreciation for the hard labor of farming, the work his father had done, but Mose had learned a trade. Folks around Jebediah County said it was more than a trade, more like a gift. Mose Dupree knew how to shape and fit wood when he came out of the womb. He could make wood curve, smooth it until it was softer than the silk worn by the wealthy, so that touching it was like a blessing. Mose could work a piece of wood until folks just stopped to stare at the wonder of it, seeing the hidden colors revealed by his artistry. When the two bachelor Kimble brothers decided to build their mansion, they hired Mose.

Gustave and Alfred Kimble had been fair men to work for, and the Dupree family had lived well for Negroes in the Pine Barrens. Mose had carved the staircase that floated on a spiral to the second floor. He built the bookcases that shifted to reveal a secret walkway. The cabinets in the kitchen and the gingerbread trim that adorned the house were the handiwork of Mose. The carpenter entertained his young son with stories of the oddity of the Kimble house, and, curious, little Jonah took to following his father to work, learning the trade of carpentry and also learning to read and write. Once the house was finished, the Kimble brothers kept Mose on. He built furniture and cabinets and counters and barns. When there was no real work, Gustave would set him to making toys for the children they hoped would come in the future. The brothers married, and Mose made boxes and ornaments for the wives.

Anna Kimble, the darkling sister whose desperation for a child was soon written on her face, nurtured Jonah. In the hour before it was time for Mose to walk home, Anna took Jonah into the library each day. Among the many wondrous colors of the leather-bound books, Jonah learned to read and do sums. He learned the Bible and he read history, so that as his knowledge grew, the town of Drexel shrank. Before tragedy struck, Jonah had read the great adventure tales of Jonathan Swift and Robert Lewis Stevenson. His mind was afire with reading. He dreamed large, imagining a world where horses talked and pirates hoarded gold that could be taken with intelligence and bravery.

After the shootings, when Greta left town with the only surviving Kimble, she took with her the good life for the Dupree family. Not deliberately. She left because she had to, but in doing so Mose Dupree lost his job and Jonah lost his dreams. Jebediah

County was not a place that drew wealthy families, and those that remained couldn't afford to hire a carpenter to make beautiful cabinets when plain ones would do as well. Mose and Jonah turned to the only thing left, farming. Neither had a talent for making the soil yield, but they worked long and hard, and grew corn, beans, turnips, melons, and squash. They had food, but no money for medicine or the simple luxury of new shoes. Hard times had fallen, and then Mose died from an infected cut. When Jonah, as a young man, was offered the job of working for the Sellers family as a yardman/butler, he took it without a backward glance. He cared for his mother until she died of what the doctor called consumption, and then he moved into a small cabin at the back of the Sellerses' family property, where he was close to his work and the long hours necessary to complete it.

From his window, he could watch Lucille, a young teen so delicate that she seemed almost ethereal when the sun brightened her pale hair. He watched her and thought of Rapunzel in the fairy tales Anna had read to him. Lucille's innocence caused him physical pain, and he watched as she grew to understand her power over men and lost that innocence. Had Bedelia Sellers bothered to ask him, he could have told her that trouble brooded on the horizon for Lucille. She was too undisciplined to handle her own beauty.

The road spun beneath the wheels of the car, and though Jonah knew he was in the present, the past gripped him hard. So much so that when Lucille spoke, he turned to her in amazement. She was an older woman now, just as he was an older man. The flesh along her jawline, so firm and perfect in his memory, sagged. The red lipstick she wore was now too garish for her age, her hair too blond and damaged.

"There won't be yard work today," she said. "The bridge club is coming at two, and I'll need you to park the cars for them. You'll have to bring Ruth back to help, so take me home and then go get her."

Jonah couldn't quite hide his amazement.

"Don't look at me like some flopping fish. It's my turn for the club, and I won't disappoint the ladies."

"Ruth isn't feeling well," he said. Ruth had never missed a day of work. He kept his gaze on the road, waiting to see how Lucille would handle that bit of news. He'd defied her twice in one day.

"Can you drive over there and ask if she's feeling better?" Lucille didn't look at him.

"Will it hurt you to ask?"

"No, ma'am," Jonah said, and in the trembling of her lip he saw again the young girl with too much beauty, and realized that she clung to the bridge club not for social reasons, but because routine was her way of praying. "I'll check on Ruth. Maybe she'll feel better now. Could be she just had a headache," though he knew it wasn't true. What ached in Ruth was so much more than her head.

He pulled to the front of the house and went around to assist Lucille out of the car. In his days as butler for her mother, Jonah had learned the manners of the gentry. Once Lucille was in the house, he got in the car and drove home, troubled anew at the shifting order of things. Twice in one day he'd driven Lucille's car without her present. Things were busting up and breaking apart. In his world, change meant trouble and damage.

It took only ten minutes to drive home, a distance that, walking, took an hour. He'd never gone back to the house that his parents had lived in. He'd built a new home closer to his work, and now Jade lived in the old house. Thinking of his daughter gave him a bit of peace as he pulled into his front yard. He found his wife sitting on the porch in her rocker, the chair drifting slowly back and forth as Ruth watched him come. There was no smile of welcome on her face, and Jonah didn't expect one. They had made a bargain when it became obvious they would not have a marriage in the traditional sense of the word. He'd never regretted what he'd given for what he got.

"She sent you to see if I'd come make the food for her bridge club," Ruth said, her mouth tightening with satisfaction. "She's so spoiled it does her good to remember how easy I make her life."

"She makes ours easy, too," Jonah said, though it would only add fuel to the fire of Ruth's hatred. He couldn't really blame his wife, except that she'd let her jealousy and anger destroy her capacity for love.

"I'll bet she makes your life real easy," Ruth said in a voice like ripping cloth. "I wonder why."

"For both of us," Jonah said. "She wants you to come back, if you feel like it."

"She don't care how I feel, she just wants me to come back and help with her party." She made a sound in her throat. "Her party! With her daughter nearly dead in the hospital and her grandbaby taken, she's going to have her bridge party. Can't nothin' interfere with her party."

Jonah let out a soundless sigh. If it wasn't the bridge party, it would be something else. Ruth had latched onto Lucille with the power of a loggerhead turtle. She gnawed and snapped and worried at everything Lucille did or didn't do. Criticizing Lucille had become the sum total of Ruth's life, except for Jade. And Jade was worth it all.

"Are you coming?" Jonah asked.

Ruth stood up. "She let you bring the car for me?" Her laugh was sharp. "She must want me bad." Her too-big shoes, cut to ease her corns, clopped on the porch as she walked across it, went down the steps, and got into the front seat.

Frank sat in his truck in the Bramlett driveway listening to the wind shuffle the pine needles. The smell of resin was on the hot breeze, and Frank wondered if Lucas was also harvesting the pines for turpentine as well as timber. Fifteen minutes had passed since he stopped the truck, thinking through what he intended to do. Huey was still in the woods with the dogs. Frank was supposed to be at the hospital but instead had chosen to visit Lucas. There were questions that had to be asked, and Huey would not ask them.

A photograph of John Hubbard was in the

mail from the Hattiesburg police department. It would arrive by Monday, but Frank already had the man pictured in his mind. Handsome, with an easy smile and a string of compliments. He was a man who could light a lady's cigarette, hold her chair, admire her with his eyes even if he said nothing. John Hubbard, a solitary man, was someone who wouldn't think twice about crossing another man's boundary line. From the evidence Frank had gathered at the scene of Suzanna's abduction, he believed that Marlena had taken her daughter and driven to the woods for a picnic with Hubbard. Someone had come upon the trio, whether by chance or design, Frank couldn't say. Lucas might be able to speak to that issue, but Frank knew that he was moving into treacherous terrain. Lucas was not a man who tolerated being questioned, not even by the law.

Through the gently swaying pine limbs he could see the second story of the house. Once, he'd seen a man move past an upstairs window. He had been only a shadow, but Frank knew it was Lucas. The Bramletts had no servants, except for Jade, who was more of an occasional companion for the child than help hired for cooking and cleaning.

He started the truck and drove to the house. When he got out he stood for a moment, listening to the quiet. Once, at a party, Marlena had confided to him that she hated the quiet. She wanted to live in town, but Lucas would not consider it. Lucas liked the isolation and the privacy, she said. Marlena had laid her palm on Frank's arm, and he'd felt the trembling in her hand. He'd wanted to pull her into his arms and hold her until she felt safe. Instead, he'd patted her hand and uttered something inane about how safe Jebediah County was. Too late, he understood that her fear came from something inside herself.

Out of the corner of his eye, he caught a glimpse of something at the fringe of the woods. He waited until his mother stepped out of the shadows. She held the single rose that had been placed in her hands in the coffin. She wore the same pale lavender dress, her face carefully made up. She shook her head slowly and stepped back among the trees.

Walking to the front door, Frank felt weary. Lucas answered his knock, surprise on his face. "Deputy Kimble, what can I do for you?"

"I need to ask some questions," Frank said.

Lucas stepped out of the doorway and motioned him inside. "We'll go to the study." He led the way through the foyer, down a hall, and into a room filled with books. Frank had a larger library, but these books looked as if they were read. A solitary chair faced a fireplace, and Lucas got a desk chair and brought it for Frank to sit in. "I've answered questions for Huey, but obviously you have more," he said, sitting down.

Frank took a seat. "The dogs struck a trail. Huey is on it now," he said, wondering why this wasn't the first question out of Lucas's mouth.

"Was there any sign of Suzanna?" Lucas asked.

"No," Frank said. "We found her Keds, but nothing else."

Lucas nodded slowly, a frown touching his face and then clearing. "Surely the ransom request will come soon."

Frank didn't answer. Originally he'd assumed the abduction was a kidnapping for ransom. Now he knew better. There would be no ransom request. Whoever had taken Suzanna had almost killed Marlena. They had not taken the child for money and left the mother nearly dead. Everyone in town knew that Lucas had bought Marlena once

120

and would likely do it again. But not Suzanna.

"If you have questions, ask them." Lucas's hands gripped the arms of his chair, the fingers digging into the leather.

"Was there trouble between you and Marlena?" he asked.

Lucas flushed. "How dare you —"

"I dare because I want to find your daughter," Frank said softly. "If Marlena was angry, defiant, we can begin looking in that direction. The choices she made in going to the woods will be different than those if she went to fish. One way to find Suzanna is to backtrack Marlena."

Lucas inhaled, gathering his control. "My marriage isn't perfect, but my wife wasn't gallivanting about the woods in an effort to get even with me. She would never do anything to endanger Suzanna, no matter if she were angry with me."

Frank nodded. "Are you in any financial trouble?"

Lucas smiled. "None whatsoever."

"If there is a ransom request, do you intend to pay it?"

Lucas hesitated. "Within reason. I have money, but much of it is tied up in land and timber. I'm not liquid, but I do have cash in the bank. What's there won't be hard to get."

Frank wrote in his notebook to keep from showing his emotion. Lucas was a cold fish. He talked about his daughter with the same calculation as he did his money.

"Do you have any enemies?" Frank looked at him, watching the flicker of Lucas's eyes as he went through the files in his mind.

"I haven't thought of that angle," Lucas said, "but I do have a few people who wouldn't mind seeing harm come to me. But would they brutalize my wife and take my child? I don't know."

"We'll check them. Could I have the names?"

"Just a moment." Lucas got up and left the room. He came back with several thin files in his hand. "There are three people I've bested in business deals." He remained standing, scanning the papers in his hand. "Oren McNeil, Kip Locklin, and Dantzler Archey."

"How did you best them?" Frank asked. Business was sometimes business, and sometimes it was very personal.

"McNeil put in a bid on some timber I got. He accused me of having inside information." His smile was superior. "Locklin tried to buy a major share of the railroad from here to Pascagoula. I squeezed him out." He hesitated, his gaze slipping from the pages to the window.

"And Archey?" Frank prodded.

"His men were coming onto land I owned and taking my timber. They were pirates."

Frank leaned forward, waiting. When Lucas didn't continue, he asked, "What happened?"

"I told my men to set some traps. They did, on my land. Archey's son brought a crew over to cut. He stepped on one of the traps. He bled to death."

Frank had seen terrible deaths, horrible agony. A bear trap that would snap bone and chew arteries was not a good way to die. He rose. "I'll check this information. If a ransom call comes, it'll probably be here, at the house. Will you be here?"

"The rest of the day," Lucas said. "Tomorrow, I have business to attend to."

The phone rang, and Lucas rose slowly, with deliberation. He went to an extension on the desk in the library.

"This is Lucas Bramlett," he said. He listened for a moment. "No, thank you, Governor. I don't believe more dogs and searchers would be helpful now. Let me ask Deputy Kimble." He looked at Frank.

Frank considered. "No. Not at this time," he said.

"No, thank you. Not at this time," Lucas said into the phone. He paused. "Yes, Governor. Yes, I will. I'll let you know the minute we find her."

Frank rose. "Thank you, Mr. Bramlett. I'll be on my way. Call if you hear anything."

10

Jade locked the door of the shop, her shoulders so tired they felt as if a small, deep fire burned beneath the skin. Her last appointment was gone, but there was still work to be done. She had to set the towels to wash so she could hang them out early. Mr. Lavallette had called her from the funeral home. Not for Suzanna, though her heart had nearly burst when she heard his voice. Old Maizy Campbell had passed, and all she needed was a hair arrangement and a bit of lipstick. Jade had agreed to stop by when she closed the shop. Somewhere in the next hour or so, she also had to get a bath, iron a fresh dress, and go to the hospital. She'd called the hospital three times, but the only information they were giving was that Marlena's condition hadn't changed. Jade didn't know if that was true or if it was just what the hospital employee had been told to say.

Desperate for any word at all, Jade had even called Lucille Longier's house, and to her amazement, had heard the sounds of a party. Ruth had answered the phone and said that if there was a change, no one at the Longier house knew of it. "And no one cares," Ruth had added with such bitterness that Jade felt fear for her mother. Ruth did not have to work for Lucille. Jade made enough money that her mother could stay home. But she wouldn't. Ruth went every day, her back rigid with hatred, yet she went.

Jade worried for her mother. For Lucille, she felt nothing. Were it not for Marlena and Suzanna, Jade would never have thought of her kinship with the domineering old woman who took her father and mother so for granted.

Jade set the towels to soak, swept up the hair from her last cut, put combs, brushes, and curlers in perfumed disinfectant, and left. The sun was still hanging on the horizon, the day still hot, when she got in her car. She drove to Rideout Funeral home and slipped in the side door. There was no sign of Junior's truck, and she was relieved. She'd spooked him, but it wouldn't last. Junior was not a man she wanted to antagonize. His eyes held a strange gleam, something reptilian. He was the kind of man who hid beneath a rock, waiting to strike when a back was turned. She went straight to the embalming room. It took her a moment to adjust to the sight of the dead woman laid out on the porcelain draining table. Cuts had been made in the artery in her neck to insert the tubes for the embalming fluid to enter her body. To allow the blood to leave, Elwood had made another cut in the body. The heavier embalming fluid pushed the blood out and down the drain table.

Jade checked the level of fluid in the gravity bottle. The process was almost complete. She could see that Elwood had done the internal stitching necessary to keep the mouth shut. The body would normally be dressed before hair and makeup, but tonight, Jade had to finish up and get to the hospital. She retrieved the makeup kit she left at the funeral home, plugged in the rod to curl the hair, and adjusted the block under the woman's head. Her goal was to make Maizy look like she was in a blissful sleep. Sometimes, this last look gave the family comfort. They could forget the suffering of a long illness or the shock of an accident.

"She looks so peaceful," they would say, and they would take that back to their homes and hang onto it at night when the dreads or a bad conscience came knocking at the door.

Jade checked to be sure the embalming room door was closed before she spoke. "Maizy," she said, looking directly into the face of the corpse, "tell me what you want done?" Sometimes Jade had to make a choice between pleasing the family and pleasing the dead, but she always asked first. She closed her eyes and waited until an image came. She saw Maizy Campbell in her yard, sunbonnet pulled down low as she worked a bed of pansies. As Jade watched, Maizy looked up, her face unadorned. "Okay," Jade said. "I know now. I'll do my best."

With a light touch she applied Vaseline to Maizy's lips to keep them closed and then added a hint of color. She took her pot of rouge and tipped her finger in it, using the merest smudge. The flesh beneath Jade's fingers was cold, but she worked the rouge until it covered the high point of Maizy's cheekbone, leaving only a faint flush when she was done. Jade got the curling rod and wrapped the hair, which had already taken on the texture of death, around it. In ten minutes, she had the hair curled and lightly combed out so that it fluffed around the sunken cheeks. She stood back, nodding.

Maizy Campbell had been a woman without adornment throughout her life. She'd never come to Jade's shop, but Jade had spoken to her in the market on occasion. Maizy had lost two children to fever and had four living. She looked as natural and peaceful as Jade could make her. Jade packed up her things and walked down the hallway to speak to Elwood.

He wasn't in a parlor, so she turned right, toward his office. Her hand was on the knob when she heard voices. She didn't want to interrupt Elwood when he was with a family, so she hesitated.

"Frank's not talking, but I heard through the grapevine the slut was with a man," Junior said. "She got exactly what she deserved."

Jade felt her body go rigid. Only her heart pumped in large, painful thrusts. She had a vivid image of Marlena sitting on a picnic cloth, laughing at a silly remark made by a man. She realized how seldom she'd seen Marlena laugh. The idea that Marlena was committing adultery, while terrifying, struck her as suddenly true. But with whom? No one in Drexel would chance Lucas's wrath.

"How do you know?" Elwood asked, impatience in his voice.

"You should have seen that picnic she had

laid out. No woman's gonna make chicken salad for a kid."

"That's slim evidence to be gossiping about Lucas Bramlett's wife," Elwood said. Jade heard papers rustle. "Let me remind you, Junior, that when you malign Marlena, you also cast a stain on Lucas."

There was a stretch of silence, and Jade could almost hear Junior thinking. It was a slow and laborious process. "Lucas should know what his wife's up to. He'd probably pay whoever told him."

A chair creaked. "Let me suggest that you shut your mouth," Elwood said in a tone Jade had never heard him use. "To suggest such a thing when a woman has been as severely injured as Marlena is begging for trouble. Lucas would not appreciate your insinuations, and if you want to enjoy the social aspects of Drexel, you'd better shut up."

Jade just had time to step back and duck behind some curtains when the door flew open. The draperies were heavy and thick, and Jade couldn't see Junior, but she could smell him. He stomped down the hall and left by the back door. She waited until Elwood closed his office door again, and then she knocked.

"I've finished with Mrs. Campbell," she said.

"Thank you, Jade. Come in a minute."

She stepped into the office, appointed with dark cherry furniture and another Oriental carpet with turquoise in the pattern. It was her favorite among all the carpets.

"I know you're exhausted, and I appreciate it." Elwood rose. He pointed to a carafe of coffee. "Would you like a cup?"

"No, thanks. I'm gone now."

"Have you heard how Marlena is doing?"

"No, sir. I'm staying with her tonight. The hospital won't give out information."

Elwood nodded. "I'm sure that's what Lucas wants. Half the town is gossiping about what happened and the other half is making it up."

Jade felt a sense of suffocation. She nodded, forced a smile, and left the funeral home. The sun was just beginning to touch the tops of the trees when she got in her car and drove home.

Jade loved her old house. Her granddaddy, Mose, had put in all the cabinets, a beautiful light oak that gleamed whenever light hit it. The beds were hand-carved, one with cherubs and angels. Jade had chosen that bed for her own, covering it with a hand-made quilt in a cherry blossom pattern, a gift from Ruth. There was a fireplace in the bedroom and indoor plumbing, something Jade had added herself. She turned on the hot water in the tub and went to the closet to select a dress. She chose a pale pink with a looser waist. Sitting in the hospital chair was uncomfortable enough without binding clothes.

While her tub ran, she got out the ironing board and iron and pressed the wrinkles out of her dress. Ruth had instilled in her the necessity of neatness. Jade didn't leave the house unless she was wrinkle-free and clean, with lipstick applied. She smiled at the thought of her mother, whose dark skin had never known cosmetics, not even lipstick. Ruth had chosen to ignore her gender. It was almost as if Ruth had chosen to become more shadow than substance. The thought troubled Jade as she hung the dress and went into the bathroom.

She looked out the curtainless window. Her house was at least three miles from anyone else, something that concerned her parents, but she loved it. She shucked off her dress and underwear and stepped into the hot water. From her vantage point in the tub, she could watch the sun slip beneath the horizon. She didn't particularly like dusk, because it marked a melancholia she didn't understand. She loved the colors of sunset, though. Leaning back against the slanted porcelain tub, she let the hot water do its work on her tired muscles. She closed her eyes and sank lower, feeling the tug of sleep. For just a moment she relaxed enough to slide into a state where half-dream images raced through her mind. She heard the tip, tip of water dripping into the tub, but it was lulling. She heard the clock strike the hour of six. She heard the sound of footsteps on her porch.

Jade opened her eyes, fear clutching at her heart. She slid deeper beneath the water, the window a point of vulnerability now. There was no telephone in the house. Jade had chosen to have the phone in her shop instead. For business. She'd never felt a need for a phone since she had a good car. The light switch was across the room, and Jade would have to leave the tub to reach it. Her nakedness would be obvious to anyone outside the window looking in. She slipped further down, until only her nose and eyes were above the water. She could only pray that if someone walked by the window, her dark hair would seem a shadow in a corner of the bathroom. But they would know where she was. The light advertised her whereabouts.

There was no other choice. She got out of the tub, water sluicing to a puddle on the linoleum floor, her body shaking from fear. The memory of Marlena's butchered body came back to her, the long line of black stitches that held her together. There was an animal on the loose.

The knock that came at the front door made her bite back a scream at the same time it brought a measure of relief. A robber or killer wouldn't knock, her rational mind told her. She grabbed a white bathrobe that Marlena had given her from the hook on the door and tiptoed out of the bathroom into the dusky bedroom. She moved silently to a front window and peeped out. Frank Kimble stood on her porch.

"Jade," he said, knocking lightly.

"Just a minute." She tied the robe tighter and went to the door, not intending to let him in. She only needed to know if something had happened to Marlena.

"I need to ask some questions," he said. His gaze dropped to the bit of throat revealed by her robe and then shot back to her eyes. A tingle of amusement touched her then, more a release from the tension than anything else, but she felt an irrepressible urge to laugh out loud. She did, and saw the incomprehension in Frank's eyes.

"You just about scared me to death," she said, taking a deep breath. "I thought someone bad was on the porch."

He nodded. "Sorry. I tried to call the shop but you'd left."

"Is there word on Marlena?" she asked.

"I'm going there next," he said. "First, I wanted to ask you some questions."

Jade stepped back from the door, aware in a new way of her robe and her slick body beneath it. Frank was a handsome man, but there was more to him than that. She had the sense that death had touched him more than once, and that he was no stranger to the machinations of the dead. It was something they shared.

"Have a seat." She directed him to the kitchen table. "I'll put on some coffee while I . . ." The word would not pass her lips. To say it would emphasize her nakedness beneath the robe. She lit the stove and put a kettle on. "I'll be back."

She hurried into the dress she'd ironed, pulling on clean panties and shoes. A decent woman always wore shoes, Ruth had drummed that into her head. No matter what she wore on her feet, though, the racing of her heart was indecent. She ducked into the bathroom, running a brush through her short hair, which was thick and curled in soft ringlets all over her head. She reached for her lipstick, but stopped. Frank would know she'd applied lipstick. He could read many things into that act, and she was afraid of what it revealed.

Before she sat at the table, she poured up the hot water. Those simple tasks calmed her. When she turned to him, her hands on the sink behind her, she managed calm. "You said you haven't seen Marlena?"

He shook his head. "I'm going there next. You're a bright woman, Jade. What do you think happened to Marlena?"

Jade knew what he was asking and skirted it. "She was attacked in the woods. Two men hurt her and took Suzanna."

"What was she doing in the woods?"

"She took Suzanna fishing." Jade met his pale gaze with a level one of her own.

"Was Marlena in the habit of fishing?"

Jade held herself very still. "Marlena isn't in the habit of checking with me before she goes fishing or does anything else."

Frank's gaze dropped, and when he looked at her again, the chill was gone from his eyes. "I know you two are close."

Jade thought about it. She shook her head. "No, we're not. I work there sometimes, and

I keep Suzanna when they need me. I wouldn't say that Marlena and I are close."

Frank shook his head. "You're sisters."

"Half-sisters," she said, her voice emotionless. "That's not something Marlena would view as an asset."

"She should."

Jade turned away from his gaze and got two cups from one of the beautiful cabinets. She poured black coffee for both of them and placed a cup in front of Frank. She put her own cup at the table and sat down. "If I can answer any questions, I will. I want Suzanna back. The truth is, Marlena didn't confide in me. Dotty Strickland is her close friend. Ask Dotty."

"I couldn't get a straight answer out of Dotty if I asked her directions to the courthouse."

Frank wasn't exaggerating. Dotty prevaricated about everything. When she wasn't doing that, she was outright lying.

"I need some help here," Frank said, his voice low. "It's been twenty-five hours since we know Suzanna's been taken. Could be a little longer. The more time that passes, the less chance of getting her back alive."

"There hasn't been a ransom call?" Jade was glad she was sitting; her legs felt dull and unresponsive. The overhead light cast harsh shadows on Frank's face. His eyes were hollowed and his nose prominent. His cheeks looked sunken, but that wasn't all from the lighting. He was tired, and it was showing.

"No. At least Lucas says there hasn't been one. I believe him."

Jade put her hands around the coffee cup. The coffee was hot, and even though the day was still in the eighties, the warmth of the cup was comforting.

"Jade, if you know anything about who Marlena might have been meeting in the woods, tell me. For Suzanna's sake."

"I don't," she said. "So you think she was meeting someone. What else do you think?"

"That she was having a picnic with her lover. That Suzanna had been sent to fish on the bank of the river. That the attackers came up, two of them, one heavy and one slender. One grabbed Suzanna and subdued her, then they both attacked Marlena."

"What about Marlena's lover?" Jade asked.

"That's what's troubling me. He left her there. That's the thing that really bothers me."

Jade saw the scenes Frank had created with his words. She saw Marlena, laughing on the picnic blanket, a handsome man teasing and touching her leg. In her mind she heard a childish scream. The man jumps up, dashing toward the sound. Marlena hugs herself on the blanket. And then she screams as two men advance towards her.

Jade shut her eyes and shook the images from her mind. "I have to say that if Marlena is having an affair, she's taking a terrible risk. Lucas will take Suzanna and leave her penniless."

"Where would Marlena meet a man?"

It went without saying that Marlena would not sleep with anyone in Drexel. Lucas had too much power. He could crush a business or put a farmer off his land. Marlena wasn't in the habit of traveling alone. She never left town without Lucas at her side. Jade lowered her head into her palms, leaning on the table. "If ever there was a woman who could use a gentle touch or a bit of laughter, it would be Marlena. If she is seeing a man, it would have to be someone who traveled through town." She lifted her face and put her hands on the table. "Have you told this to Lucas?"

"No."

"Are you going to?"

"Not unless I have to. I think the cat's out of the bag, though, Jade. Lucas isn't stupid."

"But he is arrogant."

Frank nodded.

"Please . . ." Jade stopped herself. Maybe she'd learned it from Ruth. Maybe it was just a part of herself, but she'd never asked a single person for anything. "Please don't tell him unless you have to." She saw something flicker in Frank's eyes, something hot that tingled. Then it was gone.

"Okay." Frank finished his coffee. "Would you like a lift to the hospital? I have to go and see if Marlena can talk to me."

Jade had her own car. If she rode with Frank, she'd have to get someone to ride her back to her house in the morning. "Yes," she said, despite the trouble it would cause later. "I'd like a ride."

She rose and went to her bedroom, collecting her purse, a book she'd bought, and a pillow. She returned to the kitchen. "I'm ready."

Frank followed her to the door, and as she exited, her arm brushed his chest. She stumbled, his hand catching her and holding her steady, holding her just a moment longer than necessary. She felt his grip tighten, and he drew her back to him so that they stood in the doorway, face to face, reading the wants and desires in each other's eyes.

He bent to her, his lips claiming hers as if he had a right. It happened quickly, and with such intensity that Jade had no defenses. She was unprepared for the betrayal of her own body. Pressed against Frank, she could feel his desire, and instead of shock or shame, she felt joy and a power as old as humanity. He wanted her.

His kiss was demanding, his probing tongue a promise. She was lightheaded with passion, and heavy with a need so sudden that she could not force her legs to move. She felt him bend, his arms scoop beneath her knees, and in a moment he was carrying her through the house to the bedroom. He settled her on the cherry-blossom quilt her mother's hands had made. Her shoes had fallen off somewhere, and Frank's hands were at the buttons of her dress, while hers tore at his shirt.

Jade heard it first, the sound of a car bumping over the rutted road to her house. She put a hand on Frank's cheek, stilling him that quickly. He heard it, too, and he stood, rebuttoning his shirt and tucking it in as she jumped up, straightened her dress, and found her shoes. They were both sitting in the same places at the kitchen table when Jonah Dupree stepped into his daughter's house. He looked at her and then Frank, considering.

"Evenin', Mr. Frank." Jonah's focus

shifted to Jade. "I came to give you a ride to the hospital. Miss Lucille gave me the use of her car. She said I could get you in the morning and bring you home. I thought you might be too tired to drive."

"Thank you, Daddy." Jade felt the heat in her cheeks, but there was nothing she could do. Jonah would never question her about Frank's presence, but it would lie between them like the facts of her birth, something that was never examined but never went away.

11

Dotty paced the small hospital room, checking her watch and then checking it again. Her lips had a raw, chapped look where she'd licked and rubbed them, a nervous gesture she'd almost conquered, until today. Lucas had not stopped by even once, and he knew she was there. Her dress was wrinkled, and she could smell herself, a not unpleasant odor of femininity and a low note of sex, like a fruit that has reached the peak of ripeness and is about to slip into rot. She moved to the open window. At least the sun was melting down the sky and the air was cooler. She didn't understand how a person could heal in a room that was an oven. More like they were trying to bake Marlena, except the patient hadn't broken a sweat. Dotty's dress back was soaked with perspiration, and she could feel sweat trickling down her spine. It had been a downright miserable day. And where in the hell was Jade?

The Bulova watch that perched on Dotty's wrist, held by two black silk threads, told her it was six-thirty. Jade closed the shop at five. So where was she? Dotty's temper simmered like the landscape. It would be just like a worthless nigger not to show up at all.

The door pushed open almost silently, and Dotty simultaneously saw that it was Jade and felt the last hold on her temper slip. "It's six-thirty. I've been waiting here for you to come. Where in the hell have you been?" It didn't help that Jade looked clean and refreshed.

When Frank stepped through the door behind Jade, Dotty faltered backward. She wasn't prepared for Frank. She felt a flush touch her face. Everyone in town treated Jade like she was solid gold, especially Frank Kimble. He treated her like a white woman, and Dotty could see his sharp disapproval.

"Jade was answering questions, Miss Strickland. Official questions. Something that I need you to do, too."

"Oh, of course." Self-importance was a soothing balm to her aborted temper fit. "I'd be glad to do whatever I can to help. Are we going to the sheriff's office?" Her eye was set on Lucas, but Frank wouldn't be a bad option for a little Friday night fun. Lucas had the money, and everyone in town knew Frank was a little off, living in the big old house and using only a few of the rooms. If she owned that house, she'd open it up and have a party every night. That idea was so pleasant, she smiled.

"I can ask you the questions here," Frank said.

She thought she caught some underlying meaning in his tone, but didn't understand it. "I don't mind going to the sheriff's office." No one else would be in the courthouse at this time. She and Frank would be alone. Was the man so dense he didn't realize that?

"It's okay, Miss Strickland. I have to meet Huey at seven, so I'll just ask you now and let you get along home to a hot bath. The more information I have to report to Huey, the quicker we'll find that little girl. You may have information that will save Suzanna."

Dotty had almost forgotten Jade. She saw her lean against a wall in the corner, a book held in her hand. "Would you be so good as to get us a cola?" Dotty asked her. She wanted Jade out of the room so she could have a moment alone with Frank. Marlena didn't really count for a presence since she was so drugged up she didn't know where she was.

"Good idea," Frank said, pulling his billfold out of his pocket. "Can you carry three Coca-Colas?" he asked, holding out a dollar.

"I believe I can manage." Jade's face was expressionless, as it should be. She took the money and left, her shoes clicking on the tile until distance absorbed the sound.

"Was Marlena seeing anyone?" Frank asked.

His tone was abrupt, and it annoyed Dotty. "How should I know?" It was just like Frank Kimble to think Marlena was up to something.

"You're her best friend, right?"

"She never said nothing to me."

"You're positive?"

"Look, I'm not some uneducated Negro. I finished high school, and I would have remembered if Marlena had blurted out some confession like that. She's the victim here. Maybe you should start thinking of that."

Frank studied her. Normally she liked men to look at her, but there was something about Frank that made her uncomfortable. He was crazy. She could see only darkness in his eyes. She was glad she hadn't gone to the courthouse alone with him. "If you're going to ask a question, do it. I want to go home."

"How old are you, Dotty?"

That question stung. "It's none of your business."

"You're thirty-six, right? I can check your driver's license records."

"What if I am?"

"Do you know anyone who would want to hurt Marlena?"

That question had a multitude of meanings, and Dotty was far too smart to fall into the trap Frank had set. "Of course not. The whole town loves Marlena, as far as I know. She's on every charity committee. She does volunteer work at the school and the hospital. She's practically a saint in this town."

"Someone doesn't think so."

Dotty frowned. "I don't think Lucas would like you saying that. In fact, Lucas wouldn't care for a single thing you've implied."

"I wouldn't blame him. I don't like to say it because I have a special fondness for Marlena. When Mama was so sick, Marlena took her food every day."

That tidbit shocked Dotty. It shouldn't have; Marlena was like that. She had a tender heart, and because she didn't have to worry about finances, she had plenty of time to run around town playing Florence Nightingale and Lady Bountiful, all at the same time.

"Looks to me like you've got a special fondness for that nigger gal," Dotty said. "I'd be careful, Frank. You could make big trouble for Jade, and for yourself, too. Some things just aren't tolerated in Drexel, no matter what kinds of things went on over in Eur-rope." She hit the last word hard.

"What are you saying, Dotty?"

She'd made him angrier than she intended. His eyes suddenly seemed vacant, as if Frank's soul had fled. "I'm just trying to be a friend. Perception can sometimes be misleading. Jade's a pretty woman, but there's a reason she's not hitched. She hankers after the wrong color, and this town won't sit still for it."

"How do you know what Jade hankers after?" he asked.

"I got eyes. I see what's going on. And other folks do, too. Folks who aren't as open-minded as I am."

Frank nodded. "I know you're only looking out for me, Dotty, and I thank you for it." He smiled, just his lips twisting up at the corners, and Dotty had a sudden, terrible thought, that if he opened his mouth, his teeth would be sharp and pointed.

"Are you finished?" she asked, eager to get out of the room and away from him.

"Would you say Lucas is happy in his marriage to Marlena?"

She'd been checking in her handbag for her car keys, but she stopped. She felt Frank's gaze on her neck. Chill bumps shimmied down her arms. "They seem happy to me."

"Lucas has never complained. To you."

She met his gaze, wondering how he knew. She had the craziest notion that he knew everything she'd done that morning. "Lucas never said a harm word about Marlena. Not a single word." It wasn't a lie.

"And Marlena? Did she ever say a harm word about Lucas?"

Dotty shrugged. "Just wife stuff. She was tired of cooking him a big breakfast, tired of him making all the decisions and just telling her how things were going to be." She shrugged again. "Stuff like that. Nothing serious."

"Thank you, Dotty," Frank said, and she felt as if she'd been dropped from the talons of some bird of prey.

Frank had gotten nothing useful from Dotty

Strickland, but he hadn't expected to. The nurse on call said Marlena had not spoken any more, but that tomorrow the doctor would try to wean her down from the morphine that kept her so heavily sedated.

Frank drove back to the courthouse where Huey waited, a long-suffering look on his face. "You sort of left us out there in the woods," he said, not exactly an accusation but with a hint of displeasure.

"Had a call to come back to town. Marlena partially identified the attackers. There are two of them, one heavy and one slender. They wore some type of covering on their heads."

The news cheered Huey. "Do you think the Klan might be mixed up in this?"

Frank shook his head. "Not the Klan. Lucas could have the bank close down their mortgages. They wouldn't risk that, and there's been no indication Marlena's done anything to upset those idiots."

"Maybe not Marlena?" Huey said.

Frank had a sudden respect for the sheriff. "I hadn't thought of that," he admitted. "I can't imagine those lowlifes taking on someone like Lucas Bramlett's wife."

Huey leaned back in his chair and put his feet up. "If it were anyone but Lucas, I'd give it more thought, but his dealings with

Negro girls are limited to commerce. That's not something the Klan has a problem with."

Frank sat down on the edge of Huey's desk. When the need arose, Huey could be both pragmatic and unobservant. He saw what he needed to see.

"What'd you find in the woods?" Frank asked.

Huey shook his head. "We lost the trail in the river but picked it up downstream just where you said. We went to the location where you found Marlena. We searched high and low, but we couldn't find a trace of that young'un." His worry was real. "I fear she's dead, Frank."

Frank nodded. "I know."

"But what if she isn't? What if they're hurting her?"

Frank examined the sheriff. Huey's thoughts didn't tend toward the dark side. He wasn't a man who spent time thinking about the behavior a true deviant would display. "Is that what the volunteers were saying?" Junior, Pet, and Rufus Dean were always volunteers on searches, wreck sites, floods, whatever. The two other men were John Merritt and Ammon Sullivan, local farmers who'd taken a hot day to walk the woods and search for a lost child rather than work their fields.

Huey nodded, his lips tightly compressed. "Junior thinks she's been sold into white slavery." He made a sound of disgust. "I'd rather she was dead."

Frank nodded again. "Sometimes death is the easiest answer." He took a breath. "I talked to Lucas earlier about possible suspects. He gave me some names to check out. I've eliminated two men, but there's one other to check. Why don't you give Lucas a call and tell him the result of the search?"

"Okay." Huey picked up the phone and started dialing. Frank pulled out his notebook. Of the three names Lucas had given, Locklin had up and moved his business to Texas, and Orin McNeil had a rock solid alibi — he was in the hospital with kidney stones. Only Dantzler Archey remained on the list, and he was a man hard to catch up to. That fact alone whetted Frank's appetite to find him. Darkness was falling now, and Archey would have to go to ground. Frank intended to be there when he did.

12

From the hospital window, Jade could see the lights of half a dozen houses along Jasmine Street. As a little girl, she'd been in three of the houses, where Ruth picked up ironing she did late at night to make a little extra money. At one house, Eula Lee Walden had given Ruth five dresses for Jade. Mrs. Walden's daughter, Beth Ann, had outgrown the clothes. One was a beautiful yellow-and-white-checkered sundress with butterflies embroidered all over it, and a matching yellow sweater with a butterfly on each lapel so that when the sweater was buttoned up, it looked like the butterflies were kissing. It was the most beautiful dress Jade had ever seen. She loved it and wore it whenever Ruth allowed. One Sunday, when Jade was wearing the dress, she ran into Mrs. Walden and Beth Ann in town. To her surprise, Beth Ann started crying. She looked at her mother and said that Jade was prettier in the dress than she had been.

Beneath the shame and embarrassment, Jade tasted joy. Washing dishes in the Longier home as Ruth's assistant, raking leaves in the Longier yard as Jonah's helper, Jade had never dreamed that she would have anything that a rich little white girl would want. It felt good.

Jade stared at the lights of the Walden home and thought about those days. Beth Ann had grown up to marry a doctor in Jackson, Mississippi. Her picture had run in the local newspaper, her long chestnut hair shining, a string of pearls around her neck, and her veil pulled back to reveal her smile. That was ten years ago. Most of the young women Jade's age, black or white, were married, many of them moved away. Jade had not married. In fact, had dated little. She had been bedded, because she could not halt the sexual needs of her body even though her heart was not engaged. For the most part, though, there seemed a barricade around her that most men did not care to climb. Frank Kimble was the exception, and Jade turned to examine her sister in an effort to stem the hot surge of desire that thoughts of Frank generated. She was too old to let a man make a fool of her, too old and too careful. Lust would not be her undoing.

Marlena tossed on the pillow, and Jade soaked a cloth in cold water and made a compress for her sister's forehead. Marlena's fever was high, and Jade knew the doctor was worried. He'd been in once and talked about the possibility of a specialist from New Orleans. There was a wonder drug, penicillin, and he'd given Marlena some without ill effect. He was going to give her more.

Marlena's skin was smooth and hot, so tight it felt as if her cheeks were trying to burst. Jade touched her with the backs of her fingers, drawing them across the taut skin, whispering softly, "You have to get better, Marlena. We have to find Suzanna, and we need your help. We need you, Marlena." And it was true. The doctor had reduced the morphine to a level that should have allowed Marlena to regain lucidity. She had not. Jade had heard the doctor whisper to the nurse that he thought Marlena was deliberately avoiding a return to consciousness.

Jade rewet the cloth and reapplied it. She got hot, soapy water and washed her sister's body, massaging her feet and legs, stimulating the muscles and the nerves. "Marlena, we need you here with us," she said. "Frank wants to talk to you."

Frank. Not Lucas, who had never come a single time to visit his wife. The whole hospital was buzzing about it, and some of the earlier gossip had even made its way to her four-thirty hair appointment, Mrs. Hargrove, who feigned shock at Lucas's callousness.

"Maybe he's waiting at home for the ransom call," Jade suggested, a possibility that, because it lacked malice, had been overlooked.

A nurse's aide came to the door. She was young and dark-skinned and looked at the floor when she spoke. "There's a phone call for Miss Dupree at the desk."

"Thank you," Jade said, wondering why Jonah or Ruth had called her at the hospital. She felt her heart rate increase. She walked purposefully to the desk. The nurse hesitated when she handed her the telephone. Jade was too weary to care.

"Hello," she said.

"It's me, Lucas. How's Marlena?"

She was surprised. "About the same. The doctor says he's giving her penicillin for the infection. He said he'd be back at eight. He wants a specialist from New Orleans to see her."

"I'll try to be there, but I don't want to leave the phone," Lucas said. "Has she said anything more?"

"Nothing." Jade felt a twinge of apprehension. Lucas hadn't called while Dotty was sitting with Marlena; he'd waited to talk to Jade. Lucas was a deliberate man, so what portent was behind his action?

"If I don't make it for the doctor, will you call me?"

Lucas had ordered her to do things. He'd left her written instructions on how to do things, but never once had he ever *asked* her to do a single thing. "Yes, sir, I'll call after the doctor leaves."

"Thank you, Jade," he said, and she marked down another first. Lucas had thanked her in a tone that held sincerity.

She went back to the room and her station by the bed. Marlena was dying. She sensed it, even though the doctor would not say so. Infection had set in and was waging war, and it was winning. Part of it was that Marlena had given up the struggle. Whatever had happened was so terrible that she sought escape in unconsciousness. Jade's hand trembled as it stroked her sister's hot face. Jade put one hand on Marlena's forehead and another, gently, on her heart.

"Come back to us," she urged. "We need

you, Marlena. We need you to help us find Suzanna."

Jade's hands lifted, hovering above her sister's flesh. She felt the heat of the fever from a distance, and she concentrated on cooling Marlena, thinking of a chilled stream of water and Marlena's body immersed, floating, face turned to the sun as her hair undulated around her head.

"Jade?" Marlena's voice was weak.

"I'm here," Jade said, opening her eyes. "It's going to be okay."

"They have Suzanna."

Jade didn't dispute the fact, but she didn't add more to it.

"I heard her scream. The men came. One had Suzanna. He dropped her."

Marlena wasn't crying, and she wasn't emotional. Jade felt her forehead, finding that the fever had broken. Sweat trickled down Marlena's hairline, and Jade wiped it with the washcloth. "I'll be right back. I need to find Frank Kimble. He's been waiting to talk to you."

Marlena shook her head slowly. "Tell him. I can't stay. I . . ."

Jade knew she was losing her. "Marlena." She shook Marlena's shoulder lightly, and Marlena's one good eye fluttered open, a slit of blue beneath the battered flesh. The bone beneath her eye had been crushed by the beating, changing the contours of her face. To stabilize the side of her face, the doctor had wired her jaw shut. Marlena would keep her sight, if she lived. And she would live if Jade could keep her from slipping away.

"It's good here, too, Marlena," Jade said. "We have to find Suzanna so we can both watch her grow up. She hasn't had much of a chance to live. She's just a little girl."

"She's gone," Marlena said, sighing.

"Did you see her?" Jade felt a chill slip through the open window and touch her bare arms. "Marlena, did you see her?"

Marlena's only answer was a smile. Her eyes fluttered.

"Marlena, if you leave, Suzanna will die."

Marlena's eyes opened, the bliss twisting into pain. "What?"

"Tell me about the men." Jade knew her sister was weak. She was afraid to push hard, yet afraid that Marlena would die without telling what she knew. "Did the men say anything?"

Marlena's nod was abrupt. "Mean things."

"It's okay," Jade said, holding Marlena's hand. "Tell me. You have to tell me."

"Cunt. Whore. They said I needed to be hurt."

"The other man, what did he say?"

"He held me, while the big one —" Her mouth opened into the shape of a scream, but nothing came out and her head arched backward, the throat constricting, and still no sound.

Jade moaned at Marlena's anguish. She regained her control and squeezed Marlena's hand. "It's okay, girl, they can't hurt you again. You're safe here, and I'm watching over you."

Her words seemed to calm Marlena. "Did they say anything about Suzanna?" Jade asked. "About what they intended to do with her. You have to tell me. Think, Marlena, think."

"Took her." Her chest began to move rapidly. "They said I'd pay. Whore of Babylon."

It was a phrase Jade had heard all of her life, and it had always applied to some exotic woman with bangles and a multicolored skirt who whirled when she danced and shimmied.

"Marlena, was someone else with you?" Jade felt like a traitor to her sister.

Marlena tore her hand free. "No! Not Lucas."

And that was answer enough. "I won't tell Lucas, but we have to find that man," Jade said. "He may know something about Suzanna. Who was it?"

Marlena shook her head. Her features were contorted, whether by pain or her own thoughts, Jade couldn't tell. "No," Marlena said. "No."

"Your daughter's life hangs in the balance."

Before Marlena could answer again, peace slipped over her face. Her body stilled to the point that Jade had to pinch her nostrils to see if she still breathed. She did, but when Dr. Miller and the specialist arrived at eight, the doctor told Jade she could go home. Marlena's fever had broken, but she had slipped into a coma. The prognosis was not good, and watching her was pointless.

13

Frank wasn't unaware when he crossed the county line into Greene County. There was no change in the tall, dark pines that crowded Highway 63, and there was no sign saying he'd left Jebediah County for the even more rural Greene. As a county lawman, Frank knew the invisible line that marked his authority, and tonight he traveled under the guise of an unofficial visit, an attempt to seek assistance. Playing out variations of conversation in his mind, he continued down the gravel road at a clip that would have been dangerous had a vehicle come from the other direction. There was no traffic, making it more likely that trouble would come from a deer or cow loose on the right of way. He watched carefully but didn't drop his speed. It had taken him almost two hours of phone calls to find where Dantzler Archey maintained his most permanent residence in the heart of the East

River community. The man was a gypsy. He lived in log camps throughout southeast Mississippi, and over into the fringes of Baldwin and Escambia counties in Alabama where the Mobila and fragments of the Creek Indians could still be found.

Dantzler Archey was a timber man by trade and a criminal by nature. He took what he wanted, by whatever means necessary, and his brutal nature had cost him his son. Of course, Archey didn't see it that way. From all accounts that Frank had collected, Archey was a man capable of the vicious attack on Marlena and the abduction of Suzanna. The lack of a ransom would also fit into Archey's character, as Frank understood it. If Suzanna was in his possession, Archey would feel he had the upper hand. Archey would hold what he believed Lucas valued, and he would toy with Lucas until the last possible moment. Instead of feeling concerned, this actually made Frank feel more hopeful. It would explain the now twenty-eight-hour stretch without a word about the girl. A man like Dantzler Archey would want Lucas to sweat, to touch the wounds that had been so viciously inflicted on his wife, and wonder what was happening to his daughter.

In the stalag in Nuremberg, Frank had

seen this principle at work many times. For the most part, the POWs were left hungry, dirty, lice ridden, and alone. But there was a Luftwaffe officer who took a special interest in the men of Frank's barracks. The officer would walk through the prison, hair perfectly combed, uniform immaculate, death in his eyes. He would point to a prisoner, an arbitrary choice. The man would be dragged away by the guards, and the remaining prisoners would spend the next hours in a living hell. None talked, but each knew that when the taken man was returned, he would have lost something. An eye, an ear, a finger, a toe, a testicle, a strip of flesh, a bone, a piece of scalp. It was part of the method of torture. And nothing was worse than what the men left behind imagined. More than a few were driven to madness.

As a small child, Frank had walked among the dead in his family home. In order to survive, he'd learned to turn away from certain mental paths. Never once had he asked the ghosts that haunted him what they sought. Never had he allowed himself to think of what they might do to him. In the prison, he would turn and face the wall and let his spirit leave. Once he was free of the prison, he drifted past season and continent to the crisp fall weather of Jebediah County where he would walk through the woods with his dog, Getter. Morning mist glistened in Getter's red hair, and the dog bounded ahead, eager to pick up the scent of a rabbit or deer that he would track for the simple pleasure of the run. Frank did not hunt. He woke up too often in the middle of the night to confront his dead relatives and the gory results of gunshot. Killing held no interest for him. Yet he had killed a plenty in the war. Sometimes those dead Germans rose out of the ditches where he'd bayoneted them, or stood on the killing grounds with blood pouring from the stump of an arm or leg. He had shot them, stabbed them, beat them to death with the butt of his rifle. Frank had been given two Purple Hearts, the Silver Star, and uncountable silent visits from the dead.

Frank made a curve in the road, startling a buzzard from a feast of roadkill. He slowed enough to give the ungainly bird clearance as it swooped up. Once in the air, it would ride the currents, graceful and determined. He continued on until he came to a rutted turnoff. There was no mailbox. Dantzler Archey wasn't the kind of man who got letters. Frank turned slowly into the road and began to move more cautiously. He flipped the radio on, the sound of KWKH in Shreveport, Louisiana, belting out into the starry night. He did not want to come upon the timber camp unannounced.

The timber camps were legendary places where men worked hard all day and often drank hard through the night. Wisdom dictated that Frank didn't startle the men, yet he didn't want Archey to scatter at the sight of someone he knew represented the law, even though Frank had no jurisdiction in Greene County, and Archey, like most criminals, was an authority on the law.

The camp had been located in some of the thickest forest so that the men would not have far to travel. Frank wasn't familiar with this territory, but he knew the Chickasawhay River would be close, so that the men could drag the felled trees to the river, raft them up, and float them to the sawmill in Pascagoula. Some of the more modern loggers were now cutting and loading their trees onto trucks and driving them to Drexel to the railroad spur. But some, like Dantzler, would die rather than add to Lucas Bramlett's profits.

In checking around, Frank had found that the relationship between Lucas and Dantzler was beyond rancorous. It was abscessed.

The men hated each other, and it was over more than timber and a dead son. Junior Clements, always a source of gossip, had told Frank that Lucas had gotten Dantzler's sister, Katy, pregnant. Frank remembered Katy as a frail girl with large, violet eyes and skin as pale as moonlight. Somewhere around the tenth grade, she'd dropped out of school, and the folks of Drexel hadn't seen or heard of her since.

The road narrowed and curved, and finally disappeared beneath a mud puddle that stretched the width of the road and for a good twenty yards. Frank got out of the truck and walked to the puddle, using a limb he found to gauge the depth. It was at least two feet deep, and the bottom was soft mud. He went back to the truck, turned off the radio, lights, and engine, and started walking toward the camp. In the still night he could hear a whippoorwill, a bird that old-timers said brought death. It was a sad and mournful sound, and he thought of the slender singer, Hank Williams, who lived his songs of temptation and self-destruction.

A chorus of cicadas whirred loud enough to deaden Frank's footfalls, and then fell silent. It was then he heard the click of a hammer being pulled back. Frank stopped, his hands hanging at his side. He hadn't brought a weapon, a deliberate choice that he now silently questioned.

"Hold it, mister," the voice said, and Frank knew the speaker was male and young. The words sounded as if they were being gargled before the boy spat them out. Cleft pallet? Some type of speech defect? Frank stood perfectly still.

"Put your hands up." The boy struggled with the words.

Frank obliged. He felt the barrel of the gun in the small of his back and knew that if the trigger was pulled, the best he could hope for was quadriplegic. After what he'd seen in the war, he knew he'd rather be dead.

"Move." This word flew out, freed with such force Frank almost felt it against the back of his head.

He stepped forward, moving slowly and with ease. The gun stayed in his back and he didn't try to turn around. He didn't try to explain. The boy was a guard for the camp, and as such he had no authority to make a decision. Frank knew to wait until he talked to Dantzler himself.

They walked for half a mile before Frank saw the light of a fire and the sound of men. There was laughter and the rough scratch of a bow on a fiddle.

"Zerty!" The boy called out, another word he spoke with ease. "Zerty!"

His cry silenced the men, and Frank walked into the camp with his hands in the air and a rifle barrel snugged against his spine.

"Well, look who's here," Dantzler said as he came out of the rough cabin, pulling the straps of his suspenders over bare shoulders. "Deputy Frank Kimble, come to call on us. I wonder why." Dantzler spoke to the group of four men in various stages of undress. Even from a distance of ten feet, Frank could smell them. He suspected the ground where they sat would retain their odor for weeks to come.

"I need some help," Frank said, aware of the possibility that he'd miscalculated. He'd assumed that if he simply came to ask questions, Dantzler would cooperate. Now he wasn't so certain.

"Help with what?" Dantzler walked around Frank slowly, looking at him from all directions as if he weren't quite certain what Frank was.

"There's a missing girl, Suzanna Bramlett. I know you and your men are experienced woodsmen. I was wondering if you'd help look for her. She disappeared downriver from here."

Dantzler laughed, continuing his circuit around Frank. "Now that's an interesting question, Kimble. Here's one for you. How does a man go from being a decorated war veteran to a lapdog?"

The men all laughed and Frank forced his body to relax. "I'm a sheriff's deputy," he said slowly. "I'm doing my job. No more, no less. If it were your young'un missing, I'd do the same."

"No," Dantzler said. "No, you wouldn't. I happen to know that for a fact because my young'un was murdered, and you didn't do a thing about it."

Frank had touched the canker that went straight to Dantzler's heart. "Your boy was killed twelve years ago. It happened up in Stone County, and I wasn't a deputy then. Even if I had been, it would have been in Sheriff Haven Tate's jurisdiction. I couldn't do anything there, and I can't do anything here in Greene County. You know that."

The men were silent, but the barrel of the gun was solid in his back. Frank hadn't realized the boy was old and strong enough to hold it for so long. He turned slightly and caught a glimpse of the boy in the flickering fire and wished he hadn't looked. The boy was badly deformed. What he'd thought was a cleft palette was far worse. Scars covered one side of the boy's head, binding the mouth shut on that side, pulling closed the skin of a dead eye. There was no ear, only a hole.

"Stop lookin' at me," the boy said, his voice filled with hatred.

Frank averted his gaze, looking instead at the men on the ground. They, too, had turned away from the boy.

"Tell me, Deputy Frank, why you came all the way here to ask for expert timber man advice. Seems to me your folks used to be timber men. Seems to me there are lots of timber men in Jebediah County. What's so special about me?"

Frank turned slowly, until he faced Dantzler. His gaze passed over the boy, not stopping. He looked directly into Dantzler's eyes. "There's bad blood between you and Bramlett. If there was a chance you took the girl, I wanted to talk to you, see if you'd give her back. Try to keep the lid on this whole thing before it turns bad."

"Did Lucas Bramlett send you?" The night was so quiet, Frank could hear the fire snapping and popping.

"No."

"You came up here on your own to ask that question?"

"Yes."

"And you think you can do that and just walk out of here?"

"Yes." Frank wasn't afraid. That was the one thing that Dantzler Archey could not understand, and Frank knew it was his only trump. "Do you know anything about the Bramlett girl?"

"I could kill you and no one would ever find you."

"Eventually they would. Times have changed, Dantzler. There are forensics now, evidence." He shrugged. "If you've got the girl, give her to me."

"And if I don't?"

"Then I'm asking for your help in finding her."

Dantzler laughed. "You've got a set of balls."

"Do you know where Suzanna Bramlett is?" Frank asked. One of the men to his right shifted. Frank caught the glint of light on a blade. Behind him, another man shifted. They were arming themselves. If they all fell on him at once, he'd never stand a chance. He didn't look at the men. He kept his gaze on Dantzler. No one would make a move unless Dantzler ordered it.

"Boy, go up to the camp," Dantzler said. When the boy failed to move fast enough, Dantzler cuffed him hard enough on the head to knock him down. "Half-wit," Dant-zler said under his breath. "Get up to the camp!" He drew back a foot to kick the boy on the ground.

Frank stepped between them.

"This is none of your affair, lawman."

Frank didn't answer and he didn't move. The boy scuttled out of kicking range, got up, and ran to the camp, his rifle left in the dirt.

"You'd best get yourself back to the road," Dantzler said to Frank. "Now."

"Not until I know if you have the girl." The men shifted behind him again, and Frank knew they were preparing for an attack.

"I won't give you my word on anything. I don't give my word to Lucas Bramlett's lap-dog, but you can go up to the camp and look for yourself." Dantzler brushed past him, walking past the fire and into the woods. Like well-trained troops, the men followed after him until Frank was alone by the fire, the rifle in the dirt at his feet. He considered picking it up, but instead walked toward the camp where an oil lamp burned.

The boy was in there, and perhaps he'd be waiting with a knife or a gun. Frank considered the possibilities as he walked. When he got to the door, he smelled cornbread cooking. It wasn't uncommon for the timber camps to hire a black woman to cook and wash for the men while they were out working the trees. He tapped lightly, and when there was no answer, he pushed the door open and walked inside a long, narrow room with six beds. The stench was almost unbearable. The room was a narrow tomb, without windows or any ventilation. He pinched the skin under his nostrils and walked toward a curtain that was draped across the doorway that led to what had to be the kitchen.

He could hear someone in there, possibly the boy, maybe someone else. Frank didn't believe that Suzanna was at the camp. Dantzler wouldn't give her up so easily, unless he intended to ambush Frank on the way back to his car. Frank clicked through the possibilities as he walked toward the curtain. For some reason, he dreaded pushing aside the cloth. Dantzler had set him up, and whatever Frank was going to discover was going to be unpleasant. There were few things man could do that Frank had not already witnessed, and sometimes participated in. Still, he dreaded the looking.

He could hear soft scuffling behind the curtain and the sound of a chain dragging on the wooden floor. His hand touched the cloth. He heard the sound of crying, and a soft murmur, not words but a crooning of comfort. He drew the curtain slowly, not wanting to startle what sounded like a wild animal. He stepped into the heat of the kitchen, the smell of cornbread baking, and the sight of the woman. She was naked, her body fleshless and discolored by bruises. A heavy iron manacled one ankle, and hooked to it was an iron chain and ball, the type used by prisons. The boy clung to her, a knife in his right hand and a threat in his eyes.

Frank stood, unable to move as he looked into her face, the dark hair matted and filthy, and the violet eyes filled with the light of madness.

"Katy?" he said, his voice breaking on the word. "Katy?"

"Stay away," the boy said, brandishing the knife. "You stay away."

Frank stood perfectly still, taking in the scene, letting the pieces fall into place as his body filled with a rage so searing he thought he might explode.

"Katy, get some clothes," he said, talking as if she were a frightened animal. "Get some clothes. I'm taking you with me. You and the boy."

"Stay away!" The boy stabbed into the air.

"I want to help you," Frank said, talking now to the boy because Katy had shown no recognition of his words.

"You can't!" The boy howled the words. "If she tries to leave, he'll burn me again."

Frank nodded that he understood. He inched backward, moving toward the cloth that separated Katy and her son from the men who worked for her brother. "I'll be back," he said. "I'll come back to help you."

The boy shook his head, his one eye flowing with tears. "Don't," he choked. "Don't come back. That girl ain't here."

Frank left the camp. He stepped into the fresh night air, his lungs tight with an anger he hadn't felt in years. Dantzler materialized out of the darkness.

"Just remember, lawman, you don't have any jurisdiction here. By the time you roust ole Sheriff Miller up to Leakesville, Katy and the boy will be gone. I can move them and hide them as much as I like."

"She's your sister," Frank said.

"She's a whore. She brought shame on me, and now she's paying for it, just like in the Bible."

"I'll be back for her."

"Won't do you no good. She's insane. I keep her on a chain so she won't get lost in the woods. She can't wear clothes because

176

she sets herself on fire." He laughed. "Now you get back to your truck and you get off my property, and you'd better not come back unless you bring a lot of lawmen with a lot of guns."

14

Dotty's red-nailed hand snapped the knob of the television off. She picked up her empty glass and walked to the kitchen, annoyed at the silliness of Eve Arden as Connie Brooks in her pursuit of an obviously uninterested Mr. Boynton. It was only a foolish television show, but *Our Miss Brooks* seemed a perfect parallel to Dotty's life. Here she was, stuck in Drexel, her intentions good and her talents wasted.

She reached under the kitchen counter for the bourbon, poured another shot in her glass, and got an ice tray out of the refrigerator. She added several cubes, and then some Coca-Cola, swirling the mixture with her finger before she tasted it. Normally, she didn't drink alone, but Lucas had awakened something hungry inside her. She paced the kitchen, the skirt of her dress swishing against her thighs, her skin alive to the whisper of her nylon slip. She felt every texture, every sensation, and she wanted more.

She glanced at the clock. It was eight-forty-five. At this rate, she'd never be able to relax and go to sleep. She thought about calling the hospital to check on Marlena. Perhaps Lucas was there, but she didn't believe that even as she thought it. Lucas was at his house. He would wait there for others to report to him.

Making a decision, she picked up her car keys. Drink in hand, she walked out into the still hot night, got in her car, and headed toward Lucas's house. If he was home, he might welcome a visitor. She'd had a bath and changed into her second best pair of panties. Maybe tomorrow morning she'd go into town and do a little shopping. Marcel's carried a brand of underwear that she normally didn't buy because of expense. Hell, though, she still had a little of the money left from what the railroad had given her after Joe was killed when a train crushed him. Some folks called it blood money, but she'd paid off her house, like the lawyer recommended, and bought herself the television set because she deserved some entertainment on the long nights she spent alone. The remainder of the money, which wasn't much, she'd put in the bank for emergencies. Well, new underpants might just classify as an emergency, especially if Lucas Bramlett was going to see them. Dotty had seen Marlena's underwear, had been with her when she bought it in Mobile at one of the expensive department stores. If that was what Lucas was used to seeing, Dotty intended to give it to him.

She thought about the television show she'd just watched. Eve Arden was so innocent it made Dotty's teeth ache. All her character had to do was walk up to Philip Boynton and tell him she wanted some of what he had in his pants. That would do the trick. Dotty smiled, the cool wind from the car window and the bourbon making her lips feel both numb and eager.

She wasn't going to play innocent and hard to get. That was for television stars and young girls. At thirty-six, Dotty knew the sand was running out of the hourglass fast. Maybe Lucas would want another child. She could do that, though she'd never wanted children. The doctor had said Marlena couldn't carry a child. Lucas hadn't seemed all that interested in Suzanna, but it was hard to tell. Sometimes men didn't want something until it was taken from them. Just to be on the safe side, she had two rubbers in her purse. She'd put them there before she took Lucas breakfast. He hadn't used any protection, though. She accelerated slightly as she thought of what that might mean.

When she got to the Bramlett driveway, she stopped. The gate was across the road, the chain laced through it and the big padlock clearly visible. Lucas had locked the gates. It was such an unexpected twist that she sat in the car, unable to come up with another plan of action. Climbing the gate was out of the question. She could go home and call Lucas, ask him to open the gate, but somehow she knew that wasn't smart. He obviously didn't want company, and Dotty instinctively accepted that she couldn't wheedle him into anything. She backed the car onto the highway and kept heading east. After all, it was Friday night. She had no intention of being alone.

At the junction of Highway 63, she turned left, heading in a northeasterly direction. Just on the other side of the Greene County line was a bar. There was a jukebox and dim lights and an endless supply of whiskey. She'd go there and have a few drinks, maybe dance with someone if he was handsome enough. Maybe do more if he made her feel beautiful. She was hot and horny and in need of someone to make her feel desirable.

If Lucas was too busy to tend to her needs, she'd find someone who wasn't. She'd spent the entire day nursing his sick wife, and this was the thanks she got. Well, she'd see about that.

She pulled into the parking lot of the Friendly Lounge, a place where most nights the drinking and dancing went smoothly. She parked, got out of the car, and walked through the front door, staggered for a moment by the smell of beer and cigarette smoke. She pushed into it, slowing as her eyes adjusted to the neon lighting provided by Budweiser beer and Kool cigarettes. At the end of the bar a large fan blew, plastic ribbons dancing in front of it.

"Well, if it isn't Miss Strickland." The bartender reached behind him for a bottle of Early Times and a glass. "The first one's on me."

Dotty smiled. Boo Bishop was always nice to her, and he'd never blamed her for the knife fight that cost Tommy Teel twenty-six stitches around his neck and the Friendly a shut-down of two weeks. She perched on a stool and took the drink Boo handed her.

"It's been a while, Dotty. Where you been keepin' yourself?"

She shook her head. "I've been sitting with Marlena Bramlett at the hospital. You know she's my best friend, and it's just terrible what those criminals did to her."

Boo propped up on his elbows. "I heard she was beat up bad. That someone did awful things to her."

"You don't know the half of it," Dotty said, leaning closer so that he could smell the expensive perfume she wore. She'd taken the bottle from Marlena's vanity. The condition she was in, Marlena wasn't studying about perfume and chances were she'd never wear it again anyway.

"Tell me," Boo said.

"She was cut up bad and raped with . . ." She faltered.

"With a tree limb," a man said from the darkness of a corner. Junior Clements stepped up to the bar. "It was surely bad."

Boo stepped back. "That's a terrible thing. Miss Marlena has always been nothing but nice to me. I hate to think someone would hurt her like that."

Junior took the seat beside Dotty uninvited. He leaned his elbow on the bar so that he could address both of them. "I heard she got what she needed."

"That's a vile and terrible thing to say." Dotty edged backward from Junior. He made her skin crawl. "If Lucas heard you say such a thing, you'd be sorry."

Junior shrugged. "I'm not judging her, I'm just repeating what I heard."

"Well, you'd better stop," Dotty said, miffed that Junior had stolen her thunder. "Marlena is a good person. She didn't deserve anything that happened to her, and what about Suzanna? I guess she deserved to get herself kidnapped and taken off."

Junior sipped the beer he was holding. "Wonder what happened to that young'un. Sheriff Huey's been searching high and low. Frank Kimble hasn't slept a wink." He chuckled softly. "I heard Frank learned all about tracking from some old Injun got blown apart in the war. I guess it ain't doin' him much good, though, if he can't find a kid."

"I sure hope they find her and that she's okay." Dotty put as much maternal emotion into it as she could muster. Going on the record with a tender sentiment was a good thing to do. Junior ran his mouth all over the county, so it was just as well he repeated something sympathetic. "The men who took her are gonna be sorry." That was just a fact. Once Lucas found out who was behind this, no law in the country could protect them.

"What makes you think so?" Junior asked.

"Marlena told Jade something tonight. Some way she can identify the men who hurt her." She had Junior and Boo's full attention, and she decided to stretch the lie. "There's going to be hell to pay."

"I thought Mrs. Bramlett was unconscious," Junior said. "What I heard was that she wouldn't ever be right in the head. No matter what she says, no one's going to believe her. She's gone be a vegetable."

Dotty felt a lightning bolt of fury. Junior was an oaf. "That shows what you know. She told that nigger sister of hers something. Marlena knows who hurt her, and when she's strong enough, she's going to talk."

Junior laughed in a way that made Dotty feel stupid. She stood up. "The doctor said he expected a full recovery." She was outright lying. "It won't be long before that little girl is back with her mama and daddy and the people who took her are going to prison, if they live long enough to get there."

The front door of the bar opened and Dotty swung around to see who was coming in. The neon light struck Frank Kimble full in the face, and Dotty inhaled sharply. Frank looked like he'd seen a ghost. He was that pale, and shaky looking. He ignored her and walked to the bar, taking a seat three stools away from her.

"Bourbon. Make it a double, on the rocks," he said.

Boo poured the drink and set it down in front of him, then moved back. Dotty watched, twirling the ice cubes in her drink with her finger. It had been fun, titillating Junior and Boo, but now something serious had walked into the bar. "Frank, you look all done in. Did you find out something about Suzanna?" She got off her stool and walked over to him, carefully putting one foot in front of the other in a way that made her hips undulate.

"Dotty, I'm not in the mood," he said.

She stopped in her tracks, an expression of hurt on her face. "I was just asking a civil question. You don't have to get all touchy. I have a right to ask about Suzanna. She's my best friend's daughter."

She saw something rise up in Frank and touch his lips. He almost spoke, but he didn't, and she had the sense that she'd been spared. She didn't like men who made her feel uncertain. "Thanks for nothing," she said as she went back to her bar stool and her drink.

She watched Junior walk over to Frank, thinking the coroner was about as dense as a creosote post. Frank radiated an energy that warned others to keep away. It was as effective as a sign, to everyone except Junior.

"Find anything about the kid?" Junior asked.

Frank stared at his drink, but when he finally looked up, his expression was hard and cold. "No, Junior, I didn't find anything about Suzanna Bramlett. I'm just wondering what you and Pet Wilkinson stole out of that Chevy that was parked on the side of the road. What things did you take that may affect my finding Suzanna?"

"We didn't take a damn thing," Junior said. "You ain't got no call to go and say something like that."

Frank stood up, drained his glass, and turned to confront Junior. "I know you took something, and when I find out what, I'm going to see that you pay."

Frank put a dollar on the bar and walked out, slamming the door hard behind him. Junior stood looking after him. "Bastard," he said, but he didn't make a move to follow Frank into the parking lot. "I'd bust his chops but everybody in town knows he's crazy as a run-over dog."

The August night had fallen hot and heavy. Jonah had watched the three-quarter moon rise and disappear behind a thick cover of high clouds. Before the orange glow had disappeared from the western sky, he'd

187

heard the cry of a hoot owl. Death waited in the hot, dark night. He read the signs, and no matter how he tried to interpret them, they all said that someone would die before the sun lit the eastern sky.

Jonah wasn't a man who fought against fate. He had watched his father sicken and die from what some had considered a minor injury. Mose had limped into the house, the gash in his calf bleeding profusely. Jonah had helped his father wash out the cut and wrap it with clean rags.

"It may heal clean and it may not," Mose had said. As if the ambivalence of his own words had opened the door, infection set in. Jonah had helped his mother wash the oozing wound and even tried to cauterize it with a hot poker. Through it all, Mose had never cursed or screamed. He understood that his time to die had come.

Jonah accepted life, and death, much as his father had. Jonah had worked for the Sellerses, and then the Longiers. He'd learned what they wished him to learn, such as driving a car and the fancy manners of a butler. He'd dressed as they wanted him to dress, in tails for parties and khakis for gardening. He'd been by Lucille's side through her pregnancy, her marriage, her second pregnancy, and the death of her husband. In some ways, he was as married to her as he was Ruth. That hurt his wife, and he knew it. Still, he sat on the Longier porch in the cool of the night, listening to the portents of death, waiting for the phone to ring or the headlights of an approaching vehicle to bring the news of tragedy. Miss Lucille did not need to be left alone, and over the years Ruth had made it abundantly clear that she did not need him, would never allow herself that luxury.

Jonah shifted his position on the top step of the porch and thought about his life and how it was ruled by three women. Jade was his sun. She warmed his life and brought joy and bounty. He could not look at her without a smile. Lucille was the moon, a pale light that created shadow and hid more than it illuminated. Her rule over him was as strong as the tide, and as inevitable. Ruth was the earth, as solid and permanent as the ground he walked upon. He could not imagine a day without her.

There was not a single one of the women he could lose. Without any one of them, his life would fail to cycle through the seasons. At night he sometimes dreamt of Jade living in a city like New Orleans. He saw her happy, with a husband and children of her own. To have those things, she would need to leave Drexel, and as much as he wanted them for her, he wanted equally for her to stay, to run her beauty shop and content herself with her growing wealth. He did not dream of losing Ruth or Lucille. That time had come and gone. It was Jade whose fate was not yet sealed.

He heard the floorboards of the house creak and knew that Lucille was up. He heard her come to the screen door and look out across the side field where Amos and Andy, the two old mules, grazed in the lush summer grass, their dark silhouettes visible as the moon blinked out from behind the clouds. Jonah made no move to turn and talk to Lucille. He waited for her to speak first.

"Why are you still here, Jonah?" she asked.

"The night's full of sadness. Bad moon." He pointed to the sky where the moon floated from behind a cloud. For a moment, a banner of stars was also revealed, and then all was concealed by the clouds.

"Sitting on the front step won't keep bad news from coming in my door." Her voice broke at the last. She sobbed softly. "I want my grandbaby."

Jonah remained sitting. Lucille did not show her grief easily. She was not a tough woman, but she had built walls around herself. When one crumbled and fell, it brought chaos and shame, for Lucille and those who witnessed. From long years of practice, he waited her out. Her heard her sobs subside, and then the small intake of breath that signaled her efforts to regain control.

"Ruth will be telling everyone in the black church that I kept you here with me all night."

Jonah registered the bitterness in her words. For all that Ruth obsessed about Lucille, there was some of the same going in the opposite direction. "Ruth won't say anything. She's worried about Suzanna, too."

"She hates me. She's hated me every day for the last thirty-seven years."

Jonah didn't deny it. Why should he, when it was true? "Ruth cares about Marlena and Suzanna. She helped raise that girl of yours, and she was there the day Suzanna was born. She fed her her first bottle and changed her first diaper. Ruth can act cold as stone, but Marlena is part of her heart."

"She has reason to hate me," Lucille said, and Jonah heard the slamming of the door. He was surprised to see Lucille's bare toes peeping out from beneath the edge of her cotton gown as she came up beside him and used his shoulder for support as she sat down. "Sometimes I hate myself."

Jonah sat perfectly still. Long ago, there had been a time when he would have put his arm around Lucille and let her cry herself out against his chest. She had been such a pretty little thing, so dainty and delicate. Bedelia Sellers had never said aloud that part of Jonah's job was to protect Lucille. She hadn't had to. Jonah knew. When he drove Lucille to town, he followed behind her, letting the men of the town know she wasn't to be trifled with. Those had been perfect days, and whenever he remembered them, it was always April and the sweet smell of wisteria filled the air.

"Do you believe that the sins of the father are visited upon the children?" Lucille asked.

Jonah knew that sometimes words were a trap. Lucille was quoting the Bible, but the application of those words could be treacherous. "I don't know. I never thought much of God as a vengeful god. I think he's a god of love and forgiveness."

"The Bible says that my sins will fall on my children." She hesitated. "On my grandchildren." She spoke under duress.

"Lucille, I think you paid for your own sins, just like I've paid for mine."

"And Marlena? Why has this happened to her?"

"I don't know. Miss Marlena never hurt a single soul. I don't understand this, but the Bible tells us, too, that we don't always understand the ways of the Lord." He sought to bring her comfort. There wasn't a soul alive who couldn't flay the skin from their bones if they thought back over the things they'd done. Now wasn't the time. "We need to think about what we'll do when Miss Suzanna comes home." He turned to face her. "We should have a party." He realized his mistake. "You and Mr. Bramlett should have a party for Marlena and Suzanna. You could invite all the folks who help find her."

Normally, a party would be right up Lucille's alley, but he could see that she wasn't thinking on festive times. Her face was drawn, the wrinkles more pronounced than he'd ever seen them. He looked away, knowing how much pain his thoughts would cause her.

"When I got pregnant with Jade, I only thought about saving myself," Lucille said. Her voice seemed disconnected from her body. "I didn't care what happened to her. I didn't care that she was my daughter, I only wanted to get rid of her so that I could have my life back."

Jonah had often wondered how Lucille felt when she looked at Jade. Beneath that practiced coldness, there were feelings. Lucille wasn't more or less than human. She could not look upon the beauty of her abandoned daughter and feel nothing, no matter how hard she tried. "Jade has been well loved."

"More so than Marlena," Lucille said. "I am an evil and selfish woman, Jonah. God should strike me dead right here."

Jonah felt the dull pain of heartache. The source was always Lucille. He had spent his whole life protecting her, and her worst enemy was herself. "God don't judge you like that, Lucille. You did the best you could for Jade. If you'd kept her, her life would have been much worse, and you know it."

"I know I never considered keeping her. From the moment I realized I was pregnant I began to think of ways to get rid of her. If that doctor in Mobile would have aborted her, I would have done it."

Jonah wanted to get up and run away. The idea of life without Jade was unthinkable. "That's the past," he said, trying hard to believe the words he spoke. "Jade is a grown woman. She's a good woman. You didn't do her any harm."

Lucille took several deep breaths. "Now, Marlena. Oh, I wanted that baby. She grew inside me with all the love I had for another living soul. I never touched Jade once she was born. The nurse took her away. But I nursed Marlena. I loved her, and now she may not live. She may die and Suzanna may never be found. And this is all my fault."

Jonah put his arm around Lucille. He eased her against him so that he supported her. She wouldn't cry again. Lucille wasn't a woman of tears. She'd survived by taking action, and by morning, she would have a plan. Her confessions of the night would be something to bury and forget. He rubbed her shoulder as she leaned against him, her breath soft on his neck.

"I'm tired of being alone, Jonah."

Her words caused him the first surprise she'd given him in years. "You're not alone, girl. Why do you think I'm sitting out here on this hard old step?"

Her arms went around him and she clung to him. "Thank you, Jonah."

He didn't tell her that thanks weren't necessary. A man protected those he loved.

15

Daybreak slipped into the house, bringing the pine walls to a burnished brilliance. Most mornings Jade felt as if she awakened inside some ancient heart, part of the pulse and power of glowing red blood. This morning she thought of the fires of hell as she lay atop the quilt where she'd been all night. She'd drifted in and out of sleep, waking to the nightmare of reality that far surpassed the images of her dreams. Marlena was in a coma. There were no clues to finding Suzanna. Now, it was Saturday. She had appointments at the beauty shop beginning at seven, and she felt as if her shoulders were in the grip of a cruel giant. She'd crossed a line with Frank Kimble, and that, too, troubled her. Frank was a white man. He belonged to a world that would not admit her, at least not in the rigid social structure of Jebediah County. A liaison with Frank would define her role in Drexel into something she found unacceptable. She would not be the mistress of a white man. She would not hurt Ruth and Jonah, and herself, in that way. Her whole life had been a balancing act, and though she'd slipped, she had no intention of falling off the wire at this late date.

She got up, took a quick bath, and drove to the shop. Her movements were sluggish, as if a heavy weight of water held her in place. In front of her shop was a large white oak, and as she parked, she caught the first hint of fall. It was in the rustling of the tree leaves and the cry of the birds, just the merest whisper, but it gave her unreasonable hope. Time continued, and there was comfort in that.

She unlocked the front door, went in, and began her preparations. It was just after six, and she put water to boil on a hot plate she kept in the back. She hadn't taken time for coffee at her house, but if she was going to make it through the day, she needed a hard jolt of caffeine. As the water heated, she opened the back door, inhaling sharply at the tall, well-built man standing in her doorway. Frank looked like death.

"What? Is it Suzanna?" She put her hand on her heart, a melodramatic gesture that was purely reflexive, as if she could protect that organ from pain.

He shook his head. "May I come in?"

The pulse of blood in her head made her dizzy. Despite her earlier decision, she stepped back, allowing him entrance. He walked through the shop, closed the front door, and locked it.

The kettle screamed, a shrill sound that Jade at first thought came from herself. When she realized what it was, she put coffee in the dripolator and poured in the boiling water. "I'll have us a cup in a few minutes. You look like you need one." She was suddenly afraid of what he'd come to tell her.

"I went out to Dantzler Archey's house last night. I had reason to believe he might know something about Suzanna."

Jade kept her hand on the aluminum coffeepot. It had been her mother's, a gift when she opened the shop. Ruth gave practical gifts, things of use. Jade clung to her thoughts, veering away from the direction Frank tried to lead her. She knew Dantzler Archey, knew he was a violent man. The idea of Suzanna at his mercy was almost more than she could bear.

"I didn't find Suzanna," Frank continued, "or any sign of her. I found Katy."

His tone forced Jade's head up; her gaze

found his and she trembled. Death clung to him. "Don't tell me," she whispered. "I don't want to know."

"I have to tell someone," Frank said, his eyes dark with pain. "I called Sheriff Miller over in Greene County last night. He said there was nothing he could do. He said Dantzler swore Katy was insane and he was doing his best to care for her."

Jade got two cups and poured them both black coffee, aware that she was repeating movements from the previous night. She remembered his lips, his kisses that had stoked a fire deep inside her, one that continued to burn. She waited for him to continue, finding his eyes with her gaze as she handed him a cup.

"He had Katy chained in the kitchen, naked. I think the men who work for him are using her. Maybe him, too."

She never let her gaze falter. She allowed him to infect her with the things he'd seen. She swallowed and put her untouched coffee down.

"There was a boy," Frank said, squeezing the words out. "Katy's son, I think. Her son and Lucas's. He's been severely burned, and I think Dantzler did it deliberately. I think he tortures the boy and Katy."

Jade concentrated on slowing her breath.

Sometimes, when she was alone in the embalming room with a dead person, some- one who'd been mistreated or murdered, she felt things. Like now. She'd learned to hold still and let the feelings ripple through her. Holding on to them was the road to madness. When she had regained some calm, she asked, "What are you going to do?"

"I don't know," Frank said. He looked at his untouched coffee and put it beside hers. "I want to kill him."

Dantzler Archey had once struck Jade's father in the face when Jonah had followed Miss Lucille into Marcel's fine apparel shop. Jonah had gone to carry the packages for Miss Lucille, as he always did. Archey had accused Jonah of touching the lacy lingerie. Jade had been thirteen, and she hadn't understood the full implication of what Archey had said, but she understood enough to know that her father had been accused of something shameful. She could see the stain of it spread across Jonah's face as he rose to his feet.

Jonah's hands had curled into fists, and Jade had seen hatred in his eyes. The terror of it had made her cry out and run to her father, grabbing his arm, begging him to come away. Jonah had pushed her aside, the anger making his breathing harsh. Miss Lucille had stepped between the two men. She'd taken her purse and swung it hard, slamming Archey in the face. Blood had spurted out of his nose. "Get out of this store," Lucille had said in an imperious tone. "Get out before I have you put in jail."

Archey had left, and the next night someone had shot old Jake, the mule, and killed him in the pasture. Jonah had never spoken Dantzler Archey's name, but Jade knew who'd done it. And she knew to take care when she walked to town alone. For nearly two years she'd had the habit of crawling into the ditch at the sound of an approaching vehicle. Better safe than sorry was the axiom she'd learned to live by where Dantzler Archey was involved.

The idea that someone would kill him left her feeling nothing, but the look on Frank's face caught her like a physical blow. She shook her head. "No," she said. "Parchman prison is where he needs to be. I've heard that place is worse than hell. You're a lawman, put him in jail."

Her words had the desired effect. Frank smiled, and for a moment he shook off the pall of death that had come in the door with him. She was amazed at the power her simple words held, and then she was aware of a charge in the room. The air had turned electric. Frank looked at her, and she felt as if he were slowly removing every stitch of clothing she wore. She felt his gaze move over her breasts, bringing the nipples to erect points. His gaze lingered on her flat stomach before he moved lower, twisting her insides into something that quivered with a hungry need. It happened so quickly, she was unprepared to stop it. She did not want to stop it, even if the costs were high.

"Jade." His voice was hoarse.

She opened her mouth to say something, but nothing came out. She simply stood, looking at him, desiring his touch.

In a second he was across the small kitchen, his arms around her, his mouth on hers. She pressed herself against him, seeking some relief from the terrible need that had taken over her body. His hands tugged at her dress, pulling the mint green bodice apart.

She felt as if a giant tide moved inside her, drawing her toward shore with a power she could only yield to or drown fighting. Frank's arm supported her as his lips demanded, bending her backward so that she clung to him.

His hand reached inside her dress, inside her bra, and found her nipple. In a moment it was free and in his mouth. She moaned with pleasure, her fingers lacing into his thick hair, gripping, forcing his head to her breast for more.

She turned her face and caught sight of their reflection in the long mirror that ran down one wall of the shop. His dark head was buried in her breasts, his teeth gently tugging one nipple. She did not recognize herself, her features transfigured by wanton desire. It was enough of a shock to bring her to her senses. She caught his face and held him away from her.

"Frank," she said. "Frank. We have to stop."

He grew perfectly still, his short, hot breaths on her exposed skin. He inhaled and lifted his gaze to her. "We don't have to stop."

Her tears were unexpected and angry. "Yes, we do. I do."

His reaction was immediate. He stepped back, pulling her dress together. "I'm sorry, Jade."

She was not used to contrition on the face of a suitor. Jade was a careful woman, but she was not innocent. Men led to the brink of passion were seldom contrite. "No," she said slowly, "I'm the one who's sorry." She turned and picked up her coffee, aware that her dress was torn, her décolletage revealed.

"What's wrong?" he asked, and a smile played at the corners of his mouth. "Other than the fact that your sister is in a coma and your niece has been abducted."

She felt her own lips turn up, a match for his. "Oh, I don't know. That could be part of it. Another part is that you're a white deputy and I'm a black hairdresser. I don't see any future in it except pain and heartache." She swallowed the sudden lump in her throat and clung to her smile. "Just a few little insurmountable issues to consider."

"Will you have dinner with me tonight?"

She shook her head. "That's the problem, Frank. Where would we eat? You wouldn't be welcome in the restaurants that serve me, and I couldn't walk in the front door of Amy's Café or the Fish House. They wouldn't serve me if I sat at a table."

"Oh, you would be served —"

Jade shook her head. "Because you have the power of the law, you might make them serve me. But what happens after that? I have a business here. My parents live here. I won't start something I can't finish."

Frank's smile held. "The food there isn't worth starting something over." He stepped closer and his hands touched her bare arms.

"Come to the house. I'll cook."

Jade felt the hot desire deep in her bones. She wanted to melt, but she couldn't allow it. "You can cook?" She fought to keep her balance.

"I'm a good cook. I learned in France. Someone there taught me."

She knew she should say no. She was not a woman who wanted or needed a secret life, and Frank could never be a daylight suitor. But she could not deny herself. "Okay," she said. "Just dinner." The words were a transparent lie, but she felt better saying them.

"I'll pick you up at seven."

"Unless Marlena gets better and I have to stay with her."

He nodded. "Unless I get a break in the case and have to pursue a lead."

She reached up and touched his face, felt the growth of dark beard that had felt so exciting against the tender skin of her breast. "This may be a tragic mistake," she said.

Frank's eyes smiled this time. "My life is one tragic mistake after another, but this isn't one of them. I want to know you, Jade."

"I have to get ready for the customers." She didn't have time to go home and change her dress, but she had a smock in the back that she could put on. It would be hot, but it would cover the torn bodice.

"I'm going to Hattiesburg, but I'll be back around five."

"Hattiesburg?" She felt hope. "Is it Suzanna?"

"It's the man Marlena was meeting. He's been gone since Thursday afternoon. He hasn't shown up for work or even called in. I'm going to take a look around his house, see if I can pick up a lead."

"Do you think he has Suzanna?"

"I don't know," Frank said. "I think he was there. He may have seen what happened to her. He may know more."

"Are you going alone?" She was surprised that she wanted to go with him.

"Yes." He seemed to read her mind. "Do you want to go?"

"Yes" — she closed her eyes — "but I have appointments, and I should be here if Marlena needs me. I don't even know how she's doing this morning."

"I'll be back," he said. "I'll tell you tonight what I find out."

He went out the back door, stepping into the sun and heat, disappearing down the alley. Jade put on her smock and unlocked the front door again, opening it wide. Beneath the thrill of anticipation, she felt a beat of fear. Things were changing. She wasn't sure what she felt for Frank, except desire. Talk around town was that he was mentally unstable. He'd just proven that by asking her to dinner.

Jonah stood under the branches of the oak tree and waited until he saw Frank exit the alley behind Hollywood Styles, cross the street, and head toward the courthouse. Jonah's heart was troubled, a pain that reverberated in the pounding of his head. Jade and the white deputy were involved, and Jonah saw disaster on the horizon. Not broken hearts that would mend and tears that would dry, but true tragedy. He'd seen the signs of death the evening before. He'd waited all night for someone to come and tell him who had died, but no word had come. Death hung over Jebediah County, and Jonah knew that it was only a matter of time before it struck.

Jade was courting calamity. He'd suspected it last night when he walked in on the two of them, both so interested in the coffee in front of them that they couldn't look at each other. Now he knew for certain. He'd seen Frank and his daughter in a passionate clinch. His first instinct had been to rush into the shop and save his daughter from the mistake she was about to make. He didn't do that, though. Jonah understood the power of passion, the pull of the forbidden. He could have stopped them this time, but there would be a next time, and a next, and a next, until the passion was spent or the pressures of living a secret tore them apart. Or until Jade was destroyed. The course they'd chosen did not lead to happiness.

Jonah lingered in the shade of the oak, sorting through the crossroads he'd passed in his own life. Sometimes, it just seemed he made the same decision over and over again. He'd spent the night not with his wife, but with Lucille. The memory of her toes, exposed beneath her nightgown, came back to him, an intimate knowledge of a white woman he should not have. She'd asked him if the sins of the parent would be visited upon the child. He'd told her no, but now he wasn't certain. Jade was his daughter, and she'd chosen a path that could only lead to disaster. If she fell in love with Frank, truly loved him in that way that was given only once, her heart would be destroyed. Was this the punishment that Jonah had exacted upon her?

If the town suspected a relationship between the two of them, Jade would be the object of scorn, and likely worse. Jade would suffer, not Frank. All along, Ruth had been right. Jade should have gone away. She should have moved to Detroit or New Orleans, some city where the color barrier could be stepped over by a woman with pale skin and green eyes.

He watched Jade work around the shop. She'd put on a pale lavender smock over her dress, and he knew why. Jade was thirty-five, a woman truly grown. He'd never given much thought to her physical needs. He'd assumed that she had male friends, companionship, sex. Because she was his little girl, he'd never wanted to know the details. It wasn't that he objected to Jade loving a man. Frank was simply the wrong man. Bowing his head, he realized there wasn't a right man for Jade in Drexel.

Jonah started to leave. He needed to get home to check on Ruth. Before Suzanna was taken, Lucille had made a long list of things that needed to be done before fall set in. The corncrib needed repairing, the dead pine pasture had to be turned over. Work stretched out in front of him as long and hot as the day. There was comfort in work, a sense of rightness. Ruth understood this, and it was because they shared this in common that they'd been able to live together.

Ruth would have sat up and waited for him for a while, and then she would have gone to bed, madder by another degree. When the sun crested the horizon, she would have gotten up, made coffee, and had her bath. Likely she'd gone on to work for Miss Lucille. He saw Ruth walking down the road in her too-big shoes, back ramrod straight, hate boiling in her heart. Jonah moved from the shade of the oak to the bench beside the three big azaleas. He had no energy to go home; the truth had smote him like a hammer. Ruth was a force of hatred. He'd tried to be a force of love. Jade was caught in the middle, pulled in both directions. Neither he nor Ruth had prepared her for the destruction love could bring into a life. He'd failed her as surely as Ruth had.

He heard the sound of a large, smooth engine. The hearse from Rideout Funeral Home was coming slowly down the street toward him. He recognized the large man at the wheel. Junior Clements. Jonah felt a sense of dread. Here was the news that had been foretold. Death had struck, and Junior was the harbinger.

The hearse drew level with Jonah and stopped. Junior didn't say anything, he just looked at Jonah for a full minute. Junior was the kind of man who didn't like rules, except when they governed the behavior of someone else. Jonah did not speak. It was Junior's place to do so first.

"Tell that girl of yours Mr. Lavallette's gone be needing her today."

Jonah kept his gaze focused on the black paint of the hearse door. "Yes, sir, I will." Jonah feigned disinterest.

"Don't you want to know who died?" Junior asked, exasperated.

"Ain't none of my business," Jonah said. He stood up, prepared to move along.

"That's the truth. It ain't none of your business. It shouldn't matter to you that Mrs. Amelia Covington passed this morning. She died as peaceful as a baby."

"Sorry to hear of her passing," Jonah said. "I'm sure Jade will be happy to help Mr. Lavallette out today."

"You tell her to get up to the funeral home after lunch."

"Sure will," Jonah said. "I'll do just like you say, Mr. Clements." When he was a younger man, he'd suffered when he uttered obsequious words. At fifty-five, he was a wiser man. Words were a small price to pay to keep danger averted from those he loved. Junior Clements was a man capable of violence, as long as he thought there would be no consequence.

The hearse eased down the street. Jonah considered going over to talk to Jade, but he didn't trust himself not to lecture her. He put his straw gardening hat on his head, an attempt to fight the August heat, and he started to walk. He went away from town, away from his house, away from Miss Lucille's. He walked toward the Chickasawhay River and the place where Miss Marlena had been attacked and Suzanna taken.

16

Frank turned left off Highway 98 onto Letohatchie Road. The sun blazed down on the new asphalt, making it look like liquid and leaving the smell of something burning. Frank thought about the boy at the timber camp. If Dantzler Archey had taken Suzanna, he hoped she was dead. He'd learned death sometimes came as a rescuer. He had no doubt that would be the case for Suzanna if Archey was her captor.

He checked his watch. The morning had slipped away from him in a series of unproductive leads. He'd stopped at two stores in McLain only to discover the clerks worked only on Saturday and didn't know John Hubbard, the Big Sun route man. Berger's Grocery in Beaumont had been closed, a sign in the front window saying there'd been a death in the family. Frank had continued northwest until he came to New Augusta, the county seat of Perry County. He was still thirty-odd miles from Hattiesburg, and it was almost lunch.

The road to the town square was newly paved, but the heavy log trucks had already wallowed out potholes. He drove slowly, dodging the holes. Huey had let him bring the patrol car, since he was on official business. Frank was worried about Huey. Even sitting behind the desk in his office, his face was too red, a trickle of sweat at his hairline. Frank knew the cause was Suzanna's abduction, and he also knew that part of it was Huey's real concern for the child.

Frank circled the square and continued out Highway 12 to Goode's Grocery. This was one of the stores Hubbard serviced, and Frank felt his hopes rise when he saw the store was open. The door was unlocked, the windows up to allow for a breeze, in the unlikely event of one dropping down out of the Gulf Stream. Frank pulled in beside the gas pump and waited until an elderly man came out of the store, pulling his suspenders up as he walked.

"Fill her up?" the old man asked.

"Sure," Frank said, getting out and stretching. He was wearing khakis and a starched white shirt, the long sleeves rolled up on his forearms. He'd decided against his uniform. Sometimes official trappings were a hindrance, and the car was more than enough to legitimize his questions.

"What's the law from Jebediah County doing up here?" the man asked.

"Following a hunch," Frank said. He leaned against the car. "Might be you could help me out."

"Me?" the old man asked, arching his eyebrows. "What would I know about anything that happened down in Jebediah County?"

Frank pushed himself off the car and walked casually around the gas pump. "I think I'll get myself a drink. Maybe some chips. I've got to drive on to Hattiesburg and I haven't had breakfast." He hesitated for a few seconds. "You got something good and cold?"

"There's a cooler in the store." The old man didn't look at him.

"What's your name?" Frank asked.

"Sample Corley," the man answered. He tapped the gas nozzle twice and pulled it out of the car's tank. "That'll be four-twenty-three."

Frank pulled a five-dollar bill out of his wallet and handed it over. "I'll walk in with you and get my Co-Cola." He followed one step behind Corley as they opened the screen door and walked into the store.

The wooden floor was well-worn, darkly oiled so that it caught the dim light and held it. A low hum came from the freezer box at the back of the store where glass bottles of fresh milk chilled beside brown-bottled beer. Another meat freezer was on the far side of the store, and Frank could see steaks, roasts, pork chops, sausage, and bacon already cut and laid out on pieces of wax paper. A round of hoop cheese was beside the meat. Staples, canned goods, and baking supplies lined the aisles. The rack of Big Sun chips was right at the counter. Only a few bags remained.

"I was wanting some chips, too," Frank said, "but you're out of the barbecue."

"Johnny didn't come by yesterday," Corley said, frowning. "He left me short last week and then didn't come by."

"Is that normal for the Big Sun route man?"

"Heck, no, Johnny's usually on the dot. He must be sick."

Frank didn't say anything. He got a Coca-Cola from the red box freezer, opened it, and took a long swallow. "That hit the spot," he said. "Could I get some cheese and crackers?"

"Sure," Corley said, going to the meat cooler and pulling out the hoop cheese. He cut a hunk and weighed it. "That'll be forty-five cents, and the crackers are five."

Frank nodded. "That's fine." He took the cheese, wrapped in wax paper, and got a single stack of saltines. Corley moved back to the cash register, totaled up Frank's purchases, and gave him his change.

"Do you know John Hubbard well?" Frank asked. He broke off a piece of cheese and put it in his mouth.

"Why are you so interested in Johnny?" Corley asked, suspicion in his gray eyes.

"Like you said, he missed his route Friday. Could be something bad happened to him."

Corley snorted. "Right. You're all worked up over a chip and candy salesman who don't even live in Jebediah County."

Frank grinned. "You're too smart to be a grocery clerk."

"One thing about running a store. You learn folks. No lawman from down by the state line is gonna come all the way up here to check into the well-being of someone who *might* be in trouble. What's going on?"

"Mr. Hubbard may possibly have information on the abduction of a child." Frank knew it was foolish to dance with Corley. The old man had nothing to do except exercise his caginess.

"Johnny wouldn't take a young'un." Corley's face had gone tight. "A woman, maybe. A young'un — not on your life. Johnny wasn't overly fond of the little ones."

Frank took another swallow of the cola, feeling the burn at the back of his throat. "I'm not looking at him as the abductor. I think he may have been on the scene, or nearby. Could be that he saw something that will help us."

"When did all this happen?" the clerk asked.

"Thursday, around lunch or a little after."

Corley reached under the counter and got a plug of tobacco and a pocketknife. He cut off a chunk and put it in his jaw. As an afterthought, he held it out to Frank.

"No thanks. I quit smoking in Germany. Never cared to take up tobacco again."

"World traveler," Corley said, snorting.

"Prisoner of war," Frank said, unwrapping the cheese and breaking off another piece. He chewed it slowly. "So Hubbard didn't care for children, and he liked women. How do you know this?"

Corley walked out from behind the counter and went outside, motioning for Frank to follow. Two old chairs had been set up in front of the store. Corley took one and waved Frank into the other. He spat into the dirt at his feet. "It was more or less a joke not to leave the wife minding the store on the day Johnny was due to come by. He talked to the womenfolk." He shrugged. "He had a way with them. Women liked him. He made them shine."

"Did he do more than talk?"

"Not here. Myrtle may enjoy a compliment, but she's not interested in much more. She sure enough loved to see that Chevy pull in, though. Her whole face would light up and she'd call out to me, 'Sample, it's Johnny. Get that slice of pound cake I brought him.' She'd bake a cake just for him, too."

Frank watched the old man's face. "You like Hubbard?"

"Couldn't help it," Corley said, then spat again. "He's a likeable guy. Not a kidnapper, though. Like I said, might run off with a wife, but he wouldn't take a young'un."

"You're sure of that. Why?"

"More in the way he'd look at the children when they came in the store. Like he thought they had some kind of disease. No, he wasn't a man who thought a lot of kids."

"This girl who was taken, she comes from a wealthy family."

Corley snorted and laughed. "Johnny doesn't need money. He has everything he needs, and then some. Big Sun pays him well. He's their top salesman, and he told me just a couple weeks ago that they offered to move him to the best route, up to Jackson. He's sitting pretty."

"Did he ever talk about any women in particular?" Frank asked. His Co-Cola bottle was empty, but he held it in his hand, enjoying the lingering chill.

"He was sweet on someone. The reason I know is that he stopped talking about all the other women. He usually had some foolishness going, like men do." Corley peered at Frank to see if he understood.

"Maybe you'd better explain."

"You know, like he'd talk about what this one did and that one did, which one was better at what." A slow flush crept up Corley's neck. "Not in front of Myrtle. No, he wasn't like that. Only when I was here by myself. Hell, he'd get me so worked up I'd order anything he put in front of me." He laughed, looking away. "But all of that talk stopped about six months ago. He said he had him someone special."

"Really? Did he say a name?"

Corley shook his head. "He never did. He did say the only fly in the ointment was that she had a kid." He chuckled. "He just didn't care for children, and he said this one in particular was a real brat." Another thought crossed his mind, and his eyebrows arched. "Maybe he ran off with this girlfriend and got married. Maybe that's why he didn't run his route Friday."

Frank stood up. He put the empty Coke bottle in a wooden rack beside the door. "I don't think so," he said. "If you see Mr. Hubbard, tell him he needs to check in with the Jebediah sheriff's office."

Corley leaned forward. "You're not looking at Johnny for some crime, are you?"

"Like I said, he may have information we need." Frank still held the cheese and crackers. He looked down at them as if he'd forgotten what they were. "Thanks, Mr. Corley. You've been a real help." He walked to his car, got in, and drove back toward Highway 98 and Hattiesburg.

The heat was oppressive, almost like a wet glove pressing down on her face, clogging her nose. Dotty tossed on the bed, her body itching with unfulfilled needs and hot memories. She had the terrible sensation that her skin no longer fit, that her swollen flesh was splitting.

She rolled to her back and stared at the ceiling. She hadn't heard a word from Lucas since she'd taken him breakfast, and the more she thought about it, the angrier she got. Except the anger turned back on herself and she wondered why she'd ever thought Lucas would call her. She'd provided him a service, and that was that. He never said he would call, never hinted that he might think of her in the future. She'd let things happen too fast. Fearing that she wouldn't have another opportunity, she'd never made him anticipate her. She'd been too damn easy.

Her head throbbed from the whiskey she'd drunk the night before, and even though it was late afternoon, she was still in bed, still suffering. She had a vague memory of dancing with Junior Clements and Pet Wilkinson, and the idea of it made her feel nauseous. She swung her feet to the floor and sat on the edge of the bed, woozy and sick. Whatever her sin, she always paid triple for it. So, she'd gotten drunk and danced with Pet and Junior and some other men in the Friendly. She wasn't the only woman who did such things, but she was surely the only woman who paid such harsh penance for a few hours of laughs. She glanced at herself in her vanity mirror and quickly turned away. Bags hung beneath her eyes, and the skin on her face looked parched and bloated. She couldn't remember how much she'd had to drink, or how she'd gotten home.

She struggled to her feet, the pressure in her bladder too painful to ignore. Taking short, quick steps she made it down the hall to the bathroom and sank to the toilet, her head resting in her hands. She hadn't been this hung over in a long time. She considered vomiting but she hadn't eaten in hours. If she began retching, it would quickly degrade into dry heaves. No good would come of that. She ran water in the sink, soaked a washcloth, and put it over her face. The cool water seemed to help. She finished peeing, wiped, and struggled to her feet. Water was the thing she needed, if she could drink some and keep it down. She filled a glass and drank. She found the aspirin bottle in her medicine cabinet, shook out three, and swallowed those, too.

When the phone began to ring, she considered not answering it. Then she thought it might be Lucas, and she hurried down the stairs to the telephone table in the front hallway. By the time she reached it, she was panting and about to vomit.

"Dotty, it's Lucille Longier. I'm sending my driver over to pick you up. We need to chat."

Before Dotty could say no, the line was dead. She held onto the receiver as if it were some unknown implement. At last she put it down and hurried back up the stairs. She started her bath and went to the closet to find a dress. Lucille Longier was Marlena's mother. She was Lucas's mother-in-law, and a powerful woman. Dotty couldn't be sure if she'd heard disapproval in Lucille's voice or desperation. There was no way Lucille could have found out about her sexual encounter with Lucas. No one had been behind her when she turned into the Bramlett driveway. No one could have seen her. She hadn't whispered a peep about it, and she didn't think Lucas would be running to his mother-in-law to tattle. Still, there was the sensation of cold fingers on her spine. Her stomach churned and she rushed up the stairs to her bathroom, barely making it before she heaved up the water she'd just drunk. Her life was a terrible mess. She'd never done anything bad enough to deserve all that was happening to her. She clung to the toilet seat and sobbed, waiting for the next round of vomiting.

17

Jonah squinted his eyes against the glare of the late afternoon sun as he steered the Buick down the highway. His stomach growled, and he wanted nothing more than a long shower and some clean clothes. The day had gotten away from him. Jade and Marlena had become entwined in his mind, his emotions, and the end result was dread. Something bad lurked on the horizon.

Beside him, Dotty Strickland stared straight ahead in the passenger seat, too sick to realize she sat beside a Negro as they drove through Drexel on the way to the Longier house. He'd been surprised when Lucille told him to drive to town and pick Dotty up. He couldn't figure what Lucille wanted with Dotty, a woman she was more than vocal in her disapproval of. Lucille despised Marlena's friendship with the widow. Lucille was not herself lately. She hadn't said a word to him about being late for work this morning.

He'd started walking to the Chickasawhay, a mighty long trek, but he'd been picked up by Sheriff Huey and driven to the Longier house. The sheriff had told him there was nothing to see at the river, and that Lucille would need his support and help. Jonah had not especially wanted a ride back to town, but the sheriff had looked bad, his face flushed with blood, his eyes red-veined and bulging. Rather than argue with a man who looked like a heart attack, Jonah had gotten in the car and allowed himself to be deposited at his place of work.

Ruth had made biscuits and sausage gravy, but Jonah couldn't eat. He'd noticed that Lucille's plate had also been untouched. In defiance of both of them, Ruth had served herself a heaping plate and eaten every bite, washing it down with two cups of coffee. In all of his years of marriage, he'd never seen Ruth eat like that. She'd done it for pure spite. Then she'd gotten up, yanked the sheets from Lucille's bed, and started washing, her face sullen and her eyes forking lightning whenever she looked at him. To get away from Ruth's anger and Lucille's depression, Jonah had gone down to the scuppernong arbor with two five-gallon buckets. He'd filled them both with wild grapes before he walked back to the house. That's when Lucille had sent him to fetch Dotty.

He chanced a look at Dotty, wondering if he should pull over. She was green and holding onto the door handle as if she were drowning.

"Miss Dotty, do you need to stop?"

He saw her throat working, but she gave up trying to talk and shook her head. He pressed a little harder on the gas pedal, wanting to get her to Lucille's before he had vomit to clean out of the car. He turned right on the long drive that led up the hill and accelerated again. Dotty closed her eyes and turned her face to the breeze.

When they stopped in front of the house, Jonah got out and went around to open the passenger door. Dotty's hand trembled as she allowed him to help her out of the car. Because she was unsteady, he kept his arm stiff for her to use as they walked up the steps and across the porch. Ruth met them at the door, her glare sliding from Dotty to Jonah. She didn't say anything. She un-latched the screen and walked down the hall, leaving Jonah to assist the unsteady woman into the house and guessing that Lucille waited in the kitchen. He led Dotty there.

"Mrs. Strickland, I didn't realize you were ill," Lucille said, rising from her chair at the head of the table.

"My stomach is upset. I've just been overwrought about Marlena."

"Yes." Lucille took the black coffee Ruth had poured and put it down in front of Dotty. "We've all been terribly upset. Would you like something to eat?"

"No, thank you." Dotty turned away from the table. Jonah saw her lips tighten and he felt a compulsion to help her. Instead, he stood rooted to the spot, his wife staring hatred into his bones.

"Jonah, would you get a glass of brandy for Mrs. Strickland. She looks a little peaked."

Jonah went to the parlor and poured a small amount of brandy into a crystal glass. Jebediah County was a dry county, but that didn't stop the privileged members of the community from drinking. Lucille kept her liquor in cut glass decanters in plain view, even when Sheriff Huey came by on the occasional evening. Sometimes he sipped brandy with her, reminiscing about the days when Bedelia and J. P. Sellers were still alive and the Sellerses' fortune was spent on fine liquor and food.

Dotty was holding onto the table with

both hands, and Jonah put the drink in front of her. She picked it up, sipped, and closed her eyes. Jonah felt the tension in the room, but he had no idea why Lucille had sent for Dotty. He didn't understand why he and Ruth were still a part of the moment.

Lucille licked her lips and abruptly leaned forward. Her voice was almost a whisper. "Dotty, did Marlena tell you what she was doing in the woods?"

Dotty's eyes snapped open. She picked up the drink and tilted the glass to her mouth, swallowing. She put her glass down before she looked at Lucille. "Marlena never said a word. I can't imagine."

Lucille's mouth twisted into something ugly. "My daughter may not live. My grand-child has disappeared. If you know some-thing, you'd better tell me right now. If you know what Marlena was doing in the woods, now is the time to tell."

Jonah stood against the kitchen counter, feeling the need to stop the conversation. Ruth stood fifteen feet away from him, a smile of victory on her face.

"I haven't a clue what Marlena was up to." Confrontation had brought some color to Dotty's cheeks, and she sat up straighter.

Unable to stand it any longer, Jonah stepped forward. "Miss Lucille, it's time to call the hospital and check on Miss Marlena. Could be she's feeling better and she can tell you herself why she went to the river."

Lucille sat upright. She composed her features, her gaze shifting away from Dotty. "Ruth, would you mind getting the overnight case I left in the car?"

"I'll get it, Miss Lucille." Jonah started forward. His wife hated it when Lucille ordered her around in front of others.

"No, Jonah." Lucille's sharp tone stopped him. "I asked Ruth to get it."

"Yes, ma'am." Ruth shuffled across the kitchen to the back door. "I'll fetch that bag for you, Miss Lucille."

Jonah recognized the mockery in Ruth's tone, and he waited to see if Lucille would reprimand her. The women were like three frightened cats shoved in a sack, each one clawing and scratching at the other. As soon as the screen slammed, Lucille leaned closer to Dotty.

"If you know something, or think you know something, say it now."

Dotty shrugged. "I don't know why Marlena would want to go into the woods on a hot August day. The mosquitoes would eat a person alive, not to mention the yellow flies." She tossed her hair.

Lucille reached across the table and picked up Dotty's hand. "You aren't protecting Marlena by holding back what you know."

Dotty snatched her hand away. "What are you saying? What is it you think I know?" Awareness dawned in her eyes. "You think Marlena has confided some secret to me, and you want to know what it is."

Jonah stepped to the table. "Miss Lucille," he said softly, "this isn't doing anybody any good. Miss Marlena went for a picnic with her daughter. Nothing more, nothing less."

Lucille turned on him, trembling. "My daughter may die and my grandchild is missing. I have to find out what Dotty knows."

Jonah held her gaze, willing her to stop talking. If Miss Marlena was meeting someone in the woods, the last person who should know it was Dotty Strickland. "Miss Dotty can't help you with this," he said softly. "Best not to conjure up wild rumors and thoughts." He shifted his gaze to Dotty and saw calculation in her eyes. Miss Lucille had just handed her a loaded gun. He had no doubt that Dotty would pull the trigger when it would best benefit her.

Jonah heard Ruth clumping along the

porch, the heavy bag making one step heavier than the other. "Ruth, did you think to get those old letters from the storage shed? If we can find the name of Miss Marlena's friend who was moving back to town, maybe we can find her. All I remember is her fist name. Connie. Do you remember more?"

Ruth stopped in the doorway, dropping the case so that it thumped loudly on the floor. "What are you —"

"I'll walk out to the shed with you," he said, knowing that his wife would never do a single thing to help Lucille, even at the cost of Marlena. "If we can find those letters, maybe we can find that woman. That's who Miss Marlena said was wanting to meet at the river for a picnic. Remember? She asked you to make some food."

Ruth looked at Lucille and Dotty. Her mouth opened to deny any such knowledge. Jonah moved across the room and gently took her elbow. "Let's go look." He propelled her out of the doorway and onto the porch, tightening the grip on her arm when she started to speak.

"Don't say anything," he whispered, moving her along the porch and down the stairs as rapidly as he could with her balking and pulling back.

"Take your hand off me," she demanded, snatching at her arm.

"Hold your tongue," he warned, tightening his grip until he felt her wince. "You might not care about Lucille, but Miss Marlena could suffer if you don't help me."

Ruth became more pliant, and he walked with her across the yard to the old shed that had once been slave quarters. "They're watching," he warned her, feeling the gaze of someone on his back, but he didn't turn around to look. They were in clear view from the kitchen window. "Come in here with me, Ruth. We can pretend to be looking."

"I'm not part of lying," she insisted, balking again.

He leaned to whisper in her ear, an intimate gesture that would have looked loving to anyone watching. "Ruth, you're going in there to help me, and you're going to do it willingly." He didn't recognize the tone of his own voice.

Ruth obliged, walking beside him up the steps and into the shed. Once the door was shut behind them, she turned on him, her hand swinging through the near darkness to catch him hard on the face.

The sting made tears flood into his eyes, but he didn't move. She made a noise like a wounded animal and struck him again, on the other side of the face. "You bastard," she said. She rushed him, pummeling his chest with her fists. "Goddamn you. When Jade was little, I used to make believe she was your daughter. Your flesh and blood. I wanted that to be true because I was so afraid that Miss Lucille would try to take her away from us. Back then, I wanted to believe that something good could come from your love for that bitch. Now I know Jade is no part of either one of you. She couldn't be." She drew back as if to strike him again.

He caught her wrists and held her. "Nothing happened, Ruth. I stayed over here because I thought they'd come to tell her that Suzanna was dead. Nothing more."

His wife slumped against him, sobbing. He could feel the wetness of her tears soak through his shirt, cool on his skin. "Plenty more happened," she sobbed. "You chose her over me, over your own daughter. You stayed to comfort her."

"Marlena is her daughter," Jonah said.

"And Jade is her daughter, too. But that doesn't make a difference to her. She just pretends that Jade is nothing to her. So why should I pretend Marlena is something to me?"

Jonah put his arm around Ruth and held her tightly against his chest. "Because she is, Ruth. You can deny it with words, but not in your heart."

"She's a spoiled white woman." Ruth's tone was venomous.

"Yes," Jonah said, "she is that. But she's a lot more, and you know it." His hands moved over her back, soothing and comforting, as they would a child. "She's Jade's sister. Right or wrong, Jade cares about her. She cares about Suzanna, too. And even if you won't admit it out loud, you care about them."

"I won't admit it."

In the darkness of the shed, Jonah smiled. Ruth was a stubborn woman. It was both her greatest strength and weakness. It was how she survived and how she punished. "I'm going to take Miss Dotty home. The worst thing in the world would be for Miss Lucille to reveal anything."

"What's there to reveal?" Ruth asked.

Jonah hesitated, Ruth was stubborn and could nurse a grudge to the grave, but he believed her love for Marlena was greater than her hatred of Lucille. "Miss Lucille thinks Marlena was meeting a man in the woods. She was trying to find out if Dotty knows anything about it. Rumors are bound to start now, and if Dotty Strickland sees a way to turn one to her advantage, she'll spread it all over town."

Ruth stilled against his chest. He could almost feel her thinking. "Miss Marlena wouldn't fool around on her husband. Mr. Lucas would kill her."

Jonah didn't say anything. Ruth had to know the stakes were high.

"Did Lucas know about this picnic?" Ruth asked.

"I don't know." Jonah felt his wife step away from him.

"Was she meeting someone?"

He couldn't see her in the darkness of the shed, and he unexplainably felt as if he'd stepped into danger. "I don't know," he said. "No one knows for sure, but if this rumor gets started, there won't be any stopping it."

"True or not, Lucas won't have her back. He won't have no use for soiled goods." It was a simple statement of fact.

"I'm worried about what Miss Dotty's gonna say." Jonah hadn't confessed his fears to Ruth in many years. Now it felt natural, the right thing to do.

"You should be." Ruth flipped on the overhead light. She stood beneath it, her face cast in harsh shadows. "She and your precious Miss Lucille are just alike. You'd best stay clear of it, Jonah, or you'll pay the biggest price of all."

18

Jade sat beside the hospital bed as the afternoon sunlight streamed in the open window, heating the back of her neck. Tiny drops of perspiration trickled between her breasts, and she tried not to think about the work she'd left undone. Before coming to the hospital, she'd gone home and changed into a calico shirtwaist to replace the dress that Frank had torn. The memory of Frank's hands and lips made her even hotter, but the heat of passion was mingled with a cold dread. To continue would bring trouble for both of them. Mostly for her. But she couldn't stop. It was impossible to imagine not meeting him for dinner. Such strength was beyond her grasp. Frank had hovered on the fringes of her mind for the past two years, since he'd come home. She'd seen him, watched him, listened to her clients talk about him, and all along she'd never allowed herself to go beyond a mere ripple of sexual pleasure when his name was mentioned. To pursue fantasies of Frank would make her life unbearable. He was too real to toy with in such ways. Dreaming of a house on the water in Jamaica was harmless, because it was out of reach. Frank was both too real and too unattainable. When they passed each other and their gazes met, heat arced between them. She became instantly aware of her body, of the rush of blood to her groin. She was drawn to him, but up until this point she'd been able to stay away.

A sense of doom settled over Jade, and she picked up Marlena's hand. She held it, warming it between her own hands. Marlena's was cold, a white so pale the veins were exposed. Death had touched her, maybe stolen her life, or at least marked it for a future collection. The dark angel would be back, and Jade had come to do battle for her half-sister. Marlena was too young to die, innocent in so many ways. Jade knew how Death could slip into a crib, or a bed, or a room, and steal away with the essence of life. She felt Death's presence in Marlena's cold flesh, and she held on more tightly, determined not to let Marlena slip away. Jade closed her eyes and imagined Marlena laughing in the rose garden of Lucas's home. She held large scissors in one hand and several freshly cut stems of First Blush roses in the other. First Blush was Marlena's favorite flower, a creamy white with a hint of pink at the center. The flowers were the only element of her wedding that Marlena had been allowed to have her way. Jade concentrated on this image, on Marlena, bathed in white light, holding the roses and laughing.

The hospital room door opened, bringing Jade back from her vision. A different doctor, younger, stepped into the room, his face controlled, emotionless. He walked to the bed and took Marlena's other hand, checking her pulse at her wrist. The gaze he leveled on Jade was calculating.

"Her heart is strong," he said as he released Marlena's hand. "If she wants to come out of this, she will. There's some disagreement with Dr. McMillan, but I believe the coma is self-induced, an escape."

"Her brain . . ." Jade didn't finish the sentence. Marlena had been struck ruthlessly in the face so many times that there had been fear of her brain swelling, of blood clots, of damage to the frontal lobes or percussive bruising of the brain stem. Her swollen face had begun to go down, but there was no telling how the beating had affected her brain.

"When she regained consciousness, she was coherent. That indicates there's no brain damage," the doctor said. "Had she never awakened, I would've been concerned." He started to leave.

"You believe she can wake up when she wants to?" Jade asked.

The doctor's gaze shifted to Marlena's still form in the bed. "Yes," he said at last. "I believe that she can live, if she chooses to do so. Or she can die, if that's her choice. The wounds inflicted on Mrs. Bramlett's body are severe, but not fatal."

Jade released Marlena's hand and slowly stood up. "What can I do?" she asked.

"Help her remember the reasons to live. Talk to her," he said. He started out the door and then turned back. "Where is her husband?"

"Waiting for a ransom call on his daughter." Jade didn't believe that, but it was the easiest explanation for Lucas's continued absence.

"He should be here with his wife. She needs him."

Jade nodded, even though she disagreed. Lucas could not help Marlena now. She was beyond his grasp.

"I'll have one of the orderlies bring a cot

in here for you," the doctor said.

Jade started to protest, but he was gone, his dark suit disappearing down the dim hallway. She would not be in the room when the cot arrived, thereby avoiding a confrontation she had no desire to win.

Marlena sighed, and Jade picked up her hand again. "You have to come back," Jade said. She tried to recall a happy memory, something that would tempt Marlena to choose life. "Remember the swing that Jonah built for you in the magnolia tree?" Jade closed her eyes and visualized the stout wooden plank that Jonah had drilled four holes in. He'd attached chains with bolts and then climbed the huge tree in the Longier backyard. "Remember how Daddy scooted out on the limb and attached the chains?"

Lost in her memory, Jade smiled. "Once the swing was hung, he let you go first. He pushed you so high. You were screaming. Your hair flew out behind you, and then tangled like a golden web all in your face when you went backward. You were going to brush it out of your face, but Daddy told you not to let go of the chains. Remember?"

It was a moment of perfect memory in Jade's mind. After Marlena had finished her turn, Jonah had swung Jade. She'd felt like she was flying through the treetops, but safe, because her daddy was there. After that, Lucille had come out of the house and made them stop swinging. She'd taken Marlena inside, her hand pinching the little girl's shoulder as they'd walked away.

"It was May, and we could smell the magnolias," Jade continued, focusing on the good, seeing it so clearly in her mind that she could remember the light on the glossy magnolia leaves, the deeper green of the cast-iron plant around the base of the tree. Jade grasped her sister's hand more firmly. "There's nothing in the world as sweet as sun-warmed magnolia. Smell it, Marlena. You wanted a flower for your mother, and Jonah got one. He told you not to touch the petals or they'd turn brown. You were so careful. You wanted the flower to be flawless for your mother. You said she smelled like magnolias, and she did. I remember that, she did."

"I remember."

Jade opened her eyes to find Marlena staring at her. Her blue eyes were clear and lucid.

"Don't tell anyone I'm awake," Marlena said. Her words were forced through her wired jaw.

"My God, Marlena!" Jade felt lightheaded. She started to turn away, but Marlena held her hand. Jade gently touched her face, the skin a mass of purple, green, and yellow. The left side of her face had a sunk-in look. The doctor had said it would require plastic surgery to repair. "We haven't found a trace of Suzanna. Do you remember anything?"

Marlena looked at something beyond Jade. "She's dead." The clenched-jaw delivery of the words made them even more horrific.

Jade glanced out the window. The sun was falling down the western sky, but it was only midafternoon. Frank had gone to Hattiesburg; he wouldn't be back until dark. "I should call your mother." She turned, prepared to go to the desk and make the call.

"No!" Marlena's protest was so strong Jade stopped moving. "Don't call Mother."

The thought that Marlena was not right, mentally, crossed Jade's mind. "I have to tell someone. Folks are looking for Suzanna. There's been no ransom, nothing. Do you have any idea who did this?"

"They had flour sacks with eye holes cut out, and mouths." She dry swallowed. "They grunted. They called me names. They said they were going to hurt me and make me pay for being a whore of Babylon."

Jade hesitated. "Was there someone else with you?"

Marlena's gaze was unfocused. "What difference does it make?"

"It could make a difference for Suzanna. Could he have taken her?"

She shook her head. "No."

"Are you certain? If there's any chance —"

"He didn't take her. I wish to God he did, but he didn't." She turned her head to focus on Jade. "Those men took her." Marlena's gaze brushed hot along Jade's skin.

"Marlena, you have to talk to Frank Kimble. You have to tell him everything you can remember. There's been no sign of Suzanna. They took bloodhounds into the woods but didn't find anything. They're not sure where to hunt now."

"Johnny didn't take Suzanna. When the men came out of the bushes, he didn't do anything. One man threw Suzanna on the ground. She didn't make a sound, and she didn't move." She fought for control. "The other man, the skinny one, held me. He said I was a filthy slut and the big one kicked me. Johnny just stood there. I called out to him, and he looked at me like he wanted to cry, and then he turned and ran. He didn't try to help me. He ran away and left me with those men beating me."

Marlena's lip began to tremble, but her eyes remained dry. Jade wanted to give comfort, but she didn't know how. "What can I do?" she asked.

"Kill me," Marlena said. "I put my daughter's life in danger to meet a man who wouldn't even try to help me. I don't deserve to live."

The front door of John Hubbard's house had three small graduated windows, reminding Frank of steps. He was struck by the idea that if he looked through each one, he'd see a different room. When he did look inside, he saw bare wood floors and no foyer furniture. Officer Lloyd Hafner had gone around to the back where he could force the door with less chance of observation. They had a warrant, but Frank had asked for as much discretion as possible. If the neighbors became unduly suspicious, they might warn John of the law's visit.

"It's open," Hafner called, and Frank walked around the house, noting the neatly trimmed shrubs, the recently mowed Centipede grass edged around the empty cement drive. John Hubbard was a neat man. How had he gotten involved in something as messy as a married woman?

Hafner stood in the back door, his expression pained. "Something's ripe in here," he said.

Frank followed him, their boots scuffling over the gray painted boards, through the small laundry room that led into the kitchen. The odor of sweet rot grew stronger, and there was the sound of flies buzzing, an ominous noise that awoke memories of carnage and battlefield abattoirs. For a split second the past swallowed Frank and the smell of blood clotted in his sinuses, creating a metallic taste on the back of his tongue. He put his hand on the gun at his waist as they carefully made their way into the kitchen.

A small square table with white chairs centered the room. Cabinets, painted white, were wiped down and neat. Frank spotted the source of the odor. Bananas, blackened with rot, were molding on the kitchen cabinet. He relaxed.

"Looks like ole Johnny boy hasn't been home for a few days," Hafner said. He waved his hand over the bananas, sending the flies into an angry frenzy.

Next to the refrigerator the garbage can was a source of attraction for another buzzing horde of green bottleflies. As they swarmed up into the afternoon sunlight slanting through the kitchen window, he saw their brilliant color. In the battlefield, they'd been called the death fly. The truth was, the flies didn't always wait until death came. He'd seen soldiers, alive and writhing in awareness of the fly spawn growing in their wounds. More than once he'd considered shooting the wounded men. Twice he had.

"I'll take the front room, see if we can find any evidence of where Johnny boy might have gone," Hafner said. His heavy shoes echoed on the wooden floors as he left the kitchen.

Frank would have preferred to go through the house by himself, but he accepted that he was lucky the Hattiesburg policeman was interested enough to get a warrant and come along.

"I'll check the bedroom," Frank said, walking down the narrow hallway toward the back of the house. He opened one door on an empty room and kept going until he found the bedroom. He stopped in the doorway. The bed was neatly made with a blue chenille spread, the pillows perfectly aligned beneath the bedspread. The night-stand beside the bed held an alarm clock and a magazine with a mostly naked woman in a sexy pose on the cover, a recent issue.

Frank noted the date but didn't touch it.

The room was dim. He walked to a window and raised the shade, allowing the mid-afternoon light to fill the room. He caught a glimpse of two children in the backyard of the house next door. A boy and a girl. The boy rode a tricycle around in circles while the girl sat in a swing. They seemed oblivious to the heat, and Frank watched them for a moment before he returned to his work.

There was no art or other decorative touch in the room. The walls were painted a pale blue, a restful shade that spoke of careful selection. Frank walked around the room and stopped at a highboy dresser, his gaze lighting on the picture of Marlena. She wore a red dress, the flared skirt swirling around her beautiful legs. She was laughing, holding down the skirt, happier than Frank had ever seen her. In the background was the two-tone Chevy.

Frank opened the back of the frame and removed the picture, slipping it into his pocket. He wasn't certain why he was protecting Marlena, but he was. Not from the law, but from Lucas and the censorship of Drexel. The top drawer held socks and underwear and nothing more. He put the empty picture frame there before he closed the drawer and opened the next one. Handkerchiefs, belts, fingernail scissors, needles and thread, all neatly placed and arranged. John Hubbard was a detail man.

Frank heard Hafner's footsteps approaching. He closed the drawer and waited.

"Looks like a bachelor's house to me," Hafner said. "But neat. Hubbard must be a stickler for everything in its place. My apartment is a wreck."

"Yes," Frank said. "There's no clue as to where he might have gone." He went to the closet and searched through the pockets of three pants and two jackets hanging there. A pile of dirty laundry had been kicked into the corner of the closet. Frank sifted through those. "Nothing," he said.

"Hubbard is a reliable employee of Big Sun. Hadn't missed a day in four years. They haven't heard from him since Wednesday, and his boss feels that he's met with foul play." Hafner glanced around the room. "Could be that someone came here and cleaned it all up."

Frank didn't believe that, but he had no desire to redirect the officer's thinking. "Could be," he said. "Did you check the bathroom?"

"Not yet."

"I'll take a look."

"I'll check out the spare bedroom," Hafner said.

Frank let Hafner brush past him before he walked down the narrow hallway to the powder blue bathroom. There were traces of dark hair stuck to the sink where someone, presumably Hubbard, had been shaving. Two towels were on the floor. The bathtub faucet leaked one drop at a time. Frank opened the medicine cabinet. Two prescription bottles were on one shelf along with a bottle of aspirin.

"Nothing back here," Hafner said. "You got anything?"

Frank picked up a half-full prescription bottle for phenobarbitone. The label showed it was ordered by Dr. Willard Herron and filled at Hardy Street Pharmacy only a month ago. He slipped it into his pocket with the picture of Marlena. He closed the mirrored door of the medicine cabinet. "Nothing. I think we're done here," he said to Hafner.

19

Jade sat at her kitchen table, a glass of water in front of her, untouched. She stared at the water, forcing her gaze away from the clock, which showed seven-thirty-four. Night had settled over the woods and the cicadas were singing. She'd called Frank's house six times and hadn't gotten an answer. She was desperate to talk to him, to tell him that Marlena was awake. In keeping with Marlena's wishes, she hadn't told anyone else, not even her father. She'd given Marlena her word.

She sipped the water and put the glass back. Scraping the chair across the linoleum, she got up and paced the room. The dress she'd chosen to wear was the exact color of her eyes, and a rich brocade. The low-cut V neckline swooped up to off-the-shoulder cap sleeves. It was a flattering design for her full breasts and creamy skin. Jade had bought the dress in New Orleans, and she'd never had occasion to wear it in Drexel. The full petticoat, stiffened with Niagra starch, crinkled whenever she moved. The sound annoyed her as she sat back down in the chair. When she finally heard a car coming up to the house, she thought anticipation was going to disable her. She stood up and gained control of her limbs as she went to the door and waited for Frank's knock.

The sight of him made her breathless. They stood, gazing at each other, until he cleared his throat and apologized for being late. He was tense and exhausted. She saw so much in the lines of his face.

"Marlena is awake," she said. "She doesn't want anyone else to know, but I told her I had to tell you."

The news stunned him. She saw it in his eyes. "She's going to be okay?" he asked.

Jade hesitated. Marlena would never be okay again. She would live, and she would cling to some type of life, but that was far from okay. "There's no brain damage. The physical wounds should heal."

Frank grabbed her hands. "That's good news. Did she say anything about Suzanna?"

"She doesn't remember much." Jade felt the burden of her half-sister's secrets. "She was with a man. His first name is Johnny, but she didn't say more. She doesn't believe he had anything to do with Suzanna's abduction." Jade dropped her gaze. "He didn't try to help her when the men attacked. She said he ran away." She lifted her gaze. Instead of the pity she expected to see, she found anger in Frank's eyes.

"The bastard left her there to be beaten and raped?"

"Yes." Jade put her hand on his arm, a gentling gesture.

Frank paced down the length of the porch and came back to her. "I need to talk to Marlena. Tonight."

"I tried to call you and tell you."

"I just got back from Hattiesburg." He put his hands on her shoulders, and she felt his strength. "I came here first. I wanted to see you."

"We can have dinner another night," she said.

His hands tightened. "No," he said. "I can't tell you the last time I wanted something as much as I want to have dinner with you." His left hand moved from her shoulder to her neck. His finger traced a line along her jaw. "When I was in that German prison, I made myself a promise that I'd never deny myself anything I really wanted.

We'll have dinner tonight."

"How about if I drive myself," Jade said. "I can finish getting ready, and you can go by the hospital and see Marlena. If she remembers something, though —"

"I'll call you." He glanced at his watch. "Half an hour, then?"

She nodded. "I'll be there."

He started off the porch and stopped on the second step. "You could come with me," he said.

He was telling her that he wasn't going to hide his feelings for her. She felt a heady rush of pleasure, but shook her head. "Half an hour. At your place."

The August night had come down soft, the sky a milky black with a million stars scattered through it. Under other circumstances, it would be a beautiful night. Dotty swatted at a mosquito that hummed in the car. The damn thing had bitten her twice already. By tomorrow she'd have big, ugly welts on her calves. If the fucking mosquito landed on her one more time, she was going to obliterate it. She felt a tickle on her ankle and swatted with a viciousness that made her yelp. The drone of the mosquito continued, mocking her and the ridiculous situation she found herself in.

She shifted in the car seat, trying to decide what to do. She was parked down an old logging trail across the road from the Bramlett house. Her plan had been to sneak through the woods and spy on Lucas, see if he had another woman there with him. If he was alone, she intended to go up to the door and knock. She had news he might be interested in hearing. Marlena's own mother thought Marlena was screwing around on Lucas, meeting some man in the woods. That's why Lucille had grilled her — to find out what she knew.

Dotty stretched her legs out along the seat, wondering what Lucas would make of this information. Surely he'd reward her somehow, show his gratitude because she was looking out for him. She'd put on jeans rolled up to show her pretty calves, bobby socks, saddle oxfords, and a blue-checkered shirt tied below her breasts, which exposed her excellent figure and gave her the illusion of youth. She had the curves of a real woman, and once Lucas caught sight of her, he wasn't going to send her home. They could have the whole night together. She pressed a hand to her pubis in anticipation of what he would do to her. She needed to be conquered, dominated, made to do things that were dirty. All she had to do was walk across the road, sneak through the woods, and make sure Lucas was alone.

She reached for the door handle but hesitated. Her nerve had given out. Lucas wouldn't appreciate anyone poking into his business. If he caught her, she'd be dead in the water. He might not give her a chance to tell her big news. He might be with someone else. That would be the worst, to discover that she'd been thrown over before she even had a chance to show him all her tricks. The idea that he had some other woman bent over the dining table was like lye on her skin. The not knowing gnawed at her, but fear of what she might learn held her in place. Doubt, like the mosquito that hummed around her ear, bit and sucked at her contentment. Two whole days had passed and she hadn't heard a word from him. Most men, once they got a taste of her, couldn't leave it alone. The only reason Dotty could come up with to explain Lucas's behavior involved another woman. He was getting his pud pounded by someone else. She had to take action.

She got out of the car and walked the fifteen yards to the highway where she could see Lucas's driveway across the road. The metal gate was open. Probably because he was expecting company. Dotty stepped onto the asphalt, got halfway across, and then hesitated. Headlights topped the hill to her east, and she bolted across the road and tumbled into the ditch by Lucas's gate, lying flat in the thick grass. The last thing she needed was for someone to see her. She'd be the laughingstock of the town. The car slowed, and Dotty held her breath, hoping they hadn't caught a flash of her moving into the ditch.

When the vehicle turned down Lucas's drive, she covered her head with her hands until she heard it pass. She sat up quickly and caught a glimpse of Junior's beat-up old Ford pickup. Someone was in the passenger seat, but Dotty couldn't make out who it was. She got up, dusted the dirt off her jeans, and looked up the driveway. Curiosity was stronger than fear. She darted up the driveway, staying just in the edge of the woods. If Lucas was entertaining Junior on a Saturday evening, she wanted to know why.

By the time she got to the house, Junior's truck was parked in the circle driveway and there was no sign of him or his passenger. They'd gone inside. She waited in the protection of the trees, listening. The mosquito had followed her from the car and brought several friends. Dotty slapped at her neck, bringing her hand away with blood all over it. At least she'd gotten one. Another insect bit her ankle above the sock. She slapped there. With every bite, she became angrier. Lucas didn't have time to call her, but he had time for Junior Clements, the town loser. Now she was stuck hiding out in the woods like some kind of lovesick teenager or Russian spy, except she wouldn't be anything but a bloodless corpse in another ten minutes, and all because Lucas treated her like some common tramp. She stepped out of the woods. He wasn't going to get away with treating her like that.

She circled around the truck, intending to go right to the front door and knock. The truck windows were down, and Dotty peered in, making a face at the empty beer bottles and trash on the floorboard. Something else caught her eye. The cloth was rough and printed with a faint pattern like a flour sack. Curiosity won out over disgust at the filth in the truck, and she reached in and picked up the material. She held it up, the air slipping out of her lungs as she saw the eye holes and a mouth cut into the flour sack. A brown stain was strung across it. She dropped it on the seat and backed away from the truck. She caught her breath, turned into the thick woods, and started to run.

For a long moment, Frank stood in the doorway of Marlena's hospital room. The light above the head of her bed was on, but otherwise the room was in darkness. Her face was turned to the window, which gave a view of blackness. In the soft glow of the light, Frank could make out her cheek and jawline, and he realized that from that angle, Marlena looked a lot like Jade. He cleared his throat, but Marlena didn't stir.

"Marlena, Jade told me you were conscious."

She didn't react, but her voice floated back to him. "She said she had to tell you, but no one else."

Marlena spoke without moving her jaw, and Frank remembered that it was wired shut to help the damage to her face heal. "She's keeping her word. We have to find Suzanna."

He entered the room and went to stand by the bed. When she finally turned to look at him, he had to steel himself against flinching. Her beautiful face had been destroyed.

"Suzanna is dead," Marlena said.

"Are you certain?"

"She's dead."

"We still have to find her." Frank wondered how much of what Marlena believed was reality and how much fantasy or wishful thinking. No one who'd been through the abuse Marlena had received would want her daughter, helpless, in the hands of the men who'd hurt her so badly.

"The big man had her over his shoulder. He threw her on the ground and she didn't make a sound. She didn't move." She took a deep breath, then another. "Her feet were bare. She had sand on the bottoms. She didn't move, and she wasn't breathing."

"Are you certain?" Frank saw how hard she fought to hold onto her emotions. He wanted to touch her, the way he'd touched men dying on the battlefield, just the comfort of contact. He thought better of it, though. Marlena might not view a man's touch as any kind of comfort.

"Yes," she said. "I tried to forget what I'd seen. I tried to hide from it, but I couldn't. Jade called me back. I wish I could just stop breathing and die."

"You won't ever forget, Marlena, but time has a way of taking the edge off the memory." It was beyond him to lie, but he gave her what comfort he could. "Tell me what happened from the beginning." His hand went to the pocket where he still kept her photo. If he had to, he would show it to her. She had to tell him everything.

"Suzanna was fishing. I'd set up the picnic about fifty yards from where she was, on a level place with some grass." She tilted her chin up and swallowed, and Frank saw the marks along her throat where fingers had choked her. He gritted his teeth against the anger that swept over him. When he found the men who'd done this, he was going to make them understand the meaning of suffering. He'd learned things in the war, things that no man should know about pain.

"Go on," he said. "Where was John Hubbard?" he asked, before she went too far with her lie.

"How did you find out his name?" she asked.

"We found his car parked on the road. A two-tone Chevy. I got the registration, and then I found those potato chips around the picnic area."

"Does Lucas know?"

"I haven't told him, and I don't think Huey has figured anything out."

"Tell him. Maybe he'll come here and kill me."

"Go on with what happened, Marlena. Maybe Suzanna was just unconscious."

She sighed. "Johnny and I were making out on the picnic cloth while Suzanna was fishing. She knew not to come back where we were. We told her we wouldn't bring her with us if she disobeyed." She took another breath. "I'm not a bad mother. I love Suzanna, but I had to take her with me. Lucas would never let me leave the house alone. Suzanna never saw anything. She never suspected. She could mind when she had to."

Frank thought about the headstrong little girl and understood how much she must have wanted to be with her mother to concede to a rule, any rule. In his past experience with Suzanna, he'd come to believe she deliberately set out to break any limits imposed on her.

"Did you hear anyone come up?" he asked.

"No." She hesitated. "Johnny was kissing me. He'd do things to me that Lucas wouldn't. He gave me pleasure. For the first time in my life, it was about what I liked and wanted." Her chin trembled, but she didn't cry. "What a fool I've been. I married a man more suited to be a prison warden than a husband, and I fell in love with a man who betrayed me in the worst way."

Frank did put his hand on her arm, gently. "You don't have to explain it to me."

"I have to explain it to myself," she said. "I have to understand how I could lose my daughter like I did."

"No one could anticipate being attacked the way you were, Marlena. That's out of the normal ken of anyone."

"I was her mother. I should have protected her."

"Tell me exactly how it happened," he said, knowing that he couldn't give her the absolution she sought.

"Johnny heard something in the bushes. We thought Suzanna had sneaked up and was trying to watch us. He got up. I remember, he said he was going to give her the spanking she deserved." Her voice broke, and she turned her face away for a moment. When she looked back at Frank, she was crying. "The next thing I knew, this man with a sack on his head came at me. He kicked me in the ribs. I didn't know what was going on. I screamed and tried to roll away. I was naked, and he was staring at me. He was yelling names at me, calling me filthy things. Then the other one came, and he had Suzanna over his shoulder with a sack tied on her head. He threw Suzanna down and he said, 'Let's give this whore of

Babylon what she deserves.' "

A moth fluttered against the screen of the hospital window, and in the silence of the room, Frank heard someone walking down the hall. The footsteps passed, and he took a long breath.

"Where was Hubbard?"

"I don't know. The two men started kicking me in the stomach and ribs and face. I tried to crawl to Suzanna, but they kicked me back. I looked up, and Johnny was standing about fifteen feet away. He looked right at me. He started to say something and then he turned and ran."

"Did the men go after him?"

She shook her head. "No. They must not have seen him. The skinny one sat on my head and held my arms, and the big one spread my legs and told me if I didn't quit struggling, he would hurt me bad. And he did. He hurt me."

"Marlena, did they rape you? Do you remember?"

She shook her head. "They put a limb in me. They said I was too filthy for their dicks to be inside me, so they used a limb. Then the big one got a knife and began to cut me. He said he was going to take out everything that made me a woman." She turned her head away. "I'm tired, Frank."

"Just a few more questions." He got the glass of water from the table beside her bed and held it so she could sip out of the straw. "What happened next?"

"I must have passed out. When I woke up, they were gone. Suzanna was gone, too. I crawled around looking for her. I couldn't see very well. I got up and tried to find the road. That's the last I remember. I went down the river some and then headed west."

"I found you in the woods. You were unconscious."

"You should have left me there to die."

"Marlena, did you know these men?"

She didn't answer for such a long time that Frank wondered if she'd slipped away into sleep. He wouldn't have blamed her. What she'd endured was too brutal.

"I've thought about that," she finally said. "How would they know I was a whore? If they were strangers, why wouldn't they think I was married to Johnny? Why wouldn't they think Suzanna was our daughter?" She looked at him. "They had to know me."

Her logic touched him with cold, because she was right. "Would you remember their voices if you heard them again?"

"I don't know. They were excited. If they sounded like that, maybe I could."

"Why are you so certain Suzanna is dead?"

She hesitated. "Because if they knew who I was and they knew who Suzanna was, they would never have hurt me like they did unless they'd already killed her. Once they'd killed Lucas's daughter, they figured they couldn't do anything worse, so they just did what they wanted to me."

"And Hubbard. Do you think he was involved in this?"

Marlena closed her eyes. "Please, Frank, just leave me alone." Her hand reached up and grasped the nurse call. She pressed the button. "I want morphine. Ask the nurse for it, please. Tell her I've been moaning in pain and need something." She turned her face away from him. "I'm not going to talk anymore."

20

Only the third story of the Kimble house was visible from the road, and that during the day. No lights burned in the third floor windows, so in the darkness, Jade felt as if she were riding into the unknown when she turned down the driveway. Some Kimble had loved plants. Imported camellia bushes lined the driveway and then, neglected, had grown from shrubs into dense, towering trees. The driveway was a tunnel of darkness, and Jade's headlights kept picking out shapes that moved and shifted as the car crept forward, giving the illusion that ghosts flitted ahead of her.

Jade had heard Jonah talk about the Kimble house and the many wonders that his father, Mose, had built into it. She'd never been inside, though. Never even in the yard. There had been no need for her to go there. When her headlights picked up the first floor of the rambling old Victorian, she slowed to get a better look at the intricate gingerbread trim. She finally stopped, awed by the craftsmanship that had gone into the detail. The front door opened and Frank stepped out onto the porch. He'd changed clothes and looked more relaxed, though sadder. When he beckoned closer, she drove to the steps, killed the lights, turned off the car, and got out. The momentousness of what she was about to do held her frozen beside the car. Frank came down the steps and drew her into his arms, giving her time to resist if she chose to do so.

"What did Marlena say?" she asked, knowing that she was simply stalling the inevitable. If Marlena had revealed some clue as to Suzanna's whereabouts, Frank would have gone to hunt for the little girl.

"She believes the men who attacked her knew her."

Jade was stunned. She'd assumed all along that strangers had done this terrible thing. No one who knew Marlena would hurt her in that way. No one would take Lucas Bramlett's daughter and not fear what it would cost them. "Do you believe that?"

"Yes."

His fingers clasped her elbow, and she allowed him to lead her up the steps and to the front door. She heard the paint crunch beneath her feet, and it registered that the house was well-maintained, except for the peeling porch. She went inside, stopping in the foyer. Her gaze swept up the curve of the staircase. "Jonah talks about this staircase all the time. His father, Mose, made it." She walked over and touched the wood. "It's warm, just like Jonah said."

"Your grandfather was an accomplished carpenter. He put life into the wood." Frank's hand covered hers on the banister. Jade felt something tighten in her lower belly.

"He isn't really my grandfather." Jade slipped her hand from beneath his. If she did not, she would turn into his arms and kiss him. She stepped away. "I've heard Jonah talk about the Sellers family, but he would never say much about my father. Just that he was a handsome man with a talent for music. He says that's where I get my singing voice. Then on the other side . . . to think that Lucille is my mother is bitter." She stared at a landscape without really seeing it. "I wish Ruth and Jonah were my real parents."

"None of us got to pick our relatives. We just make the best of what we're given." Frank came up behind her. He touched her arm lightly. "Are you hungry?"

"No." She hadn't come to eat.

"Would you like a drink?"

"Yes."

"What would you like?"

She hesitated. "I haven't drunk a lot. I don't know. I don't like whiskey or beer."

He touched her shoulder lightly, turning her so that she faced him. "I know just the thing." He kissed her cheek, then led her into the parlor. "Have a seat," he said, waving in the direction of a sofa and wing chairs. "I'll be back."

He left the room, and she heard him in the back of the house. Instead of sitting, she went to the mantel and examined the portrait of the lovely blond woman who gazed at her so frankly. Behind the blonde there was a darker woman, almost hidden. From the back came the sound of a hollow pop, and Frank returned with two tall, slender glasses filled with a pale gold liquid. She took one and saw the bubbles rising in it.

"Champagne," he said.

"I've never had any." She tasted it, feeling the fizz of the bubbles against her lips. It tickled the inside of her mouth. "It's good."

"But not good for you," he answered.

"Who's the woman?" she asked, raising her glass toward the painting.

"Greta Kimble, my grandmother," he said.

"And the other woman, the dark one?"

"She wasn't in the portrait originally," Frank said. "I painted her in myself. It's my great-aunt Anna."

"You painted her in?" Jade examined the painting more closely. It was impossible to tell two different artists had done the work. "It's very good." The dark eyes of Anna Kimble held her. "A little troubling, though. Why is she in the background like that, almost sinister?"

"Anna killed my father's twin. An accident, I'm sure. Then my grandfather killed her, and that wasn't an accident. I painted her the way I see her."

Jade had the sense that someone had reached out from a dark corner of the room, a grave-cold hand touching her arm. Chill bumps rippled down her back. "The way you see her?"

"Yes," he said. "I see the dead. They watch me."

"I'm not afraid of the dead," she said. She was far more concerned with the living and the cruelty they committed on a daily basis. "Why do the dead watch you?"

"I don't know," he said. "When I was younger, I thought they meant to harm me. I thought it was because I wasn't supposed to be in this house."

Jade spent hours alone with the mortal remains of those who'd crossed over. She knew their thoughts and wishes, heard their voices speak to her when their mouths were sewn shut. "But that isn't what they want, is it?"

"You aren't afraid?"

"Not of the dead," she said. She downed the champagne and held her glass out. Frank took it wordlessly and went to refill both glasses.

Jade went to examine a curio cabinet that contained tiny perfume bottles. She wanted more champagne. Liquor dimmed the small voice in her head that warned her to use caution, that told her she was starting something that could only end in tragedy. All of her life, she'd listened to that voice and avoided danger. Tonight, though, she would not.

Frank returned, and she took the glass he handed her and drank it, letting the tiny effervescent bubbles dance down her throat. Frank had brought the bottle, and he refilled her glass while she stood, one hand on his shoulder to steady herself.

"Jade, be certain —"

"Hush," she said, hearing her own voice, slow and lazy. "I don't want to be certain. I don't want to be careful. I don't want to deny myself this because it might not be the right thing." She held the fragile glass lightly, drained it, and leaned into him. She kissed him in a way that left no doubt what she wanted. When she stepped away from him, she saw the need in his eyes. Her hand went to his crotch, and her fingers found the hard length of him.

"Don't talk," she said. She started toward the stairs, leading him. "Don't make any promises or talk about tomorrow. Tonight is all we have, all we need." The champagne had done its work. She no longer heard the voice. Her hand found his penis again, and she rubbed down the shaft, making him moan, chasing away any last lingering doubts he might have had.

In the moonlight that illuminated the bed, Jade looked like a sleeping goddess. She was the most beautiful woman he'd ever known. In the Kimble library, there was a book of illustrations of the Greek and Roman gods and goddesses. As a child, Frank had loved the book. He'd spent hours looking through it, imagining Aphrodite, Zeus, and Hermes come to life in the backyard. Now, lying asleep beside him, was Artemis, goddess of the hunt. It would not take a big stretch of the imagination to see Jade with a garland of leaves in her hair, a bow in one hand, and a shaft of arrows strapped to her back, a white tunic flowing high on her thighs.

He'd never imagined Jade to be so strong, but she'd surprised him, both with her passion and with her physical prowess. There had been moments in their lovemaking when he'd felt the pursued and she the aggressor. She was a woman with ardor. The memory of it awakened his penis, and he felt the head thump against the sheet. In the darkness he smiled. It had been a long time since he'd felt such heat, such pleasure.

There had been a young woman in France. She'd taught him to cook, had educated his palate for fine wine, had made him understand that it wasn't French men who were such renowned lovers, but the women who carried them to the heights of passion. She'd taught him to laugh. Her name had been Giselle, and he loved her without reservation, because he'd never understood that love could cause pain. He'd been a young man, untouched by personal loss. He'd seen death in many forms on the battlefield. Had given death when he had to, but he'd never lost someone he loved. Until Giselle. They'd had a blissful autumn together before he'd been sent on a mission. When he returned, he'd found her body. He'd pieced together what the German soldiers had done to her, and for several weeks he'd been insane with grief and pain. He'd never thought he would love again, never wanted to. But the woman beside him had touched him in the private place where all his pain resided.

In her sleep, Jade shifted, snuggling closer to him even though the moonlit night was humid and warm. Her hair brushed his cheek, hair so fine and soft that he wanted to drag his fingers through it. Jade kept her hair short. He wanted to see it long, hanging down her back in curls that invited his touch. A rush of longing for the future made him swallow. There were moments to be shared between them, if Jade would allow it.

A breeze rustled the limbs of the big oak that grew beside the bedroom window, and Frank let his thoughts drift. Something had awakened him, a not uncommon event. He'd heard or sensed something and opened his eyes, disoriented. He didn't use the second floor bedrooms. He'd prepared this one special, putting fresh linens on the bed and quickly dusting the furniture, on the chance that Jade might stay the night. When he'd first opened his eyes, he hadn't been certain where he was. He'd felt the weight of the woman beside him, and the confusion of where he was, sensations that ignited his panic. When at last his heart rate had settled down, he could no longer tell if it was something external or something in his dreams that had pulled him from sleep. He settled back against the pillow, slipping an arm around Jade to bring her closer. She sighed, and he kissed her forehead. A slight breeze stirred the oak tree outside the window, causing the pattern of leaves to marble the bed. Moonlight rippled through the room.

He saw her then. She was standing in the far corner of the room, and as he watched, she stepped forward into the moonlight. She wore shorts and a blouse, and her feet were bare. Her brown hair hung in two braids, one over either shoulder. Blood had clotted on the right side of her head, and she touched the wound as if she didn't understand what had happened to her.

"Help me," she said. "Please, help me."

Frank knew that Marlena was right. Suzanna Bramlett was dead.

21

Jonah slowed the Buick, his gaze on the mess up ahead in the road. At last he brought the car to a stop, ignoring the noises of protest from Lucille. He couldn't go any further, no matter how much she fussed. A car was parked directly across the road, blocking it, and the Jebediah County patrol car was parked on the verge. The morning sun beat down on the tarmac, and through the heat waves, Jonah could see Huey's broad behind hovering over something in the ditch.

"What's going on up there?" Lucille asked angrily. She moved her head from side to side, trying to see. She'd needed glasses since the age of thirteen but was too vain to wear them. The good point in her vanity was that she wouldn't drive herself anywhere, so her vision hadn't proven fatal. Yet. "What are they doing in the middle of the road on a Sunday morning?" she asked querulously. "I'm trying to get to the hospital and then go to church. I need to go pray for my daughter, and some fool has left a car across the road."

"Looks like trouble," Jonah said, inching the Buick a little closer. The car that blocked both lanes was big and dark blue, almost black, a strange car he didn't recognize. He put on the brake and killed the engine. "Miss Lucille, you need to stay here. Looks like Sheriff Huey could use some help."

Huey was dragging something out of the ditch, a body, a man soaked in rainwater. Jonah got out of the Buick.

"Jonah, don't you leave me alone here in this car," Lucille said, but Jonah ignored her. He hurried to the ditch. High blood pressure reddened the sheriff's face, and relief spread across it when he recognized Jonah.

"Give me a hand here," Huey said. "I got a call that the highway was blocked, and I found this fella. He's had the hell beat out of him, but he's still alive."

Jonah grabbed one of the man's arms and helped Huey move him up beside the road. Blood was everywhere on the man's body. He'd been savagely beaten, and he lay in the high grass as if dead. The damage was severe, Jonah could see that much. Part of his scalp had been peeled back from some kind of blow, and his pants and shirt were soaked in blood. Beside him, a patch of black-eyed Susans nodded in a light breeze.

"Let me call for an ambulance," Huey said, going to the patrol car and using the radio to get help.

Jonah saw Miss Lucille start to get out of the car and he went over to stop her. "What's happening?" she asked. "Is that a dead man?"

"He's not dead," Jonah said, wondering how long it would be before he was. "He's hurt bad, though. Somebody worked him over and meant to kill him."

"What in the world is going on in Jebediah County?" Lucille put her church handkerchief to her mouth, pressing hard against her lips. "Something evil is afoot here."

Jonah looked in the direction of the injured man. Only his feet were visible, the rest of him blocked by his car. He wore brown socks and no shoes. "Stay in the car," Jonah said. "I'm gonna make sure the sheriff doesn't need more help."

Instead of walking to the patrol car, Jonah went back to the injured man. The man's eyes were open. Blue eyes that reflected the summer sky. Jonah leaned over him. "What's your name?" he asked.

"Sam Levert," the man said, gasping. "Back broken?"

"I don't know," Jonah said. He put a gentle hand on the man's shoulder, holding him steady. "The ambulance is on the way. They'll take you to the hospital where someone can look after you." The man's breaths were quick puffs of pain. Jonah thought he'd played out his hand. Why it had happened that Sam Levert, a stranger to the area, would meet his fate on the secondary highway to Drexel, Mississippi, Jonah could not say. He picked up the man's hand and held it tightly. "Who did this to you?"

"Two men. With hoods. Stopped me. Searched car. Beat me. Took two . . . hundred dollars." His chest moved up and down but he hadn't the strength to say more.

"Just rest," Jonah said, squeezing his hand. "Just lay right here and rest until help comes. Could be you have a rib punching a hole in your lung or something along those lines. They can fix it right up." He tried to think of more positive things to say, but he knew that Sam Levert would not live. He wondered if it was kinder to lie or tell the truth, let the man prepare to meet his maker. One thing he was certain about was the need to keep hold of Sam's hand. Everyone died alone, but it was good to have company during the vigil.

"Thanks," the man gasped out, and he squeezed Jonah's hand back.

Jonah heard the ambulance's siren, and he continued to hold Sam Levert's hand even though the strength had gone out of it. The hand was still warm; the first chill of death had not touched him. When the two ambulance attendants came up, Jonah looked at them. "He's gone," he said. At last he released the hand and rose slowly to his feet.

"Take him on to the hospital," Huey said, sweat running into his eyes so that he squinted.

"He's dead," one attendant said.

"Take him to the hospital." Huey ground out the words. "We're gonna have an autopsy."

Jonah helped them load the body into the ambulance and then gave directions to help them turn around on the narrow road. The siren was silent as the ambulance headed back to town.

"What about his car?" Jonah asked the sheriff.

"Shit," Huey said. "I hope the keys are in it." He looked in the driver's window.

"We're in luck. Can you get it out of the middle of the road?"

Jonah glanced back at Miss Lucille, wilting in the front seat. She'd picked up a piece of cardboard and was fanning herself, her mouth set in a grim line.

"I guess I better get it out of the way. Miss Lucille's unhappy. She wants to get on to church."

"I wish my biggest problem was an unhappy white woman," Huey said. "Now let's move the car."

Frank Kimble had told Jonah once that each crime scene told a story. Though Jonah wasn't certain moving the car was the best thing to do, he got in the front seat. Huey was the sheriff. The car was cluttered with cracker wrappers and empty soft drink bottles in the floorboard. There was an invoice from Cook Hardware in Drexel, and a cork coaster with the Friendly Lounge on it. The car started easily when Jonah turned the key, and he backed up and maneuvered until he was parked on the verge pointed toward town. He rolled up the driver's window, removed the key, and got out. Huey took the key he held between his thumb and forefinger.

"I'll send a tow truck," Huey said.

"Should I go get Mr. Frank?"

Huey considered. "That's a good idea. Frank worked all day yesterday looking for Suzanna Bramlett. I hate to call him out this morning, but he should be here."

"I'll get him," Jonah said, glad to be able to put Miss Lucille's car in motion so that a breeze would cool her. She was fractious when she got overheated.

Jonah went back to the car and headed toward Drexel. "Sheriff Huey needs me to get Frank Kimble," he said.

"I didn't realize you were on the Jebediah County sheriff's department payroll." Miss Lucille's voice dripped acid.

"That man was beaten just like Miss Marlena." He didn't say more, just let her put it all together so that it was her idea.

"The two cases could be related," she said. Her voice registered fear.

"That's possible," Jonah said. "So Mr. Frank needs to come so he can look at the scene. Maybe figure out what happened here."

"Then put the car in gear and let's go get him," Lucille said testily. "I'm 'bout to die here of heat stroke and all you want to do is flap your gums about what might be possible."

Jonah drove toward the Kimble house.

■ ■ ■ ■

The aroma of the brewing coffee crept up the stairs and into the bedroom where Frank sat on the side of the bed. Jade was stretched across the bed, a sheet pulled over her hips, but her beautiful back uncovered. Frank let his gaze drift over her. From her dark, curly hair to her red-painted toes, she was a work of art. A lifetime ago, before the war, he'd thought about becoming an artist. He had talent. Gerard Marchette, a portrait painter in New Orleans, had offered to take Frank beneath his wing, a rare opportunity to work with a real master painter. Frank had declined. Painting was a fantasy, something he kept as a dream. Real life had to do with pain and tragedy, the stuff of a lawman. Now, though, he regretted that he hadn't at least practiced drawing, because he would like to paint Jade, just as she was now with her long legs extended from beneath the white sheet, her back, tight muscle over the perfect scapulas and framing her rib cage, and the gentle knobs of her spine clearly visible. Her slender neck gave elegant support to her beautiful head, which was turned to reveal her profile. In sleep, dark eyelashes rested on her cheeks.

Her skin was flawless, one smooth, mocha expanse of perfection.

She began to stir, and he let his fingers dance on her smooth calf and up her thigh. She worked on him. They'd made love almost all night long, and now, just touching her, he wanted her again.

"I smell coffee," she said, rolling so that her full breasts were exposed, the dark areolas tipping slightly up. Completely at ease with her nakedness, she sat up.

"Would you like some coffee?" He wanted to look at her forever, just as she was, rumpled by sleep with a hint of sexual satisfaction in the lazy curl of her lips.

"I'd do anything for a cup," she said, smiling. She looked at him and her smile faded. "Is something wrong?"

He considered all he wasn't telling her. She wouldn't be shocked that he'd been visited by Suzanna's spirit, but the little girl's death would bring Jade grief and suffering. He could not bear to tell her just yet. "Nothing's wrong," he said. "I'll get the coffee."

"Frank?"

She was watching him, and suddenly he wanted her again. Like a thirst for whiskey, he wanted her in a physical way, but more. She was warm and filled with life. When he touched her, she infused him with both those things. Looking at her, he could imagine a future.

"Will you really do anything for coffee?" he asked, knowing that she was aware of his arousal.

Her eyes sparkled, that unsettling shade of green like a rippling pool. "Anything that involves hot water, soap, and a toothbrush." She reached a slender hand out and rubbed against the grain of his beard. "We could shower together."

The idea was erotic. His dick tapped the sheet that covered his lap, and she laughed. "The sleeping giant awakens," she said.

"I'll get us a cup of coffee." He stood up, aware that her gaze lingered on his bare buttocks as he walked across the room. He went down the stairs and got two cups of black coffee from the kitchen. He was headed back upstairs with them when he heard the sound of a vehicle coming down his drive. He paused, wondering who would be coming to his house so early on a Sunday morning, or any time, for that matter. He didn't have a lot of visitors, didn't encourage such. Solitude was his comfort, and he guarded it.

"Damn!" Jade yelled from upstairs. "It's

Miss Lucille's car. Daddy must be driving it."

He heard her feet thud on the floor as she ran into the bathroom. Water ran through the pipes. He held the coffee cups and did nothing. Possibilities oozed around him. He imagined himself walking out onto the porch and telling Jonah and Lucille Longier that he and Jade were getting married. He put the coffee down and went upstairs for his pants and shirt. He was dressed when a tense Jonah knocked at the front door.

"Sheriff Huey needs you down on the highway," Jonah said, his gaze shifting past Frank to the inner recesses of the house. He was looking for his daughter.

"What's going on?" Frank kept it easy, casual.

"A man's been beat to death. He was in the ditch. He died before the ambulance came." At last Jonah's gaze met Frank's. "I held his hand while he died. He said the men who beat him wore hoods."

Frank couldn't see if Lucille Longier was sitting in the car or not. "Thank you, Jonah," he said. "I'll head out there."

"Mr. Frank" — Jonah's eyes were dark and hot — "there's meanness in this town. Real meanness. Miss Marlena never hurt a soul and she's hurt bad. I don't want my daughter caught up in this."

"I don't want Jade hurt, either."

"Then leave her alone. She's got a good life. If it gets out that she's been here, with you, things will change for her. It won't be good."

Frank nodded. "I'm falling in love with Jade."

Jonah's mouth tightened into a thin line. "You think that means something? It doesn't. Love is a weapon when it's directed at the wrong person, and Jade is wrong for you. It won't be you who pays the price, it'll be her."

"Jonah, I —"

Jonah waved his hand around the house. "Your family is cursed with tragedy. Don't bring it into my home or visit it on my loved ones. Leave Jade alone."

He walked across the porch and got in his car. Frank watched him drive away, right past Jade's car without even looking at it.

She came down the steps behind him, her footsteps soft and feminine. "What did Daddy say?" she asked.

When he turned to her, he saw she was dressed, the stylish green brocade a mocking nod to morning. "He doesn't want me to see you."

She nodded. "I could've told you that.

Why did he come here?"

"A man's been beaten on the highway. Your father tried to help him, and he came to tell me so I could go look at the scene."

"A man killed?"

"Beaten to death. The men who did it wore hoods, like the men who attacked Marlena."

"This is terrible." Jade sat on the steps as if her legs could no longer support her.

He got a cup of coffee and handed it to her. Once he retrieved his cup, he sat down beside her, his arm supporting her. "No," he said, "this isn't terrible. This could be a break in the case."

22

Dotty tapped her fingers on the steering wheel of the car and waited for visiting hours to start at Jebediah County Hospital. To her aggravation, her entire life had become one form of waiting or another. This time, though, her patience was going to pay off. Once Marlena heard what Dotty had to say, she'd snap out of her coma and get busy making Lucas pay. Dotty's intention was to tell Marlena every single thing that had transpired between her and Lucas and finish it off by telling what she'd found. After all, Marlena had been her friend through thick and thin. Lucas had just been a user. Possibly a lot worse. Junior Clements was mean enough to brutalize a woman, but he wasn't smart enough to think it up on his own. Everything had clicked into place: Lucille's questions about Marlena's activities, the savagery of the beating, and Junior showing up at Lucas's home. Lucas had put Junior up to it.

Once she'd seen the flour sack hoods in Junior Clements's truck, she'd abandoned all thoughts of confronting Lucas. She'd been so badly frightened she'd gone running through the woods, cutting her ankles and face on briars and tree limbs. She'd finally made it to her car and had driven to the Friendly for a few drinks to calm her nerves. Well, more than a few. Yes, she'd been afraid last night, but today she was thinking clearly. Lucas had made his bed, and she was going to make him lie in it. He thought he could play God. He'd used her and then cast her aside. He didn't have time to give her a call to say a simple thank you. He deserved everything that was fixing to come down on his head.

She got out of the car, swiping at her leg where blood had trickled down onto her white sock. Her ankles and calves were a mess, torn by blackberry thorns and God knew what else. One side of her face had four deep furrows from a tree branch. She didn't care. Let the stupid women who were so ugly they had to get a job nursing to touch a man think what they wanted about her. They were nobodies and their judgments didn't matter. She strode through the hospital, down the yellow hall, and walked into Marlena's room without knocking. She was pulled up short when she saw Lucille sitting by the bed, holding her daughter's limp hand.

"I didn't see your car," Dotty said.

"Jonah is running some errands for me," Lucille said. Her hair was a frizzy mess and her makeup smeared.

Dotty considered the situation. Lucille looked like she'd been ridden hard and put away wet. "Is something wrong?" she asked. She cast a quick glance at Marlena, who could have been a corpse. It would be just Dotty's luck if Marlena had passed on without being able to punish Lucas. Then again, the charge would be murder.

"A man was killed last night. Beaten to death on the road to my house. It was just terrible."

Dotty felt the gut punch of good gossip. "Who was it?"

"A stranger," Lucille said.

Dotty closed the door, shutting out the sound of a cart creaking down the hallway. "That's awful. Did you get any details? Why would someone kill a stranger?"

"They should find whoever did this and shoot them like dogs. Not even give them a chance to beg for mercy." Lucille dabbed at her eyes with a handkerchief.

Dotty walked over to the bed and put a hand on Marlena's cheek. "You think it was the same men who did this to Marlena, don't you?" Her heart thumped against her ribs. If her assumption was right, Junior Clements was headed to the gas chamber.

"I have no way of knowing that." Lucille rose swiftly to her feet, her gaze imperious. "Looks like someone got after you."

"Mosquitoes." Dotty rubbed the outside of her right ankle with the toe of her left oxford. She saw Lucille's eyes sharpen and smiled at the eagerness in the older woman's eyes.

"Been out in the woods?" Lucille asked.

"Maybe. Maybe I haven't been alone out there either." Dotty liked knowing things that others didn't. "Where's your son-in-law?"

"What do you want with Lucas?"

Dotty had the upper hand with Lucille Longier. For the first time in her life, she was in control. "Now, that's really none of your business, is it? I'd think you might be wondering why Marlena's husband is never here to see about his wife."

"Lucas is where he belongs. At home, trying to find his daughter." Lucille's tone was cold. "What are you implying?"

"Has Lucas even been up here to check

294

on Marlena?"

"What's it to you?" Lucille asked.

Dotty gazed down on Marlena's lifeless profile. "It could mean a lot to Marlena. A whole lot." She stared directly into Lucille's eyes. "If Marlena ever wakes up, call me. I know things she needs to hear." She turned and left the room, smiling at the expression that she'd left on Lucille Longier's face. The rule of the Longier women was coming to an end in Drexel. With Marlena's attack and injury, Lucille had lost her position. Once Lucas was brought low, the entire social order of the town would shift.

Dotty walked out of the hospital and into a morning that had turned cloudy. At least the heat had broken. She stopped by the Coke machine in the lobby and found a nickel in her pocket. She was bone tired. She hadn't had a wink of sleep all night long. Now, though, she had two trumps to barter. She'd come back to see Marlena when Lucille wasn't there.

"Miss Dotty."

She heard the voice and recognized Jonah before she turned around. He looked worn, like old leather. "What is it?"

"Sometimes you go up to the Friendly Lounge, right?"

Anger flushed her cheeks at the audacity

of a black man asking her about her personal business. "That's none of your affair." She turned and started to walk away, taking the Co-Cola with her. If they wanted their damn three-cent deposit on the bottle, they could come take it away from her.

"Did you meet a man named Sam Levert last night?"

That stopped her. She remembered the tall man with dark hair and an easy smile. He was a married man, she'd deduced that right away. He hadn't been wearing a ring, but he was married. She could always tell. Still, she'd danced with him and let him buy her a drink. He liked her tight jeans and her saddle oxfords, had told her she was beautiful. She'd gone out in the parking lot and leaned up against his midnight blue Ford and let him kiss her and feel her breasts. He'd been a good kisser, and she'd had to break it short when Pet showed up.

"What about Sam Levert?" she asked.

"He was beaten to death last night."

Dotty felt as if her swagger had been pulled from her spine. Her knees grew weak, and she was aware of Jonah's hand steadying her. "You're lying."

Jonah didn't say anything.

"He said he was going to Pascagoula. He said —" She stopped herself.

"Who else was in the Friendly last night?" Jonah asked.

Dotty thought of the men from the new sawmill on the edge of the county. They were brawlers, but none had shown an interest in Sam Levert. Pet had been there, though, and wherever Pet went, Junior was nearby. They'd killed Sam Levert. Just like they'd attacked Marlena. Jonah was trying to steal her thunder. "Why are you asking me about the Friendly? If you need a list of customers, go ask Boo Bishop and see what he has to tell you."

"I found a coaster in the dead man's car. It came from the Friendly. I was just wondering who else was up there last night."

"I can't think of a soul at the Friendly who would harm a stranger."

Jonah stared at her. "Might be you should drive over to the sheriff's office and tell what you know."

"I don't need your help or anyone else's, and I certainly don't need your advice. I'm fine just by myself."

Jonah shook his head slowly. "Miss Dotty, I've always heard if you lie down with dogs, you get up with fleas."

"What are you implying?" she demanded. Her face was flushed with anger. "You're out of line. Just because you work for that old bag, Lucille Longier, doesn't give you the right to talk to me like that."

Jonah sighed. "I'm trying to save a little girl that everyone seems to have forgotten about. The men who attacked Sam Levert wore hoods, just like the men who hurt Miss Marlena. Now I think it could be the same two."

Dotty realized that her expression had given her away. "Mind your own damn business." She started around him, but he stepped in her path.

"Miss Dotty, you'd best take care. There's some true meanness running loose in Jebediah County. If you know something and don't tell, it'll be on you."

"If you're so damned smart, why don't you ask Junior Clements and Pet Wilkinson what they were up to last night?" She pushed past him. "You can tattle that back to Frank."

"Thank you, Miss Dotty."

Jade hung the dress in the closet and took her underthings to the laundry basket. She needed a bath, but she didn't want one. She could still smell Frank on her skin, the peculiar odor that identified him in the intimate way of a lover. She twirled around her bedroom, feeling as light as air, and as powerful as a force of nature. She'd surprised Frank. She'd seen it in his eyes several times. Once when she'd straddled him, clenching him tightly with her knees as she rode him, and another when she'd taken him in her mouth. He was not naïve or inexperienced, yet she'd still surprised him. That pleased her. In fact, most everything pleased her this morning. The only dark edge on the morning was her father's visit to Frank, and his knowledge of what she'd done. Jonah would worry for her, and that troubled Jade. She was thirty-five, old enough to make her own choices, but that didn't stop her daddy from worrying. She'd explain to Jonah that it had never been so right as it was with Frank. There was something between them so perfect that she couldn't ignore it. He wouldn't like it, but he might understand. She had no worries that Jonah would tell Ruth. He wouldn't.

Naked, Jade went to the kitchen and put on water for a cup of tea. She went into the bathroom and ran the water in the tub for her bath. As much as she wanted to, she couldn't spend the rest of the day naked and smelling of Frank. She had no illusions that it would be a "happy ever after" romance. She and Frank would not marry. That was out of the question. But she wasn't his black mistress. Not that. They were equals, two adults who shared an incredible connection. Was it love? She didn't know. She'd never loved a man, only Jonah and Ruth.

Back in the kitchen she made the tea and took the steaming cup into the bathroom with her. The window by the tub was fogged with condensation. The bath was hot, but she needed to soak. Her body was pleasantly sore, and she wanted to pamper it. She turned off the water and stepped in, sinking beneath the hot water, the mug of tea still in her hand. By rights, she should have a hangover, but she didn't. She'd never felt healthier. She came up, blinking the water from her eyes. Something wasn't right. She listened for a moment, trying to figure out what was wrong.

A strange clicking caught her attention. The kettle was turned off. There was nothing in the house to click. It took her a moment to realize it was coming from the window. She looked over and felt a jolt of fear. A hand was pressed against the glass, ring tapping the pane. Beside the hand was the foggy outline of a man's face. Two dark eyes peered at her through the condensation.

With a scream, she flung the mug of hot

tea at the window. She heard the crash of glass and a low, tearing sound that wasn't human. Scrambling out of the tub, she grabbed a towel and ran. The back door was closest, and she ran there and threw the thumb bolt into place. Dropping the towel she raced through the house to the front door. She slammed it and shot the bolt home, feeling a moment of relief. She looked at the windows she'd never wanted to curtain, terrified of what she might see. Marlena had been beaten nearly to death. A stranger had been killed. The men who'd done those things were capable of anything.

Jonah had taught her to use a gun, but she'd never owned one. She'd never imagined a time in her life when she might need to kill another human. Now, though, she would have traded anything for a pistol or a rifle or a shotgun, because she knew if someone tried to come through her door, she would kill him. If Marlena had had a gun, she might not be hurt, and Suzanna might not have been taken, and for the first time, Jade experienced a hint of the horror that Marlena must have felt, the helplessness.

"Goddamn you!" she shouted. "I'll blow your guts out if you try to come in my house."

There was only silence.

The house was old, and it creaked and groaned when she walked across the floorboards. This had always been a friendly sound to her, but now it was deadly. She moved along the edges of the rooms, avoiding the middle where the boards talked. There was a hammer in the bathroom. A heavy one, and if she had an opportunity, she would sink it into the skull of whoever was outside her house.

She made it back to the bathroom and retrieved the hammer. Her nightgown was hanging on the back of the bathroom door, and she slipped it on, trembling. There were two options available. She could make a dash for her car and hope to drive away, or she could stay in the house, hoping someone would come looking for her. She realized that if anyone came, it would be Jonah. He would come straight into danger.

Hefting the hammer, she went to her bedroom and got underwear, shorts, and a blouse. She dressed quickly, picking up her old gardening shoes because they wouldn't slow her down if she had to run. She was going to her car. From the front door she had to get across the porch and the twenty feet to the car. Because she never anticipated trouble, she left her key in the car. All she had to do was get there, lock the doors, and drive away. It wasn't hard. She could do it.

The thumb bolt slipped free without a sound, and she eased the doorknob slowly to the right. The door opened a crack, and then enough for her to ease out. Once on the porch, though, she stopped. Her heart was pounding, and nausea mingled with fear when she saw what her intruder had left for her.

The flowers were store bought, a bright orange ribbon wrapped around the stems. There were roses and sunflowers and daisies, a beautiful spray of color tumbled on the worn wood of the porch. Jade stepped over them as she ran to her car, aware that the man who'd been peeping at her believed he was paying court.

23

Some fifty years had passed since Jonah had the first memory of coming up the long drive to the isolated house where he'd grown up. Jade's home now. He was proud that he and Ruth had been able to give it to her.

Trees that had been saplings were now thick of girth. Some older trees had died, rotting back into the soil from which they'd come. As a young boy, Jonah had walked the driveway two and three times a day, going to the road to wait for Mose to come home. He always had a sense of peace when he was on the property of the old home place, and he sought that peace now, praying for guidance in the things he had to say to his daughter. He drove slowly, knowing Lucille would be fit to be tied if she knew he was running personal errands in her car. Jade was more important than Lucille's tantrums. He had to talk to Jade.

He rounded a curve by an old mimosa tree, his mind on his daughter. He was completely unprepared for the big black Hudson that came at him, careening around the curve. Jonah wrenched the wheel, and the Buick swerved into the woods, taking down a small sapling and some huckleberry bushes. As it was, he narrowly avoided a head-on crash with Jade. He looked in the rearview mirror and saw she'd slammed on the brakes, sliding in the sand until she came to a sideways halt in the driveway, her body slumping against the steering wheel. He got out of the Buick and ran to her, fearing she'd struck her head. He opened the door and was relieved to hear her sobbing.

"Jade," he said, pulling her into his arms. "Jade?"

"I'm okay," she said.

She clung to him in a way she hadn't done since she was a small girl. Anger rushed to his head, and he thought of killing Frank as he held his daughter. "What did he do?" he asked.

"He was watching through the window."

Jonah didn't understand. He'd seen Frank heading out the highway to the scene of the murder. "Who was watching?"

"A man." Jade burrowed into him.

Jonah stroked her hair and back, rocking

slightly with her. The anger was gone, replaced by a fear colder than anything he'd ever experienced. "What man?" he asked, when her tears had begun to dry.

"I didn't see who it was. He watched me through the bathroom window. He left flowers on the porch."

He felt her relax, and he assisted her in sitting upright. There were things that had to be done, but for this moment, he would hold her and keep her safe. She was his daughter, the one thing he loved most of all in this world. No one else could hurt him as she could. Jade, alone, had the power to tear out his heart.

When she had quieted and he could feel that she'd gathered her emotions, he asked, "Did anyone know you were at Frank's?"

He felt the subtle shift in her body, the shift from pliant to tense. "No one saw me," she said. "There wasn't anyone else on the roads. This isn't about Frank."

"Are you sure?"

"If you think this is retaliation . . . Have you considered that Lucille might have told?" Jade's words were angry.

"She couldn't have, Jade. She wasn't in the car with me when I went to Frank's. I left her at the hospital with Marlena, so she doesn't know anything."

She bowed her head. "I'm sorry, Daddy."

"It's okay. I would have thought the same." He hesitated. "Jade, she's your birth mother."

"And that wouldn't make an ounce of difference to her," Jade said. She touched Jonah's face with a gentle hand. "You'll never believe that about her, will you? You've always been in love with her. But in this, Mama is right. Lucille would sacrifice me or you or Marlena or anyone else if it came down to it."

Jonah felt as if her words were small pebbles pelting him in the face, penetrating to his heart. "You misjudge her, Jade."

"Do I?" There was no anger in the question. "I don't think so, Daddy. I hope you're right, for Marlena and Suzanna's sake, but I don't think I'm wrong." She sighed, and Jonah felt as he had when Lucille had first confided that she was pregnant by Slidin' Jim Preston, a New Orleans sax man who'd come to Drexel to play one of the Longier parties. Jonah had been totally helpless to influence the future. Events had escaped him, left him behind with only emotions to feel and no actions to take. He thought of an animal in a trap, the way a fox or bobcat would gnaw off a leg in an effort to escape. He felt like that, and he hated it. This was the price of love. When love was invoked, all bets were off.

"Let's go talk to the sheriff," he said.

"I don't know." Jade looked out the windshield. "Let's see how bad you banged up Miss Lucille's car. She's going to be upset."

"Miss Lucille will get upset if the rooster crows on the left side of the house instead of the right. Truth is, she'll get over it. There isn't anyone else to drive her but me."

He saw the surprise in Jade's eyes, and for a moment he foolishly felt as if everything would sort itself out.

Heat danced on the hood of the big blue Ford as Frank walked around it. There were no skid marks on the highway, no indication that the driver, Sam Levert, had stopped suddenly or lost control of his car. It would seem he'd slowed down and stopped in a reasonable manner. And then someone had jumped him and beaten him so severely that he died.

Frank studied the asphalt and tried to reconstruct the scene in his mind as Huey and Jonah had described it. Huey shouldn't have moved the car, but he understood that an elected official wasn't going to block a highway. Now, he had to rely on details observed by someone else.

The car was unlocked, a fact that made him grit his teeth. He climbed in and went through the cracker wrappers, candy bar papers, and soft drink cans on the floor. Jonah had told him about the coaster from the Friendly Lounge. He shifted through the trash again. The coaster was gone. "Damn it to hell," he said softly to himself. Huey had left the car unlocked for anyone to stop and go through. Sometimes the sheriff didn't use the brain he'd been given.

Stepping onto the verge, Frank looked around. He saw where Levert had dragged himself down the embankment and into the ditch, probably in an attempt to get away from his attackers, or else he was so disoriented by the beating that he didn't know, or care, which way he was crawling. He heard the flies and followed their sound to where they swarmed around a hunk of flesh with dark hair attached. Not far away was a tire tool, blood all over it. He picked it up carefully and put it in the patrol car for evidence, certain he'd found the murder weapon.

A scene was developing in his mind — Levert driving toward Pascagoula when he sees a car blocking the road. He stops to check it out. He's attacked, beaten, and robbed.

Jonah had repeated what Levert said about two men in hoods taking two hundred dollars. There was no prevarication in Jonah's account. He'd said the same thing twice.

Frank had done a good bit of traveling after he was released from the army hospital. He'd bought a car and driven from Norfolk, Virginia, to St. Luis Obispo on the California coast. Working odd jobs, he lingered in the West Virginia mountains, drifted through the spring beauty of the lake states, and tilled the fields of the Plains. One winter he'd driven a snowplow at the Continental Divide. The solitude and grandeur of the Rockies had almost captured him forever. Sometimes, late in the evening when the first stars came out, he could hear the rattle of the ice-covered spruce trees when a wind blew over the mountains, and he felt a longing that was hard to explain. He'd never gone back, though. He knew he never would.

After the Rockies, he traveled through the desert where he pumped gas for two months. Whenever the mood struck, he packed up and left town. Along the way, he met a lot of people, most of them okay, but enough mean ones to leave their mark. There were only two reasons he'd have stopped along a dark highway. One was to help someone in trouble, and the other would be if a law officer pulled him over. Sam Levert had slowed and stopped for a reason.

Walking through the tall grass, Frank searched for more clues, but his mind returned to the coaster from the Friendly Lounge that should have been in Levert's car. He could think of only one reason someone would take such a thing. To hide the fact that Sam Levert had been in the Friendly. The logical conclusion to that thought was because someone who'd seen him in the Friendly had set out to harm him.

Marlena's beating and Suzanna's disappearance were related to the brutal death of Sam Levert. Frank knew this, though he had no way of proving it yet. With Levert, the beating had been even more vicious, and there wasn't the sexual element that had been involved in Marlena's attack. Both attacks had been committed by men in hoods, though. Frank could almost fit the pieces together, but not quite.

From among the reseeded pines and scrub oaks that grew on paper company land, he heard the sound of someone walking. He scanned the trees and found her, standing just at the edge of the young pines that came barely to her shoulders. His mother watched him, her arms still crossed over her chest, the lone rose clutched in her hands. She didn't speak, but he understood what she wanted. To let it go. To walk away from all of it. To stay safe, and alive.

Something shiny in the grass at his feet caught his eye, and he knelt. The piece of plastic paper fluttered in the grass and he picked it up, recognizing the emblem of the Big Sun chip company as he held it in his hand. There was no way to know how long the paper had been tumbling along the ditch. It could have been thrown out by anyone, days ago. He knew better, though. John Hubbard was the center of the maze. He had to find him.

24

The front door of the Kimble house was open. Dotty stepped inside, wondering when, if ever, it would become Frank Kimble's house, or even Frank's house. Never. In Drexel, the past hovered over everything like a shroud. Folks who couldn't spell "cat" were able to recite everything that had happened to their families since they'd come over from Ireland or Scotland, or England, or Africa, for that matter. It was disgusting. No one looked toward the future because they were all so damn busy preserving the past. In the entire county of Jebediah, Dotty owned maybe one of a dozen televisions. A lot of folks didn't have a telephone. They lived in the dark ages and they liked it that way. Folks acted like Lucille Longier and Lucas Bramlett were the end-all and be-all of society. Well, she had information that was going to blow the whole social fabric of the town apart. Lucas, with his orders to bend over here and his hands grasping her hair and forcing her head down, well, he'd get his share of those activities when he was locked up in Parchman Prison. Maybe she'd even go up and visit him, flaunt a little of what he'd never have again. She had the goods on him, and she was going to tell Frank Kimble, just as soon as he got home. The slow wheel of justice would start to grind. She liked that. She'd heard it on some television show, and she liked it immensely. Lucas was going to be dust when she finished with him.

Her thoughts were distracted from Lucas as she looked around the foyer of the Kimble house. The staircase was like a graceful movement frozen in time, and she walked forward, unable to resist touching the banister. Lucas thought he had such a fine home, but there was nothing in that two-story house on the highway to compare with the Kimble house. Frank needed to have some parties, show the place off. She crept forward, knowing she was an uninvited intruder and yet unable to stop herself.

As far as she could tell, nothing had been changed in a hundred years. She peered in the doorway of the parlor and saw an old Victorian sofa in faded burgundy velvet that has once been plush. She wandered into the room, spying the cut glass decanters. A shot of bourbon was her due, she thought. Frank should have been home to offer her one. She poured two fingers into a crystal glass and sipped as she explored.

The portrait of Greta caught her attention and she walked over for a better view. The fair-haired beauty in the foreground was compelling, but it was the dark-haired woman, almost a shadow, that sent chills down her body. She stepped away and avoided looking into the dark corners of the room. She had the sudden, unpleasant sense that she wasn't alone. The house was clean, but it had the smell of a place abandoned to all but spirits.

The kitchen held little interest. The refrigerator contained milk, cheese, a carton of eggs, butter, the staples of bachelor life. Two champagne glasses were in the sink, and her interest was piqued. The cabinets were empty, except for dishes. She went back to the staircase that had first caught her eye and went upstairs. One door was open, and she went there first, finding the unmade bed that looked as if a football team had wallowed in it. A thrill raced through her and she crawled on the bed on her hands and knees, sniffing. The scent was undeniable. Sex. Frank Kimble, or someone, had had sex in that bed, and recently. She climbed out of the bed and began to search the room for clues to the occupants. It had to be Frank. She was excited by her find. Everyone thought Frank was some kind of hermit or saint. He was simply discreet. The idea thrilled her. But who had he been making the two-backed beast with? That was the most interesting question.

There were no clothes in the closet or the bureaus. Frank had to have used the bed. No one else ever stayed at the Kimble house. So who was Frank seeing? She thought of a list of the youngish ladies in town and could come up with no one that seemed right for Frank. Thwarted, she finished her bourbon and thought to go back to the decanter for a refill. Frank should have been home by now. It was Sunday, and he never went to church.

She heard a car and went to the window, a vantage point that allowed her to see the driveway clearly. She put her glass down to use both hands to move the sheers in a way that would keep her concealed. The approaching truck was one she didn't recognize. She hurried down the stairs and out onto the front porch, leaving the door open behind her. She'd just taken a seat on the steps when the pickup chugged to a stop. A handsome man with dark, intense eyes and a two-day growth of beard looked at her with cool insolence.

"Frank's not here," she said, realizing even as the words left her mouth that she sounded like someone close to Frank. It pleased her and she smiled. "He won't be back for a while. Can I do something for you?"

He grinned. "I do believe you can."

When he didn't say anything else, curiosity got the better of her. "Who are you?" she asked.

"I'm an acquaintance of your husband's. Dantzler Archey's my name." He got out of the truck slowly, his eyes never leaving hers. As he walked toward her, Dotty realized that she'd made a mistake. Maybe the biggest mistake of her life.

The switchboard operator at the Forrest General Hospital sounded haughty and more than a little put out at Frank's persistence.

"Dr. Herron won't make rounds until this evening. It *is* Sunday, you know."

"Call him at home," Frank said. "It's urgent."

"If I bother the doctor at home, I'll lose my job," the woman said, more annoyed than scared.

"If you don't get Dr. Herron on the phone in the next ten minutes, I'm coming up to Hattiesburg and I'm going to arrest you. This is an official investigation, and unless I get a call back at the number I gave you, I'll have you in jail for obstruction of justice." Frank tugged at the collar of his shirt. It was an empty threat, but he had to talk to the doctor.

"You can't do that."

"Oh, yes, I can, and I will." Frank hung up. He'd left his number on Saturday evening, when he'd first tried to reach the elusive doctor, and he'd given it again just a few moments before. He had two questions that only the doctor could answer.

If the hospital operator could find the doctor, Frank had no doubt he'd soon be getting a call. He put his feet on the desk in the sheriff's office and waited. Normally, he would be at home on Sunday, or driving around the county, as he tended to do on his off days. He was just as glad to have something to do, though. Jade had insisted that she needed to spend the afternoon with her parents. He hoped she'd tell them about her feelings for him. Jonah already knew they were involved, but it might look like a sexual liaison to him, and Frank wanted both Jonah and Ruth to understand it was a lot more than that. Sexual satisfaction was easy to find, even in a town like Drexel. It was true emotional connection that was difficult, and he had that with Jade. She made him feel anchored to a reality that held hope. He wasn't about to let that slip away, no matter that she was of Negro lineage.

The image of Jade, asleep in his bed, was a gift. Neither of them had meant to become involved. Both knew the problems they'd encounter. But what they felt for each other was beyond mere attraction. If a circle of fire enclosed Jade, he would walk through it to be with her. They would see one another again, and again, and again. But after a while, that type of bond would shatter, unless there was something stronger growing beneath it. If Jade refused to acknowledge their relationship, it would continue hot and passionate, and then die. The idea was unacceptable. His thoughts disturbed him, and he got up and paced.

Huey was at the First Methodist Church of Drexel dinner on the grounds, where he was every third Sunday. The sheriff had no great belief in God or Jesus Christ, but church was politically expedient, and as Huey was quick to point out, it didn't do any harm. Frank had no patience for the cruelty of a mob, even if it was one garbed in Sunday best and singing hymns. He left the sheriff's office and walked down the hallway to the front door of the courthouse. The afternoon had grown heavy with clouds, and he could almost feel the thunder collecting. When it finally cut loose, it was going to make the normal July thunderstorms seem like an April shower. There was a chance the phone lines would go down. That fretted him, and he walked back to the office and sat, looking at the phone.

It rang, and he jumped, a little ashamed that he was so much on edge.

"This is Willard Herron. What's the emergency?"

Frank heard arrogance and impatience in the man's tone. Well, it was Sunday afternoon, and like lawmen, doctors worked a hectic schedule.

He identified himself. "Do you have a John Hubbard for a patient?" he asked.

"I do, but that's none of your business."

"Mr. Hubbard has been missing since Thursday afternoon. He's a material witness in a beating and kidnapping. I have reason to believe he may be in trouble. Now if you've heard from him, that would relieve my mind a good bit."

There was a pause, and Frank could hear

what sounded like rushing water on the line. It was already raining in Hattiesburg; he could tell by the sound of the phone.

"I saw Mr. Hubbard about two weeks ago for a checkup. He was in good health."

"You gave him a prescription for phenobarbitone," Frank said. "What condition does he have?"

"I can't reveal that. Patient confidentiality."

"Doctor, if Mr. Hubbard has a serious medical condition, I suggest you tell me. He doesn't have his medication with him. I have it right here, in my hand." He shook the pill bottle loud enough that the doctor could hear it.

"He's an epileptic."

Frank thought a minute. He knew that epileptics were prone to seizures, and that in certain circumstances, they could die. "How bad off is he?"

"Controllable, with medication." The doctor sounded worried. "Mr. Hubbard has suffered his entire life with this illness. You can't begin to imagine what it's like, the way people react, the social ostracism. He's made a life for himself in Forrest County. Please keep this in confidence. If his employer learns of this illness, they'll fire him."

"I appreciate your concern," Frank said.

He'd seen men fall into seizures from blows to the head, wounds, or just plain fear. The other soldiers had shrunk back from them, isolating them, whispering that they had been possessed by Satan or an evil spirit. Frank didn't believe in evil spirits, or Satan, but he did believe in the barbarity of men. He knew what the doctor was saying. "I'm worried about Hubbard's life. What's liable to bring on a seizure?"

"Stress, over-breathing, loss of sleep. The cause can be emotional or physical."

"If I find Hubbard and he's alive, what should I do?" Frank needed him alive.

"Take the medication. Get him to take one. Get him to a hospital, preferably up here at Forrest General where I can tend him."

"Thanks, doc." Frank replaced the phone. During the length of the conversation, the sheriff's office had grown dark. He looked out the window and saw that the sky was an angry gray bleeding to black at the edge of the front. All hell was about to break loose in Jebediah County.

25

"I can't sit here all afternoon," Jonah said. Across the table, Lucille confronted him with narrowed eyes and a slash of a mouth. "You'll stay if I tell you to."

Jonah thought about the years that had passed, the moments shared between them. Lucille's behavior was partly his fault, because he'd allowed her to get by with her pouts and petty tyranny. He'd done it because it was one of the few things he could give her that no one else would, dominion. Up until this moment, he'd believed his love for Lucille had cost him little. He'd loved her for so long, putting her needs above all others. Now, though, Jade was at stake.

"I've already told you, someone was peeping in on Jade. I need to get over there and think up a way to keep her safe." He said it patiently. Sometimes Lucille was like a small child. She was so invested in what she

wanted that she had to be forced to compre-
hend what others were saying.

"Jade's with Ruth. You said so yourself. If
you go over there, I'll be alone. What if he
comes here, looking for me?"

That Lucille was middle-aged and past
the bloom of beauty was on the tip of his
tongue, but years of caring stopped him.
"You'll be safe. Call Lucas to come and sit
with you awhile."

"You make me sound like some kind of
invalid."

"Because you act like one." He spoke with
kindness, though he knew the words would
cut.

"I've never known you to be so cruel," she
said, blinking back the tears.

"Because I don't have time to nurse your
tender feelings today," Jonah said. "My
daughter —" He paused, looking deep into
her eyes. "*Your* daughter is in danger. I'm
going to protect her. If you'd quit throwing
yourself in front of me leaving, I wouldn't
have to point out the painful truth to you."

She rose up straight in her chair. "I don't
throw myself in front of any man. How dare
you say that?"

"Because it's true," Jonah said. "You want
what you want, and everyone else be
damned. Mostly I don't mind giving in to

you, but not when Jade may be in danger. You'll be just fine here. I'll come back when I can." He rose, thinking to touch her shoulder, show her that he cared but other obligations called him away.

"Don't walk out that door."

He sighed. "Lucille, don't make this a choice between you and my daughter." In her eyes he saw that she intended to do just that. "You'll lose," he said, trying to soften it with a smile.

"Get out!" She rose, and for a moment he saw the beautiful and spoiled young girl she'd once been. "Don't you stand there and smile at me. I won't be patronized. Not by my nigger yard man."

Physical blows could not have stunned him more. In their long years together, he'd never acted as more than hired help and she'd never treated him as less than a man. He tasted dust. "I guess we both spoke the truth today, Miss Lucille." It was the first time he'd used her title when they were in private. "We've both said cutting things, and I see they're true. They hurt, but I think we both needed to hear them." He walked across the kitchen to the screen door, letting it bang behind him. He heard her footsteps coming after him.

"Jonah, wait." She caught up with him and

clung to his arm. "I'm sorry. I didn't mean it."

Jonah felt only anger and a coldness in his chest that froze the words in his throat. He tried to shake her off, but she clung to him.

"Jonah, please. I'm sorry. I'm scared and worried." She spun him so that he faced her. "Don't look at me like that, like you hate me. I'm sorry." Tears ran down her face, streaking the makeup she'd so carefully reapplied after getting home from the hospital. "My daughter's been nearly killed, and Suzanna is missing. She's dead. I know she's dead, and I can't change it. I'm distraught. I didn't mean what I said."

"Yes, you did," he said.

"I didn't." She touched his face. "I didn't mean it."

"Ruth was right," Jonah said. "About everything."

"No, she isn't. Ruth thinks I don't have a soul. She thinks I'm a pit of evil. That's not true. I'm selfish and self-centered, but I'm not evil." She collapsed against him. "I'm not. Truly, I'm not."

His arms went around her and he held her, remembering all the times he'd held her before. In tears and in laughter. In passion and fear.

"I have to go, Miss Lucille."

She straightened, holding herself erect. "Yes, go and take care of Jade." She gave a weak smile. "I'll be fine."

Jonah nodded. "You will. Now I'm going to take care of my loved ones, my family. I have a lot to make up to Ruth."

"I'm your family, too, Jonah." The smile wavered, but she struggled to keep it in place.

"No, Miss Lucille, you're not my family."

"I am, too."

He liked that the petulance was back in her voice. She was a strong woman, and he'd never given her credit for that. He turned to leave.

"Jade is your daughter."

There was something in the way she said the words that made him turn to examine her face. She was a liar and a conniver, a woman capable of drama to get her way. "Yes, she's as much my daughter as if I'd sired her myself."

Lucille swallowed. "You did. She's your daughter. Yours and mine. I never slept with that New Orleans man."

Jonah couldn't feel his legs. He wanted to leave, to run away from her as fast as he could. "Mine?" He believed her, for it was his deepest fear come to life. He'd bought so easily into her lie about the light-skinned

Negro jazz man from New Orleans because that was what was best for him to believe. His cowardice was legion, and he saw the sum total of it.

"Ours," she said, triumphant and completely unaware of his reaction. "I lied about Slidin' Jim. I made it up, and I made you believe it. I told the lie so well that Mama believed it and so did you. If Mama had known the baby was yours, she would have had you lynched. I lied to save your life."

The urge to circle her neck with his hands was so great that Jonah, finally in command of his legs, ran down the porch. He heard her calling after him but he didn't look back. His feet hit the dirt of the yard, chickens squawking and scattering as he leaped forward. He ran as hard as he could, away from the thoughts that stabbed him like flying arrows, images of Lucille in the back of the car as he drove her to Mobile for an abortion, of her crying and saying she'd rather die than have the baby she carried. Jade, his daughter. Lucille had caught him in her web of deceit and desperation, almost making him a party to an abortion that would have killed his own daughter, and he had let her. She'd lied and withheld the truth, finally bringing it out when she thought it would serve her own purposes.

Ruth had been right. Always.

He ran toward the highway and the black clouds of a gathering storm. Sweat stung his eyes and bitterness filled his mouth. He hurled himself down the road, so that he wouldn't go back to Lucille Longier's house and kill her with his bare hands.

"Don't go into town," Ruth said, holding onto Jade's arm. They sat at Ruth's kitchen table, the rooster salt and pepper shakers, the sugar bowl, the hot sauce cruet, all neatly centered. Nothing was out of place. "Doesn't matter that they wear a badge. Those white men don't care what happens to one of us." Behind Ruth, a large electric clock ticked the minutes away. It was only a little past two, Jade noticed, but the day was growing steadily darker. Storm clouds had gathered to the west, and now they were rolling across the sky. It was going to be bad weather.

The sun slipped out from behind a cloud, and a shaft of sunlight illuminated Ruth's kitchen. Jade saw the harsh lines in her mother's face and felt the unexpected pressure of tears. She was going to hurt her mother in a way that could never be repaired. Ruth had always believed that a war raged in Jade, a war of colors. Ruth's loving care and nurturing had been designed to help Jade make the right choice, the Negro choice. And now Jade had taken up with a white man. Ruth would suffer greatly, because of her worry for Jade, and her failure to save Jade.

"Frank's not like that," she said. She would try to gently convince Ruth. "He's different."

"He's white," Ruth said. "He can't help it, but he is." Ruth's hold on Jade had unexpected strength. "Stay here and let your daddy handle it."

The idea of Jonah confronting a crazed white man, possibly one of the men who'd beaten Marlena and killed a man, was enough to force Jade out of her chair and her mother's grip. Her arm bore four distinct fingerprints that would later become bruises. "I don't want Daddy in that kind of danger. This is Frank's job. He knows how to handle it."

"Don't do this."

Jade had underestimated her mother. She knew. Somehow, Ruth knew, and this moment was where she'd chosen to draw the battle line. "I love you, Mama, but I have to do what I think is right."

"This is only going to bring suffering, to all of us."

Jade had no idea how much her mother had discerned, but she knew she had to get away. She looked around her mother's kitchen, seeing the china teacups that her mother had bought, one at a time, from Houston Mercantile. She cherished them, using them every day with care. The kitchen was immaculate, and the smell of a freshly baked pound cake still lingered. Ruth could work all day at Lucille Longier's and still come home to cook the finest meal a person could sit down to. She was a marvel, and Jade loved her unconditionally. But she knew that she could not always be the woman who lived to please Ruth or Jonah.

"I'm sorry, Mama." She picked up her keys from the counter and walked out the door. Her daddy had gone to tell Miss Lucille about the car accident. The fender of the Buick had been dented slightly, hardly discernable. Jonah had taken the car back, and he would be home soon, Jade hoped, to take care of Ruth.

When she turned onto the highway toward Drexel, she peered out the windshield at the storm. It was going to be a humdinger. Lightning forked to the west. The storm front had a black edge to it, likely tornadoes. She turned her lights on and pressed a little harder on the gas. She didn't see the oncoming vehicle until it was only a few yards in front of her. The grayish truck merged into the color of the sky and the asphalt, and it was running without lights. The vehicle startled her, and when she caught a glimpse of the driver, she veered to the edge of the road. Dantzler Archey was driving like a bat out of hell, and he had some blond in the passenger seat beside him. Jade could only imagine what kind of woman would go out with Dantzler Archey. Jade pressed harder on the gas and sped to the courthouse, where she hoped to find Frank.

26

The tension of the building storm charged the air, and the first rumble of thunder made Frank look up from the riverbank. He was in the water, walking upstream, searching for the point of exit Hubbard had to have taken. Before, he hadn't been all that concerned about the whereabouts of the salesman, thinking Hubbard would eventually turn up. He'd not wanted to focus attention on him, for Marlena's sake. Now, though, his thinking had begun to change. Suzanna was dead. He accepted that. He would not find the little girl and bring her home for a joyful reunion with her mother. The child had gone on to a different plane, a place where she waited for justice. Now he'd begun to view Hubbard as something more than a coward. He'd begun to see him as a player in the abduction. Hubbard had watched his lover brutalized and made no effort to help her.

Frank was deep in the woods, farther north along the Chickasawhay than he'd been when he found Marlena. He'd come alone, pondering the words of the Hattiesburg doctor and the possible complications of a disease that could leave a strong, virile man disabled in the dirt.

A sumac plant that looked as if it had been stepped on caught his eye, and he stopped. Beside it was the cloven print of a deer hoof. Hubbard hadn't passed that way, but he had to be somewhere in the woods. He'd never come to collect his car, and as of Saturday, he hadn't shown up on his route of small grocery stores. He'd lost the job he valued so highly.

Until Sunday morning, Frank had assumed that Hubbard was alive. The death of Sam Levert had shown the attackers were capable of murder. Hubbard hadn't tried to help Marlena, but had that saved him or had it only delayed his death? Other questions troubled Frank. Why would the men who attacked Marlena and took Suzanna allow Hubbard to live? Frank circled the issue but returned to one conclusion — Hubbard was part and parcel to the abduction. But would a man allow the woman he loved to be so brutalized without lifting a finger to help her? Had he truly loved Marlena?

Frank didn't doubt that she'd loved him, but she wouldn't be the first woman taken in by a fancy man.

He went through the series of events of the attack and abduction. Suzanna had been taken sometime Thursday afternoon. He'd found Marlena just before sunset. They'd begun a search the next day. On Friday morning, he'd followed the trail of a fast runner through the woods and into a slough that wound through the woods and eventually fed into the river. He'd assumed this was Hubbard's trail and that Hubbard was traveling without the girl. He still thought he was right about that. Once the trail had gone into the slough, he hadn't pursued it. Now he was determined to follow it through, and he had to do it before the storm cut loose a torrent of rain and washed all traces away. Hubbard had to have gone into the river, and somewhere, he had to have gotten out.

Frank came to a place on the bank where the side was crumbled away. He studied the sand and clay composite and found evidence of footsteps. Hubbard had exited here. Frank climbed out of the water and onto the bank, careful where he put his feet.

The trail was scant, the evidence a broken twig or a heel print in the soft mud that led to the north. He followed and came upon a clear set of prints. The distance between the left and right foot showed Hubbard was running. It was highly possible someone was on his tail, but Frank could find no evidence of pursuers.

Hubbard had run away without attempting to help his lover. Frank realized he should have focused on this matter before now. But the concept of a lover had left him emotionless, until Jade. He'd forgotten what it meant to love someone, to put them before all else.

Jade had awakened something primitive in him. He would dismember anyone who harmed her. Their sexual union had sealed a pact for him. He would protect her, or die trying. Surely Hubbard had felt something for his lover, some shred of desire to defend her against brutality. So why hadn't he? This was the question that would lead to the truth. In finding the answer, Frank knew he would find the person responsible for Marlena's suffering and Suzanna's death. Hubbard would tell him the answer, if he was alive.

Jade stood at the locked door of the sheriff's office and felt a disappointment she knew could be her undoing. In her life, she'd avoided disappointment. That had been the lesson of Ruth, and it was one she'd learned in diapers.

"Don't expect more of someone than they can give," Ruth had admonished her. To the point that Jade expected nothing of anyone, except herself, for whom the bar was set very high indeed. As a result of Ruth's tutelage, Jade was never surprised at the shallowness or callousness of the women who came into the beauty shop. She didn't mind if they called her by her given name in the shop and told her stories of their children and grandchildren, then refused to allow her to sit beside them in a restaurant. She expected nothing from them except payment for her services.

Mr. Lavallette was good to her, but it wasn't expected treatment. She would have worked as honestly for him had he not been so kind. Because she didn't expect him to be good, it was just one of the bonuses of life.

Ruth had prepared her well to live a solitary and self-sufficient life, but she hadn't prepared Jade for someone like Frank. Jade had never expected a man to bring her such joy, to love her with generosity and tenderness. Ruth's lessons had not touched on such bounty. In the lesson of disappointment, men were at the top of Ruth's list, and her advice had been never to expect anything good to come from a man. That went double for white men.

In learning to avoid disappointment, Jade had been taught not to dream. Frank had broken that stricture. He had burst it wide apart, and Jade found herself caught in rippling fantasy after fantasy. Most of them involved the big bed in the upstairs bedroom, or her cozy quilt-covered bed in the heart-of-pine bedroom. But there were other fantasies that played through her mind, bringing a smile to her lips. Now that her imagination had been set free, Jade luxuriated in the rich and pleasurable turnings of her mind.

On the drive to town, she'd imagined Frank sitting at his desk. She told him about the man who'd peeped in her bathroom window, the dampness of his breath against the glass as he'd stared at her. Outraged, Frank rushed to her home where he found footprints in the dirt beneath her window. He took fingerprints from the flowers that had been left on her porch, and with some effort, he found the man who'd peeped at her. She'd seen Frank dragging the man into the courthouse in handcuffs. In the daydream she wove, everything was so simple. Frank was a man of action, a hero.

The reality was he wasn't where he said he would be. She was alone, just like before. And the disappointment was bitter, because she'd never before allowed herself to believe in another person, except her father.

She walked out of the courthouse and down the stairs. Her car was parked along the curb, and she took her time going to it, uncertain what to do next. Huey would be up at the church, she knew that. She didn't want to go there and disturb the luncheon that was held every third Sunday. She wondered what Ruth had cooked for Lucille to take to the dinner. She leaned against her car. The next step to take hadn't been revealed to her yet.

Storm clouds were massing to the west, a bad storm, and she didn't know where to go. For the first time in her life, she didn't want to go home. The isolation was dangerous, her home no longer safe, and she felt the sharp pain of that violation.

This was not Frank's fault. Part of her wanted to blame him, to find an excuse to kill the things she was feeling, to avoid the disappointment that was part of believing in another person. Frank had not abandoned her. Chances were he was out looking for Suzanna, which was exactly where he should be. She could wait for him in the courthouse. He would like that, to find her there when he came back in. But she wouldn't do that. There were matters to confront, for both of them. Frank's touch had told her many things. This was not a simple matter of sex or the thrill of crossing the color line for Frank. He didn't see her as black or white. In that, he was a dangerous man, because he'd given her the gift, for one moment, of not seeing herself as colored. Such thinking was dangerous, for both of them.

The hood of the car was hot beneath her thin dress, and she suddenly thought of Frank's hands. At one point in their lovemaking, he'd grasped her buttocks and lifted her. His hands had been hot on her skin. She slid off the car and got behind the wheel. Nat King Cole's voice came out of the radio tuned to the Memphis station. "Unforgettable" was one of her favorite songs, romantic, filled with tenderness and the joy of loving. Frank was unforgettable. For better or worse, her life had been changed by him. He might disappoint her, but he had also given her the gift of dreaming. He'd awakened something inside her that had been asleep for all of her life. She was strong enough to suffer disappointment if she could feel alive, and she suddenly realized that her mother was not. Ruth, whose back was unbent by forty years of toiling in another woman's home, was not truly strong. The simple disappointments of life would snap her, and in trying to protect Jade, Ruth had also cheated her.

Jade thought of her half-sister, living in a twilight world of pretense, afraid to show a spark of life to those who claimed to love her. She decided to go there, to sit with Marlena. She could do nothing for herself, nothing for Ruth, who'd made her choices so long ago. Maybe she could help relieve Marlena's fear. She set off across town, the breeze from the open car window cooling her with a sweet and gentle touch.

The hospital was quiet on a Sunday afternoon, the parking lot almost empty. Visiting hours were not until four, and the impending storm would keep many people at home. Jade wasn't worried about visiting rules; Lucas had arranged it so she could see Marlena whenever she chose. It had not been meant as a kindness to Jade, but a convenience for Lucas, who had no intention of visiting Marlena, much less sitting with her. A lump of coldness settled in Jade's heart when she wondered how much Lucas really knew about Marlena's relationship with the potato chip salesman. After the night with Frank, Jade understood how Marlena could risk so much for a man's touch.

Before Frank, she hadn't allowed herself to understand. She'd wanted to believe Marlena foolish and willful and reckless. Now she knew, she was none of those things, but simply a woman desperate for a man's caring touch.

Lucas was not a man to show his feelings, or to value the feelings of others. He hadn't been to the hospital a single time to see his wife. Not once. A lot of things could explain Lucas's absence. Selfishness was what Jade hoped it was.

Her thoughts absorbed her as she walked down the tiled corridor of the hospital. The sight of Junior Clements coming out of Marlena's room abruptly halted her, and she barely suppressed a gasp. Junior's eyes were hungry, filled with something that swirled in the gray depths.

"Has she told you anything?" he asked.

Jade's heart thudded. "She's in a coma," she lied, swallowing the taste of iron that threatened to make her gag. Junior frightened her.

"I heard she could identify the men who hurt her?"

"Where did you hear such a thing?" Jade

asked, indignation forced into her voice.

"Does it matter?" Junior's eyes were shrewd.

"I don't know. Does it?" she countered.

"I got myself a reliable source. Someone who's been sitting up here and knows what she's talking about."

The only other person who had sat with Marlena was Dotty Strickland. "Some people lie when it would be easier to tell the truth," Jade said. "Keep that in mind, Mr. Clements."

He stepped closer, and she arched an eyebrow, waiting for him to speak. She could feel the thud of her heart in her ears, but she lifted the other eyebrow and waited.

"Are you getting uppity with me?" he asked. There was a hint of excitement in his voice.

"I wouldn't think of it," she answered, but she didn't drop her gaze. "Marlena hasn't spoken except once, on Friday. The doctor thinks she probably won't ever wake up." She was acting on instinct, protecting Marlena from Junior's interest in her.

"The nurse said Frank was here."

Jade shrugged. "He was. I told him Marlena wasn't going to wake up. Since a sheriff's deputy has already been here, I don't understand your business in Marlena's room."

"Could be old Lucas offers a reward to the person who finds his daughter. I'm right certain he will, as a matter of fact. I'd like to get that money, and if anyone knows who took the young'un, it should be Mrs. Bramlett."

"Except she's in a coma," Jade said.

"For certain?"

Jade focused only on the lie. "It would be a miracle if she regained consciousness. Go and ask her doctor if you don't believe me."

Junior nodded, one hand rubbing the back of the other where blood oozed from his skin. When he saw her gaze on his hands, he stopped, putting both in his pockets.

His right knuckles were swollen, the rough skin a light purple beneath the flaking. "How did you hurt your hand?" she asked.

"The stretcher up at the funeral home rolled into a door." He smiled. "Do you want to kiss it and make it better?"

Jade almost gagged. "I'm sure it'll be fine. Maybe the nurse will take a look at it."

His eyes narrowed and his mouth flattened. "You think you're too good to doctor my hand?"

"I'm a beautician, not a nurse," Jade said.

"You're full of sass. But I like a woman with a little spunk." He leaned closer so that his breath puffed on her cheek. "It sure is pretty out there where you live."

Jade felt as if the wind had been knocked out of her. He was telling her he'd been at her home. He was toying with her, wanting to frighten her. She lifted her gaze calmly. "Yes, it is pretty. My granddaddy bought that land a long time ago. There's an old cemetery behind the house. Sometimes, at night, just before I go to sleep, I hear the dead waking up." She saw the doubt in his eyes. "They tell me stories," she said softly. "I don't always want to hear, but when they want to talk, there's nothing to do but listen."

"You're lying." He did not step away, but he leaned back from her. "You think you can scare me off, but I'm not afraid of ghosts." He laughed. "I sort of like 'em. Dead people are just dead. Nothin' more."

She could see he'd regained his nerve. Threats of ghosts would not keep him away from her property any longer. "The dead tell me their secrets."

"You're a feisty little gal," he said, showing yellowed teeth in a grin. "I might bring you another present. I got some cash. Maybe you could put on a show for me."

Her mouth was dry and she could find no other words to ward him off. He'd peeped at her, and now he was admitting it because he viewed her as helpless. This was sport for him, and he enjoyed it. Fury coursed through her. She was about to respond when a nurse hurried toward them.

"It's Mr. Lavallette on the telephone. He says he needs you to drive the hearse, Mr. Clements. There's a body needs to go to Pascagoula. That man who was beaten to death. The family wants him brought home."

"I'll be seein' you," Junior whispered softly to Jade. "You and your pretty little sister. Real soon."

He brushed past her, and she forced her legs to hold steady as she watched him walk down the corridor. She had a visceral urge to plant her knee in his crotch, but she didn't move. Jade felt the nurse's stare, but Jade held her tongue. Talk would only make matters worse. She had evidence of that. There could be only one person who'd been telling tales on Marlena. Dotty Strickland. Jade had a grim desire to make the woman pay for running her mouth.

She tapped lightly on the door of Marlena's room and entered. The blond head was turned away, the once bright hair, in need of washing, flattened to Marlena's skull. Jade heard the sound of soft sobs.

"Are you okay?" Jade asked. She closed the door firmly. "Be careful. The nurses are out in the hall. They'll hear you."

Marlena worked at holding back her tears.

"What happened?" Jade asked. She got a clean washcloth, wet it under the tap in the bathroom, and wiped Marlena's hot face. "What did he say?"

She inhaled, shuddering with the effort. "He pulled the covers back and looked at me," Marlena said. "I had to pretend that I was asleep."

Jade gritted her teeth. Junior was a pervert. He'd been spying on her and now he was exposing Marlena's poor, beaten body to his view. He was bolder, too, acting as if there was no recourse that could be taken against him. Jade thought of Frank and felt true fear. If Junior suspected she'd slept with a white man — she halted her thoughts.

"Did Junior say anything?" she asked.

Marlena sniffed. "No. He just pulled the covers back and pulled up my gown." More tears leaked out of her eyes. "He just made this grunting noise, like a pig at a trough." Her voice rose in hysteria. "I can't stay here. You have to take me away!"

"Take it easy," Jade urged. "He can't hurt you here." She didn't believe the words even as she said them, but she had no idea where

Marlena could go that would be safe. Now she understood her sister's desire to stay comatose. Waking up brought only pain and danger. Junior Clements scared her. Junior was capable of cruelty, and lately he had an air about him that was different, as if he thought himself above the law. She looked at Marlena. "Was it Junior who hurt you?" The expression on Marlena's face was answer enough.

"Jade, you have to help me." Marlena glanced around the room as if escape were hidden behind the draperies. "I can't stay here! I can't pretend any longer! They're going to find out I'm awake!" Marlena's eyes were wide. Her fingers dug into Jade's arm, clutching in terror.

"I don't know what to do," Jade said. She couldn't leave Marlena alone in the hospital. There was no safe place for them. At least not when Junior got back from Pascagoula.

"Take me somewhere safe, where no one can find me. Not Lucas or Junior or anyone." Marlena's voice dissolved into tears. "I'm afraid."

"Okay," Jade said, putting an arm around Marlena's thin shoulders. "I'll think of something."

Dotty tried to hold her weight off the jouncing truck seat, absorbing some of the punishment with her arms. There was nothing around them but trees, a thick wall of them with their gray-black trunks and bitter green needles. They were deep in the woods in a place Dotty had never imagined, going into the dense forest and away from town. Dantzler was driving like a maniac on the narrow dirt road that was little more than a pot-holed path. Outside the windshield, the sky had taken on a dark gray cast with hints of green in the center of the front. Bad weather, really bad weather, was about to hit.

The truck hit a deep hole, and Dotty's head bounced into the roof of the cab. She let out a yelp, and Dantzler's fist flew across the seat and backhanded her in the mouth. She tasted blood but didn't say anything. She'd learned in the first few minutes that trying to talk only brought more slaps and slugs. The man beside her had no interest in anything she had to say.

"Ole Frank's going to be surprised when he gets home and finds you gone without a trace," Dantzler said, chuckling to himself. "He'll be hunting that little girl *and* you."

Dotty felt the tears slide down her cheeks. Frank wouldn't know she was gone. The one thing that might have tipped him —

her car — had been left in the old garage behind the Kimble house. Frank might not find it for days. No one would know she was missing. She lived alone and hadn't made any plans to meet anyone. She had no job, no place of employment for someone to miss her. Marlena was in a coma and couldn't tell anyone she was missing even if she knew. Worst of all, Dotty realized she'd made a terrible mistake. She'd been at Frank's house ready to tell him that Junior Clements had abducted Suzanna Bramlett, and she'd been dead wrong. She was locked in a truck going forty miles an hour down a pig path with the kidnapper.

The tears ran into her split lip and she wanted to cry out with pain, but knew better. She cowered against the passenger door and prayed for deliverance.

"I'm not Frank's girlfriend," she said, the words a little distorted by her now swollen lip.

"Did I ask you a question?" he asked.

Dotty knew she had to make him understand before it was too late. "Frank doesn't even like me. He won't care that you have me."

Dantzler stopped the truck. He slowly pulled his belt from the loops of his pants. "You want to play games?" he asked. "I've got a few I really enjoy." He was laughing as he reached for her, his fingers knotting in her hair, dragging her across the seat and clear of the truck, her cries bouncing back from the trunks of the huge pines.

27

Jonah sat on the back steps of his home, sweat draining from every pore. It was a sick sweat, the smell of shame in it. He stank, and he felt nothing except contempt for himself. He could not face his wife. Thirty-seven years of neglect had weighted his marriage down in a bog of hurt. He'd never committed adultery; that was not his sin. His was worse, because he had put Ruth always last in the trinity of his allegiance. Before Jade had come home with them, Lucille had always come first. He saw that now. Yesterday, he would have denied it. Such an accusation would have angered him. Lucille had lifted the veils from his eyes, and he saw plenty now. His relationship with his wife was built on resentment and anger. She had the right to it, but he did not. Jade had become his first priority, with Lucille dropping into second place, and then Ruth. Always at the last, Ruth. Shame swept over

Jonah and he put his head in his hands and wept.

"What are you doing sitting on the back step crying?" Ruth asked him from inside the screen door. He hadn't realized she was in the house. She was so quiet, like a wraith, and that was his fault, too. He'd taken the softness from her, drained it out of her as surely as if he'd put a siphon in her.

"So much time has gone by," he said, not bothering to hide his tears from her. "I'm an old man now."

"You're crying for your lost youth?" Her tone bespoke her impatience with him.

"No, Ruth, I'm crying for the years that I was a fool, for the time I treated you poorly and was so stupid I wouldn't admit what I was doing."

He felt the screen door touch his back as Ruth pushed it open. It slammed softly. She came onto the step and sank to a seat beside him. She didn't touch him. She hadn't touched him in years. That was another thing he'd stolen from her, from both of them. His tears had dried, but the pain of remorse was wicked cruel in his heart.

"So you finally woke up?" she said. Her eyes were soft, the anger finally gone. "It's a hard fall, Jonah. I know it hurts."

"Maybe I need to hurt. I've hurt you

plenty over the years."

"Yes, you have." She said it without anger.

"Ruth, I didn't mean it."

"Most folks don't mean to bring suffering to others. Still, it happens. When you love, you risk pain."

He thought about her words. "Do you still love me?"

"I don't know," she said. "I've spent so many years hating you, I don't know what's beneath that. Hating you was the only way I could survive. Hating you and Miss Lucille." Those last words were spoken with bitterness. "You never saw her for what she really is."

"I did today." He would not tell her that Jade was his daughter. It wasn't his cowardice about not knowing that he wanted to hide. He'd believed every syllable Lucille had told him, because he'd wanted to believe the baby she carried belonged to another man. As a young woman, Lucille had been free with her body, and so he'd never questioned her story of a Negro lover from New Orleans. He'd met Slidin' Jim at the Longier party, had seen the man's charm. Knowing Lucille the way he had, he'd never questioned her lie. Lucille had tricked and manipulated him like a wooden puppet. Jade was his daughter. Lucille had hidden that from him for thirty-six years. Ruth would never know. He wouldn't taint the one thing she loved with all her heart. "I saw Miss Lucille for what she's become, over the years. I saw her, and I saw myself." His head lowered. "I'm ashamed."

"The truth can be harsh," Ruth said. "But when you turn that light on yourself, I'm forced to see the woman I've become. That's not pretty to me or anyone else." She sighed. "I haven't looked in a mirror in better than ten years. I can't bear to look at myself, an old dried up woman burning with hatred."

"You can look, Ruth." He touched her cheek, feeling skin that was unfamiliar to him. Ruth's face was soft, belying the hardness he'd come to associate with her. He turned her face so that they gazed at each other. "There's a lot to see besides hardness. There's goodness and a real love for our daughter."

"I wanted to love you, Jonah, but there wasn't any room for me in your heart."

He closed his eyes. The damage he'd wreaked was worse than any Lucille might have done. He had no excuses. He'd had a woman who loved him and wanted him. Lucille had been alone.

He stood up. "Where's Jade?"

"She went into town to talk to Frank Kimble about the peeping Tom. I told her not to. I told her the white law didn't care what happened to a black woman."

Jonah thought his heart could get no heavier. The idea of Jade and Frank tore at him. Jade would suffer, as he had suffered. And the end result would be that anyone else who dared to love her would suffer, too.

"Is there something between Jade and that lawman?" Ruth asked.

Jonah didn't answer instantly. He thought about it. He'd neglected his wife for many years. Now he wanted to protect her, but to do so, he'd have to lie to her again. That was a road he wouldn't travel twice. He wouldn't lie to anyone, especially not himself.

"Frank says he cares for Jade," he said. "She was with him. Last night."

Ruth moaned and swayed on the step. "Jesus save us." She clutched at her dress front. "Sweet Jesus up above, please help us!" she cried out and bent double.

Jonah put his hands on her shoulders and steadied her. "It's going to be okay, Ruth. You were right to want to send her away. That's what we'll do. We'll send her to New Orleans, help her set up a shop there. Everything's going to be okay. It's not too late for Jade, and it's not too late for us. I've got to go and find her, tell her." He rose to his feet, kissed Ruth's cheek, and started walking to town.

Frank wiped the sweat from his eyes. The air was heavy with humidity, as if the storm clouds were a blanket holding in place all the warmth of the earth that attempted to rise. His eyes stung from the sweat, and he blinked them. He caught movement in the gray blur of the tree trunks and reached for his pistol. When his eyes cleared, he saw Joseph Longfeather standing among the trees. Instead of fatigues, he wore the aqua-and-white-striped shirt he'd been so proud of. A red bandanna was tied at his neck, his hat pulled low over his eyes. He smiled and disappeared. Frank's shirt was soaked with sweat, but he strode through the woods, confident of his trail now, sensing he soon would have his quarry.

The trail had taken him to an old logging path choked with briars and the remains of pines too straggly for the mills. He'd traveled for better than five miles, winding ever eastward, away from the river. The dense trees had given way to rutted and barren land. The loggers had had their way with the pines, and with them they cut everything that stood in their way. A few lone blackjacks had escaped, growing out of privet and briars.

When the logging trail fed into a more traveled path, Frank felt a swell of elation. He stopped to wipe the sweat from his brow and run his fingers through his slick hair. There were tire prints in the sand. A vehicle had come this way and in the not too distant past.

He chose north and kept walking, following the path. The clouds hung low and dense, and thunder rumbled like an angry god. The few trees around him began to quake and shimmy as a hard wind swept through their tops, and Frank tasted rain seconds before the first fat drops began to fall. In the distance he heard the sad howl of hounds, and he picked up his speed.

A thin wisp of black smoke curled on the horizon. A cook fire, Frank reckoned, since it was too hot for any other kind. He headed for it.

Bile rose in Dotty's throat as Dantzler prodded her forward toward the gathering of men who stood, scratching and hawking at her approach. She'd given up trying to talk. Dantzler Archey was an animal. He'd beaten the backs of her legs to a fiery red with his belt, and the skin felt puckered and inflamed. As she walked toward the men she held her skirt so that it didn't brush against her angry flesh. He would pay. He would pay dearly, just as soon as she figured out where she was and how she could get home. They'd driven at least ten miles into the woods. She was in a place she'd never been, and she hadn't seen a house or a store or anything the whole time. The right heel on her favorite patent leather shoes had broken, and Archey had tossed it into the woods with a laugh. Now she hobbled like some kind of cripple.

The men watching her were obviously half-wits and mutes, and she hawked up a ball of phlegm and spat it on the foot of the closet one. Behind her, Archey laughed. "Boys, this here's Frank Kimble's woman. She needs to be brought to heel."

Dotty kept her chin up, but she felt her gut turn to liquid, and she had the horrible sensation that she might mess herself.

"Where'd you git her?" a tall, toothless man asked.

"Oh, I found her. You know, finder's keepers." Archey pushed her forward, and Dotty gagged on the stench of the men.

"Are we gonna keep her?" The man's eyes

glistened, and a string of spittle laced his lips.

"For a while," Archey said, grabbing her arm.

"For all of us?" the man asked.

Archey hesitated. He looked at Dotty and then back at the men who'd all taken a step forward. "Maybe," he said. He pushed Dotty forward, away from the men, and she stumbled on her uneven shoes and fell to her knees. Had Archey not grabbed her arm and pulled her to her feet, she would have fallen there and been unable to help herself.

"Come on," he said, roughly dragging her beside him. He paused and turned back to the men. "Get the truck started. We're going to the still tonight. We got a delivery to make, and then we're gonna have us some fun."

His fingers closed over her arm and he pushed her ahead of him. Dotty lost her right shoe completely and kicked the left one off. Up ahead, she could make out what looked like an unpainted cabin. She caught her balance and walked beside Archey, the sharp roots and broken limbs stabbing into her soft feet.

"What are you going to do to me?" She was beyond fear now. If he touched her — if any one of those filthy, stinking men touched her — she would die.

"Shut your yap," he said. He opened the door and pushed her inside. The door slammed behind her and she heard metal running against wood. She turned and saw the large links of a heavy chain in a hole in the door. The room was almost totally dark, only a dim light slipping through a few chinks in the wood. She made out beds, and from the stench she knew the men outside slept here.

In a far corner of the room was a curtain. She crawled toward it, praying that it led to an outside door. She'd always been afraid of the woods, afraid that she'd get lost and that some wild animal might attack her. That, now, was a pleasant dream. The nightmare was Archey and his men. She had to get away from them, and even if she starved to death in the woods it would be better than the fate he represented.

Behind the curtain she heard something dragging. A chain. She froze. What if there was some animal chained behind the curtain? A wolf, or a panther, or a bear. She could hear her blood coursing in her ears, but she heard the chain again. It moved slowly across the floor. Slowly. She inched forward, her fingers feeling the worn wood floor, the grit embedded in the unfinished lumber. If she ever got out of this, Dantzler Archey would pay. She'd get a gun and she'd shoot him. First in the balls. After he'd bled and begged a while, she might shoot his knees, cripple him good so even if she let him live, he'd realize he'd always be a cripple. After a while, if he hadn't bled to death, she'd finish him off with a blast right between the eyes.

She hung on to her plans for revenge as she moved forward to the gingham curtain, to the thing chained behind it. She stood up and walked to it, pulling it back with one quick jerk. The woman standing at the stove was naked, her body covered in dirt and bruises. Clinging to her side was a boy, his face distorted by horrible scars.

Dotty felt something in her throat. She lifted her hand and felt the column of her neck, felt the bulge there that choked off her air. She couldn't stop staring at the woman and the boy, and they, in turn, stared at her. She stumbled backward, unable to breath because her throat was jammed. She fell back across one of the beds, and the jar of the fall broke the scream loose in her throat.

Once she started screaming, she couldn't stop.

28

The hospital was still and quiet, the fluorescent lights a feeble attempt to illuminate what should have been day. Jade paced down the corridor to the front door and stopped. The storm was imminent. She opened the door and tasted metal on the air. Lightning forked a mesh of spidery veins across the heavy gray sky, and Jade ran for her car, parked beneath the water oaks in front of the hospital. She'd made it only a few feet when the clouds opened up. Rain dropped in a solid sheet. Beneath her feet, the ground trembled in the grip of booming thunder. Another bolt of lightning split the sky, and Jade ducked just as a limb in the oak tree burst into splinters, showering around her. The smell of sulfur was strong. Beside her, the trunk of the water oak sizzled in the downpour. A gash ran twenty feet up the tree where the bark had been peeled away by the lightning.

Jade fumbled with her keys, unnerved by the worst storm she could remember. She got in her car, her hands so wet they slipped on the steering wheel, and drove slowly around the hospital to the back entrance, the place where the janitors and orderlies gathered to smoke and exchange gossip.

Jade maneuvered the Hudson so that the passenger side of the car was closest to the hospital door. Before she could get out, the hospital door opened and a tall black man stepped into the rain, a bundle of sheets in his arms.

Jade reached across the car and opened the passenger door, and the man eased Marlena into the seat.

"Thank you, Tom," Jade said.

"Good luck," he said. He turned and went back inside the hospital, his clothes thoroughly soaked.

"Where are we going?" Marlena's face peeped from beneath the folds of the white sheets. She forced the words through her rigid jaw.

"Someplace safe," Jade assured her, though she had no idea what to do. Her only thought had been to get Marlena out of the hospital, away from Junior Clements. Jade couldn't take Marlena to Ruth and Jonah's and endanger them. Her own house, a place she'd once considered safe from harm, had been violated. The shop was no better.

"Where will it be safe?" Marlena asked, despair chattering in her tight voice.

Jade thought of one place where Marlena would be completely safe. She put the car in gear and eased through the puddles to the road. "Don't worry," she said. "I know a place."

When Jade turned right, Marlena looked at her. "Don't take me to Mother's. Please. I can't go there."

"I'm not," Jade assured her. "We're going to Frank Kimble's. No one will ever think to look for you there."

"Frank's?" Marlena said the word as if she didn't understand its meaning.

"It's perfect," Jade said. "No one ever goes there. Frank doesn't even use the upstairs at all. He —" She turned to look at Marlena, who was staring at her. "It'll be fine."

They passed the bank and the corner drugstore, where a lone man stood on the sidewalk in the rain. Jade pressed the accelerator harder. They left the town behind, lost in the curtain of rain. The clouds seemed to sit on the horizon, a dark, angry presence that promised no let up.

Lightning forked again, and Jade heard a

loud pop. Marlena cowered in the seat.

"It's okay." Jade reached across and touched her sister's chilled arm. Marlena felt as if she were already dead. "It was Junior who attacked you, wasn't it?" she asked.

Marlena looked out the window, her face blank.

Jade pressed the gas more firmly, until they turned off to Frank's house. In a flash of lightning, the third story was illuminated above the trees.

"The Kimble house is haunted," Marlena said softly.

"The dead can't hurt you."

"Not like the living, that's for sure."

Jade slowed the car at a turn in the driveway and stopped. "Are you positive you don't want to go to your mother's?"

Marlena slowly shook her head. "Not there."

"Why?" Jade eased the car forward.

"She'll call Lucas. I'm his property. I see that now. All along, that was my value to Mother. I could be sold to a wealthy man."

They pulled up to the front steps and Jade got out and ran around the car to help Marlena. "Can you walk?" Jade asked as she stood beside the car, rain stinging her exposed skin. It was a summer storm, but it held within it the coldness of winter.

"I'm going to find out," Marlena said. She let Jade swing her legs so that her feet were on the ground.

As Jade pulled her up, Marlena faltered and almost fell. Jade grabbed her hips and steadied her. "Marlena, I can't carry you, but I could drag you on a sheet."

Marlena shook her head, the rain running into her eyes and mouth. "I can do it. Just help me." She put her arm around Jade's shoulders. Together, they moved slowly to the house and up the steps.

The front door stood open, and Jade half-dragged Marlena into the foyer and across the wooden floor to a chair in the parlor. She eased Marlena into a sitting position and knelt down at her knees, reaching up to touch the pale face that looked like death. Jade stifled a gasp when she saw that the sheet wrapped around Marlena's body showed a creeping red stain.

"Let me look," Jade said, easing Marlena back and pulling the layers of sheet away. Three stitches had pulled loose, and blood oozed from the opening. Jade closed her eyes.

"What's wrong?" Marlena asked, too weak to even right herself.

"You've pulled out some stitches, but it

doesn't look too bad." Jade rose before she lost control and began to weep. She was terrified. She'd moved Marlena out of the hospital to an isolated place where she might bleed to death.

"I'll be back in a minute." She hurried into the kitchen. For a long moment she grasped the lip of the cold porcelain sink and held on. She'd acted on instinct, and now she was afraid. Before she could continue, her fear had to be conquered.

She thought of the time Ruth had cut the palm of her hand with a butcher knife. The wound was laid open like a split made in a roast. Blood poured across the kitchen table, dripping onto the floor. Ruth washed the wound and them applied a pressure bandage, but the blood could not be stopped. Jade had been ten, and she watched Ruth sway and fall to the floor. Terrified, Jade had run to get Jonah, and after that everyone said she'd saved Ruth's life.

She took a deep breath. She could take care of Marlena. Frank would be home soon enough. Once he was with them, he'd know what to do. Until then, she had to stop the bleeding and get her sister to rest, maybe drink some soup, something hot to ward off the chill of the rain.

Jade had no idea where Frank kept scissors, or even if he owned any. She opened drawers until she settled on a large butcher knife. When she went back to Marlena, she cut one of the sheets into long strips and fashioned a bandage she could tie around her sister's hips, applying pressure to the incision. She had to keep the wound from opening further.

Once Marlena was trussed and sleeping on the sofa, Jade went to the kitchen and began to search the cabinets for something to eat. She found coffee and a single can of tomato soup. She made both, glad to have something to do to keep busy, glad she had hot food to offer Marlena. While the coffee was brewing, she went to the telephone in the kitchen and called the sheriff's office. There was no answer. She hung up and went back to the kitchen. Her gaze fell upon the butcher knife she'd used to cut the sheets. It was a sharp knife, well-balanced in her hand.

She put it on the counter within easy reach.

The roof of the cabin sounded like it was going to collapse under the onslaught of rain. Dotty sat on the floor in the kitchen, the only light coming from a hole around the woodstove exhaust.

"It's going to be okay," she said softly. She held the naked woman's foot in her lap and carefully worked at the manacle lock, using a bobby pin from her hair and a nail she'd found and sharpened. The boy buried his face against the woman's thigh, hiding the severely burned portion as if he were ashamed.

"I'm going to get you free from here, and then you're going to help me get away," Dotty said, glancing into the boy's one good eye. "Right?" It was taking everything she had not to fall on the floor and scream. She could barely look at the boy or the woman.

"We can't leave," the boy said, clinging tighter to the woman. "Zerty will hurt us more. He'll hurt us bad."

"He will not," Dotty said. "That bastard is going to pay for what he's done. Now, I'm getting out of here and you're coming with me. You know the way." She looked at the boy, glaring. "I'll take her, too, because no living creature deserves to be chained up like this."

"She's my mother," the boy said.

Dotty stopped her furious work on the ankle. "What?" she looked up at the woman, noticing for the first time the beautiful violet eyes that were so empty. "What's wrong with her?"

The boy shook his head. His words came out with a struggle, but he managed. "She couldn't live being afraid all the time, so she just left. In her head. It makes Zerty furious, because now she doesn't even cry when he hits her."

"That evil motherfucker." Dotty pried the last bolt on the ankle band free. The skin beneath the manacle was raw and infected, but there wasn't time to worry about that. Dotty threw the metal to the floor and scrambled to her knees. "We're going to have to get out of here on foot, but we can do it."

"Where will we go?" the boy asked.

She studied him, aware that she'd assumed he was slow-witted because of his looks. "To town. To Drexel. Do you know the way?"

He shook his head. "Zerty never let me go to town. He says I'm a freak and I have to stay in the woods."

Dotty stood up slowly. She could feel panic knotting in her chest. "You are a freak, but we have to get away from here. We have to go. We can't stay here." Her voice was rising, and she saw the look of dismay on the boy's face. She stopped talking and walked over to the woman. If she stayed, she would become this creature. She knew it. Her body shook as she inhaled. "What matters is that we all get out of here. If we can get to the road, we can get a ride."

"It's about ten miles through the woods," the boy said.

She nodded. She touched the woman's chin, lifting her face. For a second she stared into the vacant eyes. The woman didn't blink or flinch. She simply wasn't there. Dotty gently brushed back a strand of the woman's matted hair. "Dantzler Archey is going to pay for this," she said, and her voice was strong and firm. "That bastard is going to pay."

She walked to the wall where the exhaust pipe for the wood-burning stove came through. "Here," she said, tapping it with her knuckles. "This will be the easiest place to get out." She picked up a piece of kindling. "We'll have to knock the boards down."

29

As Frank approached the old house, a pack of dogs came out from under the porch, teeth bared and hackles raised. In the barren yard, they looked like plague animals. During the war, Frank had seen starving dogs and starving people. One female hound, her ribs and spine prominent, had teats dragging to the ground. The dogs snarled rather than barked, and he wondered how the animals managed to stand upright they were so poor. He stood in the yard, the rain a physical force as it pelted him. His shoulders and face were numb from the stinging deluge.

The door of the unpainted shack opened a crack and a gnarled hand signaled him closer. He took three steps and waited, the dogs more agitated than before. He'd seen hungry dogs feasting on the bodies of the dead. He held perfectly still.

"Who are you?" a voice called out.

"Deputy Frank Kimble with the Jebediah County Sheriff's Department."

The door opened wider and an old man stepped onto the porch. "Yeah, he said you'd be comin'."

Frank nodded. He didn't move forward. The old man was no threat, but there was no telling who else was in the house. If Hubbard was there, and if he was desperate, it would be a stupid thing to threaten him.

"I'm looking for a man called John Hubbard. He's wanted as a witness to a kidnapping and rape." He wanted to give the old man every chance to understand what he was involved in.

"So you say," he said. "Hubbard says differently."

"I'd like a chance to hear his side of the story." The rain was so loud, Frank found that he was yelling.

"Can't do it," the old man said. "He ain't here no more."

Frank felt the tension leave his shoulders. The hand that had crept up to his waist, where his gun was tucked in the holster, dropped back to his thigh. "Where'd he go?" he asked.

"I took him into town. About an hour ago."

"Into Drexel?" Frank asked, surprised.

"Yep. Took him to the drugstore and let him out. He's a sick man."

The dogs had relaxed, but they hovered under the edge of the porch. Frank took a step closer so that he could hear the old man easier. The dogs growled a warning.

"Could I come up on the porch and talk to you?" he asked.

"I don't have much truck with the law," the man said.

"I'm only looking for Hubbard. A young girl was kidnapped. There's a big reward for her return. If you help out, you could claim some of that money."

He'd spoken the magic word. Money. The old man stepped fully onto the porch. "Git, you mangy dogs!" He stomped hard on the porch and the dogs scattered. "Come on up here," he said. "Tell me about the re-ward. How much is bein' offered?"

Frank smiled as he took the four wooden steps up to the porch. Stepping out of the rain was like entering a new world, one where his senses had the luxury to perform properly. "A good bit of money. The missing girl is Suzanna Bramlett. So, what did Hubbard tell you?"

The old man wore coveralls and no shirt. He pulled at one strap and rubbed a hand over his unshaven face. "Said some men attacked him and his girlfriend in the woods. Said he had some kind of condition where he fell out. When he came to, everyone was gone."

"Who was he going to see in Drexel?"

The old man shrugged. "How much money can I git?"

Frank pulled his billfold from his pocket. "How about five dollars for now?"

The old man took the bill and studied it. "That ain't much re-ward."

"It's all I have on me now," Frank said. "When the girl is recovered, there'll be more."

"Johnny didn't say who he meant to see. He just said he had to get to Drexel and make things right." He pulled his lips in over toothless gums.

"How long was Hubbard here?"

"Let's see. He came in sometime Friday. Looked like hell."

Frank nodded. "Where'd you find him?"

"Wanderin' down one of the old loggin' trails. He didn't have a clue where he was. Said he had a car, but we looked on the road and never saw it. I wasn't sure if he was lyin' or not."

"He has a car," Frank said. "Did he say anything about the girl?"

The old man shook his head. "Nary a word about a girl. Talked about a woman. The first day he was here, he was sick. He had some kind of fit, and when he was over it, was like he was havin' a nightmare. He screamed about some woman."

"What's your name?" Frank asked.

"Lemuel Dearman," the man said. "Where do I collect my re-ward?"

"Once the girl is found, I'll be back around with it."

He nodded. "I'll be here." He started back in the house and then turned back. "You can sit here if you'd like, but it's gonna be a spell before that rain lets up."

"Do you have a vehicle?"

The old man snorted. "Cost more than five dollars for me to drive in weather like this."

"Take me to my car down by the river, and I'll drive back out here later and give you ten more," Frank said.

The old man smiled. "You got a deal."

The wind and rain roared around the Kimble house, shaking the windows and rattling the shutters against the outside walls in a manner that made Jade remember the stories about the house. She sat in a wing chair, the butcher knife clutched in one hand, the house in total darkness. The power had gone out ten minutes earlier, probably from a tree falling on the line. The phone was out, too. She'd gone back out in the rain and pulled her car to the back of the house. Her intent had been to hide it in the old shed in the back, but once she got the doors opened, she'd found another car. Dotty Strickland's car. And no sign of Dotty. Her first reaction was anger, that Dotty had come to Frank's house waving her ass under his nose, but that anger had quickly given way to concern. Dotty was not a woman to set out on foot for anywhere.

Jade watched her sister's pale face in the constant flashes of lightning and tried to sort through the possibilities of what had become of Dotty. Someone might have come to the Kimble house and picked her up. But that didn't address the car hidden in the back shed. Jade had the terrible sense that if she walked up the beautiful staircase Mose Dupree had imbued with a life of its own, she would find Dotty's body in one of the unused bedrooms. To halt the macabre thoughts, Jade bit down on her bottom lip until she tasted blood.

She'd given up on calling Frank at the sheriff's office even before the phone went out. It had to be a tree on the line. The other possibility, that someone had cut it, was terrifying.

She felt panic like a clenched fist. She had to remind herself that Junior Clements had gone to Pascagoula to deliver the body of the man killed on the highway. He'd be gone for most of the rest of the evening. She picked up Marlena's chill hand and held it, tracking her thoughts in another direction. Jonah and Ruth would be worried sick about her, but there was no one to worry about Marlena. Jade wondered if she'd even been missed in the hospital yet. Tom and the other janitors would not tell. They could not risk their jobs.

She thought of Lucas, his handsome face so devoid of anything tender. Would he even acknowledge that his comatose wife had walked out of a hospital and disappeared? Things were not right between Marlena and Lucas. They were so bad that Marlena had not even wanted her husband called and told about her recovery. Guilt was a possible answer, but so was fear. Lucas was not a man who would take his wife's infidelity with calm understanding. And Marlena had not wanted her mother called. Jade pondered that. Lucille had always been domineering and controlling. She'd packaged

Marlena and sold her for her, Lucille's, betterment. Lucille would be more than angry at Marlena's behavior, behavior that could, and most probably would, cost Lucille her comfortable lifestyle. Lucas would not support ingrates.

A gust of wind knocked the shutters against the house with such force that Jade started. She released Marlena's hand and stood up, pacing the room. It was near the end of August, a time of stifling heat, but the ferocity of the storm had blown in a chill that went straight to her bones. She decided to go out the back door and see if she could find some dry wood to light a fire. The flickering of a fire would be cheerful and provide some heat for Marlena.

The compress bandage she'd rigged up had staunched the bleeding of Marlena's wound, but Jade knew a doctor was needed. There was a greenish cast to Marlena's skin and a coolness to her forehead that bespoke death. Since arriving at Frank's, she'd slipped into a stupor. She could answer when spoken to, but her responses were monosyllabic and monotone. As soon as Frank returned, he would take Marlena to Dr. McMillan. As soon as Frank returned, things would be okay.

She picked up one of the towels she'd gotten to dry Marlena and held it over her head as she opened the back door and dashed across the yard to the shed. If there was dry wood, it would be stacked in the shed. As she entered the darkness, she felt a rush of apprehension. She paused in the darkness, listening. The storm was so loud she couldn't hear anything except the whine of the wind and complaint of the trees. She moved slowly into the shed and stopped again; the sense that someone watched her was so powerful that her skin prickled and danced.

There was no person in Jebediah County that frightened her except Junior Clements. Dantzler Archey, who lived God knew where, also scared her, but both of those men were gone. She'd seen Dantzler driving out of town, and she'd heard the nurse tell Junior that Mr. Lavallette needed him to drive a body. There was no need for her skittishness. She stepped firmly into the darkness and made her way around Dotty's car to the back wall of the shed. She bent over and felt along the wall, hoping for some dry wood and praying that there would be no rats in it.

Her fingers found a log as big around as her upper arm, and she picked it up. She found another and grabbed it, too. She could tell it was good, dry wood. Frank had probably cut it the winter before, and it had aged and dried in the shed. She found a dozen more pieces and stacked them in her arms. Just as she stood up, she felt a puff of warm breath on the back of her neck. She froze, the wood clattering to the floor as she let it drop. Her fingers curled around one stout piece.

"I told you I'd see you soon," Junior Clements said, his voice disembodied in the darkness of the shed.

Jade didn't speak. Her response was the fire log that she swung with all of her strength. It caught Junior a solid lick. He cried out in pain and stumbled backward. Jade threw the wood at him and darted out of the shed.

"You goddamn nigger bitch! You'll pay for this. You and that white slut."

Jade rushed into the back door, flung it closed, and threw the thumb bolt into place. She leaned against the door and panted. Remembering that the front door was unlocked, she ran through the house, slammed it, and threw the lock.

"Jade?"

Marlena's voice was weak. Jade began checking the windows, making sure the locks were turned. Of course, Junior could simply break the glass.

"Jade?"

"I'm coming," Jade said. She hurried to her sister and knelt beside her. She had to hide Marlena. "The storm is getting worse. I found a safe place." She spoke quickly, trying to keep the panic out of her voice.

"What's wrong?"

"It's the storm," she said. "Marlena, I'm going to help you to the pantry." She could move a chair there, close the doors, and maybe Junior wouldn't find Marlena.

There was the sound of glass breaking in the front parlor.

"Jade, what was that?"

Jade grasped Marlena and picked her up. "It was a tree limb crashing through one of the windows," she said. Struggling beneath the weight, she carried her sister through the kitchen and to the small pantry where glass jars of preserves lined the wall. She dragged a chair from the kitchen table and eased Marlena into it.

"Stay here," she told her. "Don't say a word."

"There's someone here, isn't there?" Marlena's voice was dead. "It's Junior, isn't it?"

Jade tasted the terror. "He hurt you, didn't he?"

"He's back."

Jade saw her sister's lifeless expression in a flash of lightning. "It's going to be okay," she said. "Stay here. Don't make a sound."

"He's going to kill us both."

"No, Marlena. He isn't." Jade stepped out of the pantry and closed the doors.

30

Rain swept over the highway in slanting sheets, and gusts of wind pulled at the patrol car as Frank drove back to Drexel. Lemeul Dearman had let him off near the river, where he'd left the patrol car. The old man had not gotten his truck above five miles an hour, and now Frank made up for lost time. He had the sense that things were happening all around him, things that would impact him for the rest of his life. Through the dense rain, he saw shadows moving among the trees. The dead were walking, but he had no time for them. One thought drove him — to get back to town.

A puddle of deep water pulled the car toward the shoulder, and he wrenched the wheel, going into a sideways slide. When he finally righted the car, he was sweating. As he dropped over the crest of the last hill, the gray, abandoned town came into view. The dread that gripped him intensified.

He drove through town and went to the drugstore where the old man had dropped Hubbard off. The store lights burned dimly, and Frank parked and ran inside.

There was no sign of Hubbard. The store was abandoned except for the elderly pharmacist, who stood on a wooden platform behind the back counter where the drugs were kept.

"Mr. Hart, did you see a stranger? A man about six feet, dark hair and eyes, probably needing a shave."

Percy Hart pulled on his left earlobe and frowned. "Fellow came in here a little while ago. He looked mighty bad, if that's the fellow you're looking for. He asked to use the phone and then left."

"Who did he call?" Frank asked.

"I couldn't be sure. Herman Nyman came in about that time and needed some medicine for his croupy young'un. I didn't hear the call, but it was Lucille Longier who drove up and fetched him."

"Lucille?" Frank didn't hide his surprise. "I thought Jonah did her driving for her."

"Me, too, but it was Lucille. I noticed because she came close to taking out that pecan tree by the store. You might get Huey to have a talk with her about getting some glasses or staying out of the driver's seat."

"Sure. I'll do that. You say she picked up the stranger?" Frank asked, though he'd heard Percy the first time. He hoped for more details.

"That's right. He was soaking wet, and he got right in the front seat with her."

The questions that lined up in Frank's mind were disturbing. How would Lucille know John Hubbard, her daughter's lover? Why would she drive, alone, into Drexel to pick Hubbard up?

"Is something wrong?" Percy asked. "They took off before the worst of the storm hit. I'm sure Lucille made it home safely or we'd have heard something by now."

"Thanks, Mr. Hart," Frank said before he ran back out into the rain.

Dotty had never heard a storm like the one that battered the small cabin, but her mind wasn't on rain and lightning. Precious time was ticking away. If Archey and the men got back before they could escape, she wouldn't have another chance. The fate that loomed in front of her was hell, and she wouldn't accept it without a fight.

With the boy's help, they'd torn a hole in the wall that was almost big enough to get out. Almost. And time was running out. Dotty took a piece of wood and slammed it into the exhaust pipe. It loosened but didn't fall. "Help me," she said to the boy.

They struck the pipe together, knocking it loose from the stove. Dolly grunted with exertion as she helped the boy push it to the ground outside. They now had an escape route.

"Go on," she said to the boy.

He hesitated for a moment and she pushed him roughly. Her hands were blistered and raw, her fingernails torn to the quick. "Get out there," she said. "We have to move."

"It's raining hard," the boy said.

"At least they won't be able to track us," Dotty responded coolly. "Now get out there or I'll leave the both of you. I can only imagine what he'll do to you for letting me get away."

The boy slithered through, and Dotty grasped the woman's arm. Dotty had pulled the curtain down from the doorway and wrapped it around the naked woman. "Let's go." At first the woman resisted, but Dotty glared at her. "Get your ass out that hole," she said. "If it were up to me, I'd leave you, but that boy of yours wouldn't help me if I did."

The woman, so thin she only needed half the space, disappeared. Dotty glanced around the kitchen. There was a pone of cornbread and she grabbed it, tucking it into the top of her dress. They'd need something to eat. The woman looked like she'd blow away in a good wind. More food would be nice, but there was nothing else to take. Dotty crawled out the hole. The boy and the woman stood in the rain like animals, patiently waiting.

"What now?" the boy asked.

"Head out toward the road," Dotty said. She thought for a minute. "No, that's where they'll look. Is there another way?"

The boy nodded. "The river's about four miles to the west. We could go downstream. With this rain, the current will be fast."

Dotty wiped the rain out of her eyes. The boy was hideous and the woman was dead weight. She'd been condemned to hell with half-wits and the deformed as companions. "Is there a boat?"

"A small one. And paddles."

"Let's go," Dotty said. She didn't ask him where the river would take them, or how long they'd have to ride the current before they reached civilization. The harsh cost of survival could be paid only one leg at a time. First, they had to get to the boat. She let the boy lead, followed by the woman, and she took the rear. Rocks and sticks stabbed into her feet, but she ignored them.

They passed a shed where saws hung, the double-handled blades used by two men to bring down the big trees. She snatched one off the wall, and though it was awkward, she kept it with her. Boats were often chained to trees, and Dotty had no intention of letting a tree get in her way to freedom. Though the rain muffled the sound, she thought she heard a truck door slam. The afternoon had bled into night, or perhaps the storm was so dense that it blotted the sun. It didn't matter. She liked the night. The darkness cloaked her from the gaze of her enemy. She put her hand on the woman's thin shoulder and urged her into a jog. The boy picked up the pace. She slogged through mud and briars, the saw dragging and bumping behind her. She held onto it with grim intention. If push came to shove, she'd saw Dantzler Archey's legs off at the crotch.

Jonah stood at the edge of Lucille Longier's yard in the pouring rain. He'd never seen a storm like this one, the sky so dark that late afternoon had turned to night. It felt as if the whole world was turning liquid. Everything in Jonah's life that had been steady and reliable was falling apart. Mostly it was his view of himself that had shifted and shattered. He wasn't the man he thought himself to be. It was only by providence that his daughter was alive and well. And now, no matter what it cost him, he would see to her welfare. Even if it meant crawling back to Lucille Longier and begging for the use of her car.

The problem was the car was gone.

Headlights cut across the yard, and he stepped deeper into the shrubs. It was Lucille's car, and he could see that it was her behind the wheel. Someone else was in the front seat. A tall man.

He watched as Lucille parked, got out, and went around to open the door for the man. He wobbled as he got out, and braced himself on the fender. Lucille supported him as she helped him through the rain and onto the porch. He settled into a rocking chair, and she hurried into the house.

Jonah debated what to do. Lucille would never give him the car if he asked in front of another white person. She probably wouldn't let him use it at all. But he had to find Jade. He'd called the shop and gotten no answer. He'd tried to call Frank's house, but there was trouble on the line. Sheriff Huey wasn't to be found, and Jade had disappeared without a trace. He needed the car to hunt for her. With each passing moment, his need grew stronger.

The man on the porch slumped over as if he'd fallen asleep or passed out. Jonah stepped out of the shrubs. He walked across the yard, the rainwater rising over the tops of his shoes. He was almost to the porch when Lucille came out of the house, a glass of amber liquid in her hand. When she saw him, she stopped. Her empty hand went up to her mouth, as if to cover her expression of surprise.

"What are you doing here?" she asked, a tone of reprimand in her voice.

"I came to borrow your car," he said.

"Have you lost your mind?"

He shook his head. The man on the porch looked up, but his expression was uninterested. He was in torment, sunk far too deep in his own worries to give a care for anyone else.

"No, ma'am. Jade is missing, and I need to find her. I don't have a car, so I came to get yours."

"You think I should loan you my car?" She sounded amused.

"Jade is your daughter. I'm not asking to borrow your car. I'm taking it." He went to the driver's side and checked for the key. It was in the ignition. "I'll bring it back as soon as I can."

"If you take that car, I'll call the law on you."

"Go ahead. I can't find Mr. Frank or Mr. Huey anywhere. If I could have, I'd get them to look for Jade."

He opened the door and got in.

"I'll have you charged with car theft."

Jonah looked out the window. He saw the shell of the woman he'd loved for most of his life. The good part of her, the tenderness and caring, was long gone. He's spent his life loving something that was only half alive.

"You do what you have to do, Miss Lucille. As soon as Jade is safe, I'll bring the car back."

He started the car, backed around, and left. In the rearview window, he saw Lucille bending over the man, holding the glass for him to drink. It was only as the view disappeared around a bend that he wondered who the man was and why Lucille was so solicitous of him.

31

Jade crouched beneath the kitchen cabinet, the butcher knife clutched in her hand. Junior had made it into the house. She'd heard him in the parlor, had tracked his progress through the dining room and into the kitchen as he'd walked around the table, his breathing harsh and eager.

Now, he was upstairs, and she fought the impulse to crawl out of her hiding place and run. She couldn't leave Marlena. If Junior found her, she had no doubt he would kill her. Jade shifted in her hiding place, her knees complaining along with her back. She was jammed around the drain pipes, contorted into the only space where she could protect Marlena. If Junior tried to go into the pantry, Jade intended to kill him.

Bitter thoughts were her company as she listened to Junior's tread. She'd played right into his hands. His threats and intimidation at the hospital had been intended to achieve one thing, a rash action, and she'd done exactly as he wished. She'd taken Marlena, the only witness to his brutality and the abduction of a child. By moving Marlena to an isolated house, with the phone out, she'd put her sister in imminent danger. If Marlena died, no one could testify against Junior.

Thunder rumbled across the sky, and Jade felt the house tremble. The winds had shifted, coming out of the south now. Rain still drummed against the windowpanes, but it wasn't as heavy. The storm was letting up. She imagined running out of the house to her car, driving through the puddles in the road, water splashing up in a muddy wing as she raced for safety.

She couldn't leave Marlena, though. Eventually Junior would find her, and he'd finish the job he'd started in the woods four days before.

What little hope Jade had harbored that Suzanna was alive was gone. She thought of her niece, a child who'd never known unconditional love, or much love of any kind. Marlena had cared for the child, but she was deficit in the area of love. She'd never known tenderness or concern from Lucille, and she had no store to share with Suzanna. The child had lived unwanted and emotionally neglected, and now Jade accepted she was dead. She squeezed her eyes shut, willing the tears away. She would grieve for her niece later, when she and Marlena were safe.

There was the sound of something crashing on the second floor, and Jade thought again of running. If Junior searched the second and third floors, she might have time to get to town and get help. But once she started her car, he would realize she was gone. Then he would know Marlena was helpless in the house. No. She couldn't risk leaving, but she had to think of a place where she'd have the element of surprise. Popping out of the cabinet was a poor choice. The first strike of the knife would be at his calves. Not really a lethal point unless she was lucky enough to sever an artery.

She eased the cabinet door open and crawled out. She kept the knife with her, the blade glinting in a burst of lightning. She stepped into the pantry, where Marlena slumped in a chair. Jade touched her cheek, feeling only a hint of warmth. She was alive, but for how much longer if she didn't get medical care? Jade found a sheet in the laundry and draped it over her. It wasn't much of a disguise, but on first glance she looked like a piece of furniture.

The sound of footsteps on the staircase drifted through the open pantry door, and Jade felt panic rise in her lungs. Junior was coming back down, and he was trying to be stealthy. Jade closed the door to the pantry and tiptoed into the dining room. There was a sideboard by the parlor door. If Junior came in through the parlor door, she'd have a chance. If he chose to come in from the foyer door, he'd see her almost immediately.

She used a dining table chair to climb onto the sideboard, then flipped the chair over so that it clattered onto the hardwood floor. She heard Junior pause. He gave a low chuckle.

"I'm tired of this game of hide-and-seek. Now come on out like a good girl, and maybe I won't hurt you."

She felt her heart in her ears, a thudding sound that blocked out everything else. The hand clenching the knife was numb. She held her breath and waited, listening to his footfalls move slowly through the parlor toward her.

"Where's that slut?" Junior asked. "Give her to me and I'll let you go."

Jade's breath came in tiny, shallow puffs. She waited, intent only on the sound of his approach.

Through the crack in the door, she could

see him, a dark bulk. He stopped in the doorway, suddenly alert. Lightning lit the room, and for an instant, Jade thought he was looking directly at her. She thought her heart had stopped, but it bumped painfully against her ribs.

He took another step into the room.

Jade tensed, ready for the pounce. Another step. Maybe two.

Junior looked from side to side in the darkness. He turned in her direction, as if he could scent her. "When I find you, I'm going to hurt you bad," he said as he walked forward.

Frank passed the Buick doing seventy-five, and the fan of water that sheeted over his windshield almost wrecked him. The Buick was moving fast, too. He recognized the car as Lucille Longier's. He got the patrol car under control, did a U-turn, and headed after the Buick with his lights flashing. In the heavy rain, he'd been unable to see who was driving the car, but if Hubbard was in the vehicle, he was going to jail.

The Buick pulled to the side of the road, and Frank got out and walked to the driver's side. He was surprised to see Jonah, alone in the car.

"Mr. Frank, I have to find Jade."

Jonah's words sent a chill through Frank. He leaned toward the window. "She said she was going to spend the afternoon with you."

"Some man peeped in on her. She went to town to talk to you."

Frank didn't move. He felt the rain beating down on him, the drops sliding down his face and into his mouth. He heard the motor of the Buick running beneath the sound of the rain. He saw Jonah staring into his face, but he was removed from all of it. "When did this happen?" he asked.

"This afternoon, about one o'clock. She went up to the sheriff's office and she never came back. I can't find her anywhere."

"Did she recognize the man peeping at her?"

Jonah shook his head. "She didn't say she did. She was scared."

"She might be with Marlena. Have you tried the hospital?"

"No. I'll check her house again and then the hospital. Where are you going?"

Frank met his gaze. "She might be at my house."

Jonah turned his face so that he stared at the road. "If she's there, bring her to the hospital."

"I will."

Jonah stepped lightly on the gas and the Buick drew away. Frank stood in the rain a moment before he got in the patrol car, his body processing the emotions that rippled through him. Once behind the wheel, he pressed the gas pedal to the floor, sheets of water flying to each side. He passed Jonah and saw the look of worry on his face, but he didn't slow. Hubbard wasn't important any longer. Nothing mattered except finding Jade and making sure she was safe.

He was almost at the Drexel city limits when he cut off the highway, speeding down the narrow dirt road, ignoring the standing water that crossed it. Halfway through the water, the car shifted, sliding to the right. He pressed the gas harder and swung the wheel. He came out of the slide, hit the asphalt of Highway 13, and drove, mud flying everywhere behind the car.

He turned down his drive going too fast, and he had to brake to avoid hitting a tree. In his headlights, the camellia bushes looked like towering walls of black. Limbs slapped the car as he swerved around each curve. When the house came into view, it was dark. Tree limbs were scattered around the yard, and in the lessening rain, the house looked washed and faded. He pulled to the back and saw Jade's Hudson with a sigh of relief.

The shed doors were open, a fact that tickled his mind, and when they banged wide in the wind, he saw Dotty's car hidden in the dark recesses. Dread touched him. He slammed on the brakes, killed the motor, and raced toward the dark house.

Jonah sat in the car, the windshield wipers swishing across the glass. In the Buick's headlights, he saw the trunk of the sweet gum tree that had fallen across the road. It was a big tree, at least four feet in diameter, and a saw would be required to remove it. For some reason, he was reluctant to leave the Buick. It wasn't the rain that bothered him. He couldn't put his finger on it, just a feeling of dread. He had to find out if Jade was okay, and he tried to reason with himself that she'd headed home and then found her way blocked by the tree.

He picked up the flashlight that he kept in the glove box and got out, the rain singing against his skin. He stepped over the tree and continued the walk to Jade's house. At the edge of the yard, he stopped. The house was dark and silent, foreboding even. Rain ran off the tin roof like a waterfall, and he could remember the sound of it inside the house, when he'd been safe with Mose and his mother. Now, the house looked dangerous.

He gripped the flashlight like a club and walked up on the porch. When he twisted the doorknob, it came off in his hand. His heart pumped staccato. He eased the door open and walked inside. If his baby girl was in here, hurt, he had to find her. At first he heard only the drum of the rain on the tin roof, but his ears adjusted, and beneath that was a slow rhythmic creak. He listened in the darkness, trying to place the sound he recognized almost like a part of his body. He'd heard it all his life, all his childhood. He knew it, suddenly. He clicked the flashlight on and swung the beam to the corner of the room. Pet Wilkinson sat in his mother's old rocking chair, a grin on his face and a piece of flour sack cloth on his lap.

"Where's your girl?" Pet asked, then reached to his side and picked up a stout wooden club. In the flashlight's yellow beam, his features were white, his eyes feral.

Jonah clicked off the flashlight.

32

Dotty held the paddle in the water, steering the boat as the boy had told her. Down the long miles of the rain-swollen river, she'd become adept at using the paddle as a rudder. Paddling wasn't necessary; the current was swift, and she'd learned to search for and avoid eddies that could grasp the boat and suck it down to the bottom.

The rain had lessened, but the boy still used his hands to bail the boat, which either had a leak or was filling with rain. The woman was curled in a fetal position in the bottom of the boat, her face opalescent in the occasional flashes of lightning. The boy had covered her with the curtain, and Dotty didn't know if she was alive or not. Dotty could do nothing for the woman one way or the other. She had to focus on holding the paddle like a rudder, even though her hands were blistered and cracked. Just before they'd made it to the river, her left foot had slipped on a root and now her little toe dangled precariously, held on by a hunk of flesh. She'd almost severed it. Once she got back to town, Dantzler Archey was going to suffer. She turned her face into the rain as her thoughts curled hot and angry. She would live because she wanted to make sure he paid for all he'd done. Whenever she felt ready to drop the paddle and quit, when her shoulders burned with exertion and her foot throbbed with pain, she visualized Archey, naked and staked to the ground as she poured honey over his penis and waited for the ants to find him.

"Go left," the boy said in his strange voice.

She might not have understood him except she saw him waving in a burst of lightning. She repositioned the boat paddle and felt the small wooden craft swing toward the left bank. She'd given up trying to imagine where they might be on the river. It shifted and curved, and she'd lost all sense of direction and only hoped they were still on the Chickasawhay. The boy had told her there was a small community on the river, a place called Merrill. The river was running swift and fast with the rainwater, a virtual flood.

"Slow down!" the boy cried.

She used the paddle in backward arcs,

frantically trying to halt the swift progress of the boat. If they overshot the landing there would be no paddling against the current and they might end up, starved to death, in the Mississippi Sound.

"Look!" The boy was trying to stand up in the boat, making it rock from side to side.

"Sit your ass down!" she cried, swinging the boat in a half circle. She saw it then, the white arms extended, the back floating gently on the current. Naked and beautiful, the slender spine disappeared into the dark waters. It was a child's body.

She maneuvered the boat so that she was beside it. She could hear the skull knocking gently into the side of the boat just as the rain stopped. She knew she should reach out and catch the fan of dark hair that floated like silk on the water, but she couldn't bring herself to touch it.

"Grab it," the boy said. He was hunkered down in the bow, ready to crawl toward her and help.

She shook her head. "No," she said.

"Get it," the boy demanded.

She couldn't force herself to touch the body. She shook her head, even though the boy couldn't see her.

She felt the boat rock again and knew he was coming to the stern. She didn't protest but held the paddle in the water so the boat stayed beside the body.

The boy crept to the side, his hand snaking fast and clutching the hair. Grunting from the exertion, he began to pull the body into the boat. Dotty grabbed an arm and then a leg and helped him haul the cold, dead thing into the bottom of the boat, where it fell beside the boy's mother. Dotty felt nothing at all. It was the body of a small person, a child, but in the darkness she couldn't tell the sex. She didn't want to know. She waited for the boy to get back into position in the bow, and then she steered the boat back into the current.

"Shouldn't be far now," the boy said, and he spoke quietly, because the rain had stopped and silence had fallen over the river. "We're in the forks," he said. "Take us left."

The boat seemed to glide on the still water. The current was swift, but without the noise of the rain, it seemed they moved across glass. The clouds were shifting in the sky, and an occasional glint of moonlight illuminated the water like a silver pathway before the clouds thickened again.

"More to the left," the boy said, urgency in his voice.

She adjusted their course so that they were

only fifteen feet from the overhanging limbs of the bank. A strong wind had picked up, a wind from the south, blowing against them, slowing their progress to a lazy crawl. The clouds slipped away from the moon, and suddenly the river shimmered in the lunar glow. She looked down at the child in the bottom of the boat. Suzanna Bramlett rested beside the boy's mother. The crazy woman had taken the curtain that was her only protection and draped it over the child's body.

Dotty burst into tears. Her wail of despair echoed off the riverbanks and the wooden pier that rose out of the shadows of the bank like a whisper of hope.

Jade timed her jump, and when Junior walked close to the sideboard, she leapt upon his back with an inhuman shriek. She held the knife aloft and drove it with all her force into his neck. The blade struck his collarbone and glanced off with a jolt that numbed her arm to her elbow.

Junior gave a roar of pain and rage and began to whirl. He bumped into the table and ricocheted to the sideboard, where his weight caught Jade's lower leg and ankle with such a burst of pain that she almost loosened her grip around his throat. He shook like a bull, and it took all of her strength to hold on to him, her arm around his throat and her knees gripping his hips. She raised the knife again, just as he lurched into the wall. The blade sliced his cheek, opening a gash from the corner of his eye to his lip.

"I'm gonna kill you," he raged, and ran full tilt across the room, aiming to smash her into the fireplace.

Jade stabbed again, this time hitting his right eye. She felt him stagger. He took two more steps and dropped to his knees. She brought the knife down into his back as she slipped off him. He fell to the floor and began to crawl.

Panting, Jade started to retch. She heard someone calling her name and she staggered away from Junior. She couldn't kill him. She couldn't. Now that he no longer threatened her or Marlena, she could not finish him off, though it shamed her to realize it.

"Jade!" Frank burst into the dining room from the kitchen. The storm had ceased and moonlight flitted through the window, illuminating her as she stood, hunkered over and gasping, the taste of vomit bitter in her mouth.

"Jade!" Frank was beside her, pulling her against him as she sobbed.

On the floor, Junior moaned.

"He's still alive," Jade said. "He's still alive." She started to cry. "I can't kill him."

Frank helped her into the kitchen. He pulled out a chair and eased her into it. His hands on her shoulders were strong and warm. Kneeling beside her, he stroked her back and murmured in a tone that comforted her.

In the dining room, Junior thrashed into a chair. It fell to the hardwood floor, the sound echoing in the still night. "Help me," Junior cried in a voice that shook.

Jade could no longer check her sobs. Frank's arms circled her and shifted her so that she leaned against his chest.

"Go on and cry," he said softly. "That's the best thing now. Just cry it out."

While Junior struggled in the dining room, knocking furniture over, Frank stroked her back and hair as she cried. His strong hands softened the horror of the past hour. Junior Clements had meant to kill her and Marlena. She'd stabbed him several times. Even now, he writhed across the floor of the Kimble house, slowly dying. Jade clung to Frank as she sobbed.

When the worst of it was over, Frank touched her face. "Is Marlena okay?"

"She's in the pantry," Jade said.

Frank rose and walked across the room. Jade watched as he opened the pantry door and saw what looked like a sheet-covered chair. He uncovered Marlena's sleeping face, touched her cheek to discern if she was still alive. He tried to wake her, but without success. He returned to Jade. "You have to get Marlena to the hospital," he said.

"You take us." Jade knew she sounded weak and frightened, "Junior's still alive. I can hear him whimpering."

"You have to take Marlena. Now." He grasped her shoulders and forced her to look at him. "I have something to do."

Something glass crashed to the floor in the dining room. Junior was moving again.

"What are you going to do?" Jade asked.

Frank touched her cheek. "You don't need to worry. Not ever again. Now let's get Marlena in the car and you go. When you get to the hospital, call Sheriff Huey. Find him wherever he is and get him over there." He kissed her cheek. "And find your daddy. He's worried sick."

Dotty felt hands lifting her from the boat, and she had no energy left to fight against them. Her foot bumped the pier, and she cried out.

"Holy shit," a man's voice said.

"Get the other woman. Is she alive?"

"I can't tell. The girl is dead. Been dead a while."

Dotty let the man carry her across the creaking boards of the pier. The sound of his footsteps stopped in the sand, and she leaned her head against his chest and let go of the last tenuous threads of consciousness.

She came to again in the backseat of a car, the driver a silhouette in the front seat. Beside him and looking back at her was a woman.

"She's awake," the woman said, punching the man on the shoulder.

"Who are you?" Dotty asked.

"I'm Bill Fairly," the man said, slowing so he could glance back at her. "This is my wife, Emmy. We're taking you to the hospital in Drexel."

"Where's the boy and the woman?" Dotty tried to sit up, but the woman in the front seat put a hand on her chest and pushed her back down.

"Stay still 'til we get you to the hospital," she said.

"Where are they?" Dotty felt a surge of panic.

"They're right behind us," the woman said. "They're in another car." She turned so that Dotty could see her profile, the sharp nose and the makeup-free face that was brown and wrinkled from the sun. "Who's the dead girl?" the woman asked.

"Suzanna Bramlett," Dotty said. "Lucas Bramlett's daughter. We found her floating in the river."

"That's the little girl's been missing." She stated a fact. "I knew she was dead."

"Who's the woman and boy?" the man asked, his voice less sympathetic.

"I don't know their names," Dotty said. "They helped me escape."

"Escape?" the woman asked, casting a glance at her husband that clearly questioned Dotty's sanity. "Somebody been holding you prisoner?"

Dotty leaned back against the seat, the motion of the car lulling, even though she didn't want to give in to it. She didn't know these people, couldn't be sure if she could trust them or not. But she was too tired to fight any longer. Too tired to protect herself or the boy. She closed her eyes and slept.

The way Jonah figured it, he had two advantages. He knew the house from attic to crawlspace, and he wanted to live. The rain had stopped, and the silence that settled over the house seemed magnified. As soon as he turned off the flashlight, he moved to the right, easing into the front bedroom that Jade had converted into a sewing room. He hugged the walls, knowing that the boards in the center of the room would creak with his weight.

"Dupree," Pet said, "you might as well come on out. I ain't leavin' until I find out where that gal has gone. You can tell me and make it easy, or it can go hard. Either way, I got to know where she is."

Jonah didn't utter a sound. He shifted down the wall, moving around the sewing machine and then the chifforobe.

"I ain't got all night," Pet said. "Somebody's waitin' on me."

That would be Junior, Jonah thought. Pet didn't have the initiative to do anything on his own. He was working at Junior's behest.

"The storm's gone by and they'll have the power on soon enough," Pet said. There was a whine in his voice. "Just tell me where Jade went and I'll be gone."

Jonah gripped the flashlight. He'd made it through the front bedroom and was halfway through Jade's. The house was built in a circle, with one room leading into the next. He slipped into the bathroom, and then the kitchen.

"Listen here, nigger. You best tell me what

I want to know or you'll be more than sorry."

Jonah prayed that he would keep talking. In the darkness, that was the only way he could locate Pet. He hadn't moved. He was still in the front room, probably still in the rocking chair. Pet was not a ball of fire at any job, not even intimidation.

Jonah stepped wide over an old plank in the kitchen that moaned and complained whenever anyone trod on it. He'd avoided it most of his life, especially when he was trying to slip home after a late evening. He eased through the dining room and stood in the doorway to the parlor. Since the storm had stopped, the night was so quiet he could hear the frogs down at the pond, which was over a mile away. He listened for the creak of the rocker. He heard one soft movement of the chair.

He didn't hesitate. He lifted the flashlight as he ran into the room. He brought it down in a vicious swing that connected with flesh and bone. Something wet and solid hit the floor. Pet Wilkinson made a sound like a sigh, a soft exhalation, and then he fell to the floor. Jonah stood in the darkness, his breath ragged and his heart hammering. When he could finally move, he bent to the body. There was no pulse, no sign of life.

He felt along the body until he came to the head, which was split open and sticky with blood. He'd caught Pet right at the temple. He couldn't have hit him more perfectly had he aimed.

Jonah stood up, wiped his hand on his pants, and hurried out the door. Jade might be at the hospital, and Junior Clements was looking for her.

As he drove to town, he thought about Lucille's car. Well now, if she wanted to have him arrested, they could add a charge of murder to his sins. He hadn't intended to kill Pet, but he had. He had no regrets. Pet had come to hurt Jade, had probably hurt Marlena. Now he would never hurt anyone again.

33

Frank watched Jade's headlights bounce down the puddled driveway. She was alive, but he knew she wasn't undamaged. Fear changed a person. The things that had happened were forever in her mind, darkling images cast by a shadowed moon. Jade would have visits in the night from Junior Clements and Suzanna. She would suffer, and she had done no wrong.

When her taillights disappeared from view, Frank walked into the dining room where Junior Clements was bleeding out. A blood trail covered half the room, soaking into the wood floor, mingling with the blood of the past. Frank straddled him, listening to the bubbling sound of air mingling with the blood in his throat.

"Where's Suzanna Bramlett?" he asked.

"Fuck you." Junior could barely manage the words.

Frank picked up the knife Jade had

dropped on the floor. He pressed the point under Junior's chin, inserting the blade a quarter of an inch into the tender flesh.

"I'm going to split your tongue from under your chin," he said. "Where is Suzanna?"

Junior made a soft gurgling sound, and Frank pressed the blade slightly deeper.

"She's dead," Junior gasped.

Frank removed the blade. "How long has she been dead?"

"From the first. She kicked my balls. I didn't mean to, but I broke her neck."

Marlena had been right. Suzanna had been dead from the first few minutes of the attack. Frank lowered his face closer to Junior's. "Who told you to attack Marlena?"

The rate of Junior's bubbling increased. He tried to look away but had lost control of his head.

Frank removed his gun from his holster. He shifted down Junior's body so that he was standing on either side of Junior's knees. He pointed the gun at Junior's testicles. "Suzanna kicked 'em, and I'm going to blow them off if you don't tell me who paid you to hurt Marlena."

He gave Junior a moment to reflect. "I know it was either Lucas or Lucille. Which one?"

Junior tried to lift a hand, but the effort was too much for him. He rattled and moaned.

Frank waited another thirty seconds and then cocked the gun. "Junior, you're going to die. I'm telling you right out. It's justice for what you've done. Suzanna didn't have a choice. Neither did Marlena. It would have been kinder if you'd killed her. The promise I make you, is that I can make it quick, or I can make the last half hour agonizing."

"It was Ms. Longier. She wanted us . . . to scare Marlena. She was fucking that route man."

Frank understood, even though it sickened him. He saw the whole picture, and in the center of the web was the queen spider, willing to eat her young to preserve her kingdom.

"She sent you there to frighten Marlena. John Hubbard set it up. He had Marlena there so you and Pet could frighten her. And then it got out of hand. You killed Suzanna so you decided to have your fun with Marlena."

He gave Junior a chance to deny it, but Junior had nothing else to say.

"Then you had a taste for it," Frank supplied. "You pulled your car across the highway and tricked Sam Levert into stopping and you beat him to death for his money."

"Call an ambulance," Junior begged. "I don't want . . . to die."

Frank knelt to examine his wounds. Two were superficial, but two were serious. The eye wound posed a real potential for infection, but it was the cut to the kidney and gut that would eventually kill Junior. Eventually. Gut wounds were always the worst.

Frank read the story of the wounds. He saw how Jade had jumped on Junior's back and fought for her own life and her sister's. Junior's breath was fading. Soon he would be dead. Not even the miracles of modern medicine could save him. Frank sighed. "You brutalized Marlena, and you killed that man on the highway because you liked the way it felt. But you didn't count on Jade, did you?"

"Help me," Junior whispered.

Frank sensed someone else was in the room. When he looked up, his grandfather stood at the edge of the table. Blood leaked slowly from Gustave's temple where the bullet hole was ringed in powder. He held the gun in his right hand, and he nodded at Frank.

Frank rose slowly to his feet. He stared at

Gustave, finally understanding what must have happened on that night so long ago when Anna and Alfred were killed and when Gustave took his own life. Gustave had not killed his sister-in-law. He had not fired that first shot, or the second. Greta had. She'd killed her sister-in-law, and then her brother-in-law. Gustave had not acted in madness when he put the gun to his own head, but had merely put an end to things that could not continue. He'd taken the blame and left his wife free to raise their baby.

Moonlight broke through the clouds, flooding the room with light. The gun glinted in Gustave's hand. He nodded once more.

Frank grasped his pistol as he stood over the dying man on the floor. Junior looked up at him with a plea in his one remaining eye. Frank aimed at Junior's heart, cocked the .357, and fired. The badge Frank wore would protect him from murder charges, if anyone was foolish enough to care that Junior was dead. Frank knew his action would protect Jade from the stain of Junior's death, from the dreams that sometimes came when the night was deep and quiet.

He walked out into the yard where moonlight swished in the leaves of the trees and darkened the dense green of the camellia leaves. A sweet breeze with the promise of fall tickled the trees into a whispery sigh.

Jonah sat in one of the two chairs in the waiting room, his head in his hands and his body still shaking. He wanted to vomit, but there was nothing to come up. He needed to call Ruth, but he couldn't trust his voice to hold firm and not frighten her. In his mind was a single image that looped and relooped. Two sounds, that of his flashlight smacking into flesh and bone and the soft plop of brain onto the floor, echoed in his heart. After that, his hearing had stopped. Even now, sitting in the hospital with nurses and Dr. McMillan running back and forth, he heard nothing.

Jade was safe. She was in an exam room with a nurse cleaning blood from her. She wasn't hurt. Not physically, anyway. Her could see in her face that she was frightened and upset, in shock. The doctor had given her a sedative to calm her. Marlena was in the second exam room, and from the faces of the nurses, he could see that things weren't good for her. Lucas paced the hallway, his expression blank. Jonah was unable to read any intention in his face.

The emergency room doors burst open.

Jonah didn't recognize the man who stepped through the door with a blond in his arms. It took him a moment to realize the blond was Dotty Strickland. She looked like she'd been run over with a truck and then skinned.

"What in the hell is going on?" Dr. McMillan yelled as he came out of the room with Marlena to find another crisis in his hallway. "Take her in here." He pointed to the doorway to surgery and disappeared behind the man carrying Dotty.

The double outside doors opened again and Jonah stood up. He fought the muscles of his face to keep them from showing emotion at the young boy who walked in, his face so badly scarred he looked inhuman. Another man entered carrying a woman who weighed no more than seventy pounds and looked like she'd been beaten all over. She was wrapped in some type of cloth, and he saw the wound on her ankle that looked as if she'd been chained.

He was about to sit back down when a third man entered, carrying the body of a child. Her brown hair, dry now, fluttered silkily around the man's knees. For a moment Jonah thought her alive, but then he saw her face where death rested in the blue-tinted skin and the sightless eyes.

"Suzanna!" He cried the name and stepped forward before he could stop himself. The man froze. Jonah felt himself pushed aside, and he turned to see Lucas striding past him, his gaze on his daughter's body. Lucas said nothing. He stared at his dead child, turned, and walked away, his footsteps tapping on the hard tile of the hospital floor until they faded into nothing.

34

The August sun seemed to drink the life out of the landscape as Frank parked his car in front of the house on the hill with the wraparound porch and cool shade. It was midmorning on a Monday. A flock of chickens scattered around his feet as he walked to the steps. Lucille was home. He knew it. She had no way of leaving because he'd told Jonah not to return the car.

Frank knocked at the front door and waited. When no one answered, he walked around the porch to the side door that fed into the kitchen. Lucille was sitting at the table, her back to the door.

"Mrs. Longier," he said, tapping at the door. She didn't move or register his presence.

"Mrs. Longier," he said, knocking harder. When she failed to move, he opened the screen and walked into the room. He stepped around to face her. Her blue eyes were gazing out the kitchen window at an old shed. She seemed to be watching something of great interest, but when Frank looked out the window, he saw only the heat devils dancing in the yard and a few butterflies skimming the last of the summer flowers.

The hard rain the night before had left the earth saturated. The sun had come up hot, vaporizing the moisture and creating a bowl of humidity over the town. Frank wiped the sweat from his brow as he turned back to the woman who had masterminded her daughter's violent rape and the death of her grandchild.

"Suzanna is dead," he said simply. "You're to blame for it."

"How dare you say such a thing."

Somewhere between his entrance and his accusation, Lucille had regained her composure. He looked into blue eyes that held fire and ice. "I dare because it's true. You paid Junior and Pet to fall upon Marlena. John Hubbard helped you set it up. By the way, where is Hubbard?"

"I have no idea who you're talking about." She smiled. "I'd offer you coffee, but my servants seem to have abandoned me."

Frank had wondered if he would feel any pity for Lucille. Now he knew. None. Not the first scrap. She was unrepentant. "I wouldn't count on Ruth or Jonah ever coming back. Except to return your car, of course."

"I want him arrested. He's a thief."

"Let's talk about the money you paid Junior."

Lucille's mouth twisted up on one side. "Frank, you come from a long line of people with defective genes. Insanity is hereditary, you know."

"How much did you pay them?"

"You grandfather murdered his brother and his sister-in-law, and then turned the gun on himself. Now you've killed Junior Clements when he was lying on the floor wounded. Everyone in town knows you're nuts. The kind ones say 'shell-shocked.' Everyone knows that's code for insane."

"Did you tell Junior and Pet to frighten Marlena? Was that the plan? Or did you simply want her destroyed because she threatened your security?"

"Rumors around town are that you killed two of your own men who were wounded. Some say it was an act of kindness. Others, though, say you didn't want to be bothered carrying injured men. Which was it, Frank?"

He watched her and saw the corruption that ran to the bone. She would do anything to protect herself. Anything. Sacrifice her daughter, her grandchild, anyone who happened to be convenient. Her words were cotton puffs tossed at him. She'd never had the power to injure him, only those who loved her.

"You're going to prison, Lucille. You'll die there, if I have anything to do with it."

She laughed. "You're a fool, Frank. Who's going to testify against me? Junior and Pet are dead. You killed one and Jonah killed the other." She laughed again at his expression. "Huey called me and told me. He thought he was being kind and taking care of an old woman." She stood up. "You have no evidence that I had anything to do with what Junior and Pet did."

Frank's smile was slow. "Really."

"Really," she said, taking a step toward him.

"You forget about John Hubbard."

"Who?" She arched an eyebrow in mock confusion.

"Marlena's lover. The man who set the whole thing up. The man who was here at your house last evening." Frank grinned. "You're going to jail, Lucille."

"Where is this Hubbard?" Lucille frowned and looked in every corner of the room. "Produce him, Frank."

Frank had the first inkling of concern. Hubbard was somewhere in the area. His car was still parked on the courthouse lawn. He had no way to get out of town.

"Where is he, Frank?" Lucille demanded.

"We'll find him," Frank said. He rested his thumb over the pistol in his holster.

"I don't think you'll find him." Lucille stepped closer to Frank. "No, I don't think you'll find this John Hubbard. If he ever existed, I think he's gone." She straightened the collar of her dress. "You have nothing to link me to any of this."

"We'll find Hubbard and he'll talk."

"No, Frank, let me tell you what's going to happen. And you can take it to the bank. Lucas is going to bury Suzanna on Wednesday. On Thursday, he's going to file for divorce. On Friday, Huey is going to charge Marlena with reckless neglect in the death of his daughter. She never should have had that child in the woods while she was having an affair."

"Huey won't do that." Frank's voice lacked conviction. He knew he was lying. Huey wasn't a bad man, but he was a weak man, and in the face of Lucas Bramlett's insistence, he would do what Lucas wanted.

Lucille met his gaze. "You don't even believe that."

"And what about you?" Frank asked. "What will you do without Lucas's money to support you?"

"What makes you think I won't have money?"

Frank tasted only bitterness. He would do what he could to protect Marlena, but that would be too little too late. In killing Junior, he'd destroyed Marlena. He looked at the old woman, still handsome in a cold way. "How long do you think Lucas will support his ex-mother-in-law?" He watched with great satisfaction as the truth of his words stung her. "He'll divorce Marlena and he'll dump you. I hope you didn't give Junior all your money, because it won't be long before you're begging in the streets." He started to turn away, but looked back. "I won't ever stop looking for Hubbard. And when I find him, dead or alive, you're going to prison."

Dotty sat in the backyard swing, her foot swathed in bandages. She held a drink in her hand and used her good foot to push herself gently to and fro. The heat was unbearable. She had a terrible fear that gangrene would slip beneath the white bandages and nibble at the rest of her foot, creeping up her leg.

"Shit," she said, sipping her bourbon.

"Am I morbid or what?"

"Is it true that Zerty's in jail?" The boy came out from behind the tree. She'd learned that his name was Luke.

"He's in jail and he's going to rot there." She sipped the bourbon. "If he ever does get out, I'm going to hang him from a tree limb, gut him, and let the wasps have him."

Luke's hand traced his sightless eye. "Would you really?"

"Do you doubt it?" She'd do worse than that if Archey ever got out of the pen. "Where's your ma?"

"Inside." The boy's voice faded.

"She's going to be okay," Dotty said. When the boy didn't respond, she stopped the swing and touched his shoulder. "She'll be okay. She just has to believe that no one is going to hurt her again."

"Does she have to go away?"

Dotty thought about it. A strange bond had formed between the three of them, and she was reluctant to let the doctors in Mobile have Katy, even though she'd been assured that a stay in a sanitarium, with proper care, would be the best thing for her. "We'll give it a try," she said. "If Katy doesn't do well, or if she seems unhappy, we'll get her out."

"Promise?"

Dotty nodded. "I promise." She stood up and Luke handed her a crutch. "What about you?" she asked. "That doctor said he could do skin grafts. Lucas has set up a fund for you and your mom so there's money." She thought of Lucas and felt a flush of fury. Lucas had established the medical fund only after being threatened with exposing the fact that Luke was his child. Frank had handled the delicate negotiations, and she felt a smile building at the thought of how that conversation must have gone. "What about it?" she asked.

The boy shook his head. "No."

"What are you going to do?" Dotty asked.

"What are *you* going to do?" he responded.

She laughed. "I don't know for certain."

"Can I stay here?" He looked down at the ground.

Dotty felt the tears in her eyes. Seemed like most folks couldn't get away from her fast enough. Her husband, Joe, had stepped in front of a train, and sometimes she thought it might have been deliberate. Luke was different, though. Folks stared at him like he was a freak, and it made her mad enough to fight. For the first time she could remember, she was willing to fight for someone other than herself. Luke liked being with her, and if it was because no one else would have him, that didn't matter.

"Sure," she said. "You can stay here as long as you like. We'll figure out together what we're going to do."

35

Jade stood in the cold, tiled embalming room at Rideout Funeral Home. The door was open. She was the only person in the back rooms. Junior Clements was dead. His body had been shipped back to Laurel, a burden for his relatives and all who knew him. Jade looked at the small body beneath the sheet on the table. It was the last thing she could do for her niece.

She took a long breath and blinked back her tears. Suzanna was gone, forever free of the pain and suffering of this life. Jade imagined her playing in a garden filled with sunshine and flowers, laughing in a carefree way she'd never owned in reality.

Jade walked to the table and lifted the sheet. A gray pallor had settled over the child's features. She'd been in the water too long. Lucas had ordered a closed casket, one of the few such services in Jebediah County. He did not want the community to look upon the tragedy of his only child. Jade got her kit of makeup and carefully touched a light pink gloss over Suzanna's lips. She put the child's head on a block and combed the long chestnut hair, removing the tangles and finally braiding two pigtails. From the pocket of her smock she took two bright red ribbons and tied one onto each braid. She wondered if her niece would speak to her. She waited, but the room remained silent. At last she picked up Suzanna's cold hand.

"I know what's going to happen." Jade stroked her niece's forehead. "Your mama never meant for anything bad to happen to you, but she's going to pay anyway. When she goes off to Parchman, I'll go with her." She closed her eyes and fought to control the trembling of her body. Frank had been silent when she told him her plans. They both knew that Marlena would be convicted. There was no jury of peers for Marlena. Everyone in Jebediah County either feared Lucas or owed him money. He would get the verdict he wanted, and Marlena would die if she was abandoned to the state penal system alone. Jonah had been tight-lipped at Jade's decision, and Ruth had broken three of her cherished cups. Frank had listened and then nodded. Jade's heart had fluttered at the possibilities in his smile.

She bent closer to her niece. "I want you to know that I won't leave your mama alone. She loved you, Suzanna. She just didn't love herself enough."

Jade kissed the dead girl's forehead, so cool and smooth. "Your troubles are over now, child. I'll think of you running and laughing in the sunshine." She pulled the sheet up, covered Suzanna's face, and walked out of the room.

ABOUT THE AUTHOR

Carolyn Haines was born and raised in Mississippi. The author of the Sarah Booth Delaney mysteries and several other novels, she lives in Alabama, where she writes, teaches, and tends to her horses.